The Swampers, The Demon Spell, and The Vampire Maid

Hume Nisbet

Esprios.com

THE SWAMPERS

A Romance of the Westralian Goldfields

by

Hume Nisbet

TO DAVID CHRISTIE MURRAY, NOVELIST.
I BEG TO DEDICATE THIS ROMANCE
WITH PROFOUND ADMIRATION FOR HIS GENIUS.

PREFACE.

I HAVE to thank the following gentlemen for the prompt and hearty assistance which they have given me in books, maps, and personal information about West Australia and its Goldfields at the present hour. Having taken full advantage of such valuable information, I trust that the reader will find this romance correct in its local colouring and statistics. To Mr. Albert F. Calvert, M.E., F.R.G.S., &c., &c., Author of "The Exploration of Australia"; "Western Australia and its Goldfields"; Editor and Proprietor of The West Australian Review, for his magnificent and exhaustive works and maps. Also to those other friends, Messrs. Critchill; Ernest H. Gough; Graham Hill; Philip Mennell, F.R.G.S., &c., Author of "The Coming Colony," "Dictionary of Australian Biography," &c., &c., and Editor and Proprietor of The British Australasian; also to Mr. John Wilson, first Mayor of Kalgourlie. To all these gentlemen and others who have supplied me with information I beg to offer my most grateful thanks.

I must appeal to the good sense of my West Australian readers, and trust that they will not try to see real personages in my fictitious creations. Kalgourlie is as yet a small, if it is a rapidly-growing town, and each resident is known to his fellow-townsmen. The peculiarities of mankind are so mixed and generalized that it is not at all difficult for a reader to fix an original for my fancy study in any spot where men and women congregate. This habit, so unfair and crippling to an author's liberty of action, I must particularly warn you against indulging in. I built the "Chester Hotel" entirely at my own expense, and as my own speculation. The material was not Hessian, but a finer web of stuff which I spun from my own brain. Sarah Hall, Rosa Chester, Anthony Vandyke Jenkins, Bob Wallace, and my other characters, all came from the same source, and are as Mercutio says:

"The children of an idle brain, Begot of nothing but vain fantasy."

Therefore you must take them as such, and not localize or incarnate one of them. On this privileged ground I strictly take my stand.

Regarding any mild criticism that I may have written throughout these pages concerning the fair City of Sydney, I have no apology to make other than that perhaps my various visits may have been timed unfortunately when the inhabitants were suffering from some insensate epidemic. Perhaps they have lucid intervals between these public and social epidemics of folly and unreason, and that during these intervals they act like their neighbours, Victoria, Queensland, and South Australia, but if so, I have not had the good fortune to land amongst them at such happy intervals; therefore I can only speak as I find people, and the natives of Sydney have not impressed me so favourably as their neighbour colonials of Melbourne, Brisbane, and Adelaide have done, either for their probity, generosity, or common sense. As for that worm "Puffadder," with his blasphemous, brutal, and poisonous organ, I do not think any self-respecting colonial will care how much a reptile like this is criticised or censured. He may spit out his venom, but he would do that under any circumstances, particularly when his victim's back is turned upon him. His unsexed contributors may also snarl and yelp, while his senile admirers, who have debauched the little brains which originally they may have possessed, with his absinthe doses, doubtless will gnash their gums and cry for gore, but as "Walker, London," remarks: "That is noth ink."

My story is before you, sympathetic or hostile readers, and I trust it may interest you with all its faults. The characters are purely imaginative, but some of the incidents are drawn from facts, and in the descriptions I have done my utmost to be exact and realistic.

THE AUTHOR.

CONTENTS

I.	THE DEN OF THE MODERN WIZARD
II.	A CONFIDENTIAL CONVERSATION
III.	THE NEW ESTABLISHMENT
IV.	TREASURE TROVE
V.	JACK MILTON AT HOME
VI.	JACK MILTON'S ESCAPE
VII.	THE INTERVIEW
VIII.	COUSINS
IX.	JACK MILTON WAITS
X.	AN UNPLEASANT DREAM
XI.	ON THE WALLABY TRACK
XII.	ANTHONY VANDYKE JENKINS
XIII.	THE PROSPERITY AND FALL OF JENKINS
XIV.	JACK MILTON MAKES FOR THE WEST
XV.	THE DREAM MINE
XVI.	ROSA'S SECOND MARRIAGE
XVII.	TRACKED
XVIII.	THE OLD, OLD GAME
XIX.	JACK MILTON IS TAKEN IN CHARGE
XX.	ROSA GETS INITIATED IN MINING PARLANCE
XXI.	JACK MILTON AND HIS COLOURED FRIENDS
XXII.	TO KALGOURLIE
XXIII.	THE SWAMPERS
XXIV.	CHESTER TAKES A MONTH'S LEAVE
XXV.	JACK MILTON'S DISCOVERY
XXVI.	THE COURTSHIP OF BOB WALLACE
XXVII.	MEETING OF JACK AND ROSA
XXVIII.	JACK MILTON AT KALGOURLIE
XXIX.	"WHERE THE WEARY CEASE TO TROUBLE AND THE WICKED ARE AT REST"

The Swampers

Chapter I. The Den of the Modern Wizard.

PROFESSOR MORTIKALI sat in his inner sanctum waiting for customers.

It was a hot day, during the early portion of the month of March, 1896, and although the Professor had all his blinds drawn down, and occupied the coolest corner of the Arcade, still he could not shut out those intense waves of Sydney heat that swept in, between the crevices of the doors and windows, although he managed to shut out a good deal of the intense light.

Never had such a hot season been in the memory of the oldest colonist as this heat wave of 1896. From January 1st to the 24th it had ranged from 112 degrees to 129 degrees in the shade in New South Wales, and people had dropped dead wholesale throughout the colony. In many of the inland townships the people had been panic-stricken, and fish were killed in the creeks and lakes by tons upon tons. It had cooled off a little by March, yet there were days, and this was one of them, when the heat fury of January seemed to repeat itself.

The Professor liked shadow, for he was a modern wizard and his business did not require much light; indeed the less light that was thrown upon it, the better it was conducted; therefore, it was not often that the green venetian blinds were drawn up.

The Professor was at present resting on his oars, for it was the slack hour of the day, the hour when no one, unless absolutely forced to come out, would care to face the terrific sun-glare of mid-day.

The Professor was of that peculiar craft which flourished so much during the earlier centuries, and has more or less flourished ever since under various disguises. He belonged to the tribe of the witch of Endor, that profession of seers and fore-tellers whom King Saul tried to put down in his vigorous and virtuous years, and afterwards weakly consulted in his decline; the same craft which that modern

The Swampers

Solomon, King James I. of England, so rigorously hunted to death, and which might have died naturally only for the efforts of the Pschychological Society, and that able editor of Border-land, the discoverer of the fourth dimension.

It is not a profitable profession in merry old England, where the police imitate the tactics of Kings Saul and James, and take as much delight in making raids, as lively terriers do in hunting out rabbits. But in progressive New South Wales, where convict laws still hold sway, and men are hanged for attempted murder, while judges dictate to jurymen, as the celebrated Jeffreys used to do, where even the judges themselves consult the witches; fortune-telling and witchcraft thrive wonderfully, even in the midst of the universal depression which of late has fallen upon the. colonies.

In the Sydney of to-day you may see, amongst other closed places of business, the shutters up of many public houses and bars; the reason of this is that they have been raided by the police, because the proprietors have been selling poison undiluted to their customers, and although the colonised stomach can stand a good deal in the way of vitriol, and blue-stone, yet when the landlord omits to give his customers even the flavour of brandy, rum or whisky, then his fate as a landlord is decided.

They are a proud and conservative race, the New South Welshmen; they cannot stand the slightest approach to a joke about their country. You may abuse England or London as much as you are disposed to an Englishman, and he will only laugh unctuously, but you must not take the same liberty with a New South Welshman. His harbour is the most beautiful harbour in the world. If you admit this, yet suggest that the buildings might be just a little more classic, he will grow pale with passion and cut you dead. If you venture to hint that morality in its aesthetic quality is not so strictly observed amongst the politicians and tradesmen as it might be, he will consider it time to regard you as a dangerous person and a fit subject for the martial law that hangs first and tries afterwards, and is still in such active force in that sun-laved colony.

The Swampers

They aim to be very high-toned in Sydney, and imitate as nearly as they can the manners of fashionable London; therefore if an accomplished swindler or thief comes amongst them and knows his business thoroughly, he is nearly sure to be successful, for the veneer being all that they aspire to themselves, so are they satisfied with it in their visitors. In Victoria and Queensland the inhabitants are less conservative and much more level-headed.

Professor Mortikali was a wonderful man in his way, and pursued various branches as a livelihood. On his brass plate was written: "Professor Mortikali, Psychometrist, Pneumatologist, Futurist and Magneto-Electric Healer." He called his establishment the Egyptian-Mystic Hall and Health Sanatorium, and had on his bills a wide range of subjects, from character delineating by Phrenology and Physiognomy, Fortune-telling by Cards, Palmistry or Astrology, with the art of healing all diseases by Hypnotic treatment.

There are hundreds in the same line of business throughout Sydney, and all apparently flourishing more or less, despite the dull times. In the Arcade were three rivals, while along the principal streets every fifth or sixth shop bears the sign of a Futurist, or an Astrologer, with all the paraphernalia exhibited in the windows which one expects to witness in the windows of a wizard.

In the newspapers also of this enlightened and conservative country, along with singular gems of poetry, in the form of memoriam verses, you may read every day, advertisements like the following: "Wanted, a loving, clairvoyant, test-lady, with means preferred, as life partner, by Magnetic Healer, etc.," and yet no one laughs either at the verses or the advertisements, they have become so accustomed to both. But they get terribly vicious if any stranger attempts to criticise their politicians, or their professionals.

Professor Mortikali had his front window artfully set out, a plaster cast of the hand of Deeming the murderer, with casts and photographs of actors, clergymen, and other distinct types were displayed. A phrenological head stood on a stucco pillar, and the complete skeleton of a baby dangled inside a glass case, specimens of snakes and tape worms were coiled in bottles, or dried and stuffed, and grouped about, while the invariable alligator, which Hogarth has accustomed us to in his pictures of the Quack, was likewise displayed.

A curtain, half-drawn back from the doorway, revealed the image of a gipsy holding out her hand to be crossed with silver, while at a little counter sat an attractive-looking girl, costumed in black velvet, scarlet facings, and glittering metallic discs, such as we were used to gaze on at "fairs" in our youthful days. There was no attempt at advancement, or dressing up to date in this establishment. The old-fashioned arrangements appeared to answer the purpose perfectly, the same amount of rouge and powder on the face of this attractive handmaid to the wizard, the generous display of snowy neck, and the usual surroundings of curtains, herbs and stuffed monstrosities, they were all there, while inside waited the Futurist and Faith-Healer.

At this precise hour of mid-day the Professor and his handmaid were both similarly occupied in discussing their lunch. Hers was a slight refection, as befitted a Sydney nymph of her light and powdery nature. A couple of tarts, and an ice-cream, which she had procured at the next door. The ice she had finished first, before it became quite liquid, and now she was leisurely discussing the fruit and pastry.

Inside the sanctum the Professor was having a heavier meal, as befitted the nerve wear and tear of his occupation; an underdone beef-steak with a chunk of bread and a tankard of colonial beer, vulgarly called "swanky."

The Professor was a man well advanced in years, of an ordinary height and inclined to run to stoutness. He wore his iron-grey tresses long, so that they fell over his back in a lank and straggly fashion, his beard and moustache also were grey and mangy, while his rubicund complexion, commonplace features, and very small eyes, reminded one somehow of a mendicant friar of the Middle Ages.

The Swampers

His small eyes were crow-like and rather vacant in their expression, and what linen he displayed was of the dirtiest and most rumpled description. His garments also, although at one date black, had evidently been purchased at a second-hand establishment, and were both frayed and rusty as well as badly fitting, and being originally of the dress-suit order, gave him the appearance of a broken-down waiter at a poor restaurant.

He was not a wholesome-looking object, while he wolfed his steak as a dog might devour its meal; the steak was badly cut and indifferently cooked, the intense heat of the atmosphere, the perspiration running from the Professor's forehead and cheeks in dirty rivulets, and his dirty hands helping the fork. Ignorant, low-bred, square-pointed fingers, unclipped nails in deepest mourning, and, added to this, that vacuous mouth, with the slobbering lips taking in the steak with such evident unction, and the solitary unwashed tooth emphasizing that moist unction, rendered this hypnotic disciple of "Border-land" rather gruesome than pleasant.

As he sat, he scratched his head sometimes with his dirty nails, sometimes with his greasy fork; he also fumbled suggestively about his half-opened waistcoat as one is used to see tramps do when they fancy themselves unobserved; altogether, this Sydney interpreter of "Border-land" lore gave one the decided impression of that drawing in Punch, by Harry Furness, of the man who wrote about Pears' Soap. "Two years ago I used your soap, since when I have used no other." Harry Furness's model was attentuated and unkempt, but fancy a professor of mystic lore, in a badly-fitting waiter's dress-suit; the knees baggy, and the vest over tight. The angry buttons threatening to sever. Burly as a friar of old and soft as a retired bantam boxer, with a vacuous countenance, and crow-like eyes, always on the goggle, and you have the Professor, or ancient wizard up to date.

Supplement this with the awful heat of a Sydney mid-summer day, an underdone steak cut in colonial fashion, and cooked ditto; the natural perspiration and fumes of an unwashable tramp, decked up

The Swampers

in an old dress suit, and you may realise the picture of this High Priest of the temple of mystery without further description.

He had just finished his gorge and imbibed his last drop of colonial "swanky," when the hand-maid popped in her head, and shedding a tiny stream of pearl powder, which after all sweetened the apartment a little, announced in brassy tones: "Are ye done, Perfessor, for there's a laydy a-waiting ter consult yer?"

The Professor bundled his plates and beer-mug to a side table, where he covered them with an old newspaper, then dusting the crumbs aside with his hand, and wiping his hands again on the tails of his coat he produced a greasy pack of cards, and said with calm dignity: "Yes, Matilder, show the party in."

The party entered, a young woman of about twenty-five, fashionably dressed and according to the season, in virgin white, with a Donna-like bunch of snowy ostrich feathers in her hat, and a cloud or dust-veil about her face; she was slim-built and graceful in figure, and the Professor, who loved the fair sex, took notice that she had a wealth of golden-brown hair under the drooping feathers.

"Sit down, my dear," he said with a smirk on his sweaty and greasy red face, and the party sat and silently looked at him through her cloud. "Is it your fortune ye want to know? By the cards or by the hand?—or are you in any other trouble that a man of my experience can help you? Girls will be girls, you know, my dear, therefore you may safely give me your confidence, for it won't be abused."

He bared his lonely tooth and regarded her with a senile smile, while his crow-like, vacant gaze tried to get behind the cloud.

The visitor laughed softly yet enjoyably, then after a pause she replied, removing her white gloves at the same time:

"No, old man, I don't want any confidence business. I only want you to tell my fortune by my hands and by the cards."

The Swampers

"It's unlucky, they say, to do both at one sitting, yet, if you turn round and go to the door and cross back again, that will break the charm. Which will you have first?"

"My hand, Professor; tell me what I've done and what I'm going to do, and then I can ask you other questions when we come to the cards."

She held out her hands, palms upward, to him, while he took a magnifying glass, and after giving himself a preliminary hitch and scratch, he stooped over them to examine.

Shapely hands they were, with tapering long fingers and fleshy palms, which had hard and well-defined lines running across them. "You are married," the Professor said after a pause. "Well, what of that?"

"No more than you think of it yourself, my dear. You have had some troubles in the past, and have had some adventures; but your marriage has not been a happy one, there are no children, and you'd like to be free of your bond." "Yes, and shall I?" "I see a death here, and a little trouble, but your line of life is clear." "Shall I be married again?" "Yes, and have much prosperity in the future." "That'll do, when will it come off?" "How old are you?" "Twenty-six." "You'll be married again before you are twenty-eight." "Budgerrie for you, old man; now let's try the cards." She rose abruptly and went to the door, returning in a moment, while the Professor arranged his cards.

"There's an old fellow waiting for his fortune, at the door, Professor. Will you take him or me first?" she asked as she returned.

"Ladies first, of course," answered the Professor gallantly, again baring his solitary tooth. "Drive ahead then, for I am in a hurry," said the young woman curtly. "Shuffle and cut." After she had done so, he began to read:

"There is a dark man here close beside you, your husband, I should say, but you turn your back on him—you take hearts, do you not?"

The Swampers

"Yes," replied the young woman. "There's a diamond man facing you, that is the one you fancy." "Go on."

"You'll get that diamond man, but the club man will cause you some trouble; there's a death here — —" "To the club man?" eagerly. "I don't know yet. Shuffle again and I'll tell you."

Thrice did the cloud-veiled woman, with the strong white hands, shuffle the cards, and then he answered her curiosity and desires.

"Yes, the club man will pass from your path, and the diamond man is the winner." "Thank Heaven for that!" as she paid him his fee and went forth, brushing by the white-haired customer who was waiting his turn.

She did not look at the white-haired customer, and she was too closely veiled for any one to see her features, yet he glanced after her through his blue glasses in a curious way as she went out of the doorway, then he sought the Professor.

A tall and singularly powerful-looking man he was, this second visitor, dressed in thin grey serge, smooth faced, and with a shock of white hair that fell about his shoulders after the style of the ex-Premier of New South Wales—that leonine and doggerel verse writer, Sir Henry Parkes. Indeed for a moment the Professor thought that this much-married politician must have shaved, and mounted blue glasses as a sort of disguise, but he soon recovered himself, with the assurance gained from knowledge that this eminent man would never sink his personality, no matter what position he chose to take up, therefore he became composed and ready for his visitor. "I want my future read," said the stranger. "By the palm, or by the cards?" "The hand will do." He stretched a sinewy hand out to the Professor's magnifying glass. "You've experienced troubles in the past." "Yes."

"But you have a singularly open and confiding as well as a generous nature. I may say that you are a man who has been imposed upon by false friends, and may be again if you are not particularly careful.

The Swampers

You— —" "What a confounded old fraud you are to be sure, Jeremiah Judge."

The stranger, as he uttered these words, his left hand still lying under the Professor's magnifying glass, removed with his right hand the blue spectacles and snowy wig, and revealed a hard-faced but handsome young man, with short cropped black hair, and glittering black eyes. "Fancy me being sucked in by anyone!"

The Professor fell back on his chair, confounded, his crow-blue eyes almost starting out of his head as he uttered the feeble cry: "Jack Milton, by George!"

The Swampers

Chapter II. A Confidential Conversation.

"YES, you genial old humbug, I've come back once more to do some business in Sydney."

As he spoke, Jack Milton, as he had just been called, leaned back in his chair and regarded the pneumatologist with a benevolent, yet contemptuous air of patronage.

"Still trying your best in your small way to do the public, I see, Jeremiah, and doing it shabbily at that, per usual."

The psychometrist got upon his ambling legs, with a gushing air of welcome illuminating his steaming face, and parting his vacuous mouth.

"My dear, dear boy, who'd have expected to see you here? I thought your time wasn't up for another twelve months; how have you done it?" "Ah! I behaved myself and kidded the sky-clerk, therefore got my ticket." "What was the little item?"

"A mere trifle in the past, something I did in Melbourne long ago, and which I had forgotten, or I should not have gone there quite so openly, but the 'Tecks' remembered me and laid me up by the heels for a spell; however, it wasn't an unmixed evil, for being in lavender gave me the repose that I required, and put the Sydney scenters quite off my track."

"Good—very good," chuckled the Professor, rubbing his hands together and gazing admiringly on the powerful figure before him. "You'll find hosts of friends who are glad to see Jack Milton amongst them again, and none more so than your 'umble servant."

While the old humbug was speaking, the young man carefully replaced his white wig and blue spectacles, and became once more a kind of benevolent replica of a clean-shaved Sir Henry Parkes.

The Swampers

"I have made an appointment with my lawyer to meet me here, Jeremiah—or as you call yourself now, Professor Mortikali. I thought it safer than at his own office." "Much safer, and more secluded." "So I thought." "But how did you find me out, Jack, eh?"

"Well you are not exactly the kind of coon to give an 'agent' much trouble, if he wanted to get on your tracks; I knew you'd be up to some business of this kind where spirits or mesmerism had a share in it——" "Call it hypnotism, Jack, or psychometry." "Yes, that's exactly how I spotted you, old boy. I looked out all the sign-boards, as I came along, for the most jaw-cracking words. I knew your weakness for that sort of thing. Palmist or Futurist wouldn't be good enough for you, therefore when I came to Professor Mortikali, Psychometrist, Pneumatologist, &c., I felt sure I had run my fox to his hole, and I wasn't far out."

"No, Jack, you'd make a first-rate detective, if you wasn't better than that, a first-class——"

"Crib-cracker, eh? It takes a thief to catch a thief, but I don't belong to that race who can utilize their experience to snare their own kind. I have always been and always shall be grit to my pals. Is this much of a trade?"

He looked about him with a little disgust, and at the shabby Professor with a humorous air of pity.

"Fairly," observed the pyschometrist. "I hold my own; this is the slack time of the day, but at night they come up wonderful, considering."

"You haven't got a fashionable class of customers I can see, or you'd be better togged up. Never mind! I'll put you up to something good before many days are over our heads."

"No, Jack, no, I'd rather not!" cried the Professor nervously. "I don't mind helping you when the game is safe, but you are so reckless, my dear boy, and don't at all consider personal safety. Now you see, I'm doing small things, and the police don't touch me at 'em, but one never knows where he'd land, if this business spread out into many more new branches."

"Bah! The business I'm going to set you up is strictly in your own line, Psychometry and the other P. H.'s. You're too cramped here. You want bigger and more fashionable premises, and to get yourself togged up more like an orthodox medical Professor, and less like a broken-down waiter, and I've spotted the shop that'll suit you to a nicety. Do you know that place where 'Brisco'the jeweller used to be, in George Street?" "With the bank on one side, and the pawn-broker on the other?"

"Exactly. Would those diggings suit you to open a branch establishment of the Faith Healing and Fortune-telling fake?"

"What d'ye mean, Jack Milton? D'ye know them 'ere premises will cost in rent and taxes near to a thousand a year?" "Well!"

"And the fixing of them up properly, with furniture, carpets and sofas, &c., &c., will come to nigh five hundred quid."

"You've hit it pretty nearly, I should say, to do it properly," replied Jack calmly. "You'll want some attractive-looking girls, with a little more style than this one here, and some respectable toggery for yourself Yes, you'll need all that money, and more perhaps, till business comes in." "Yes, and who's a-going to pay for all this outlay."

"I will, my sage psychometrist. I think there are vast possibilities in this business of yours if properly worked in this city, and as I happen to have the sponduloux, or will have if my lawyer, who'll be here presently, isn't a fool as well as a rogue, I'll set you up and be your sleeping partner. I'm going to make a boom in the prediction business. We'll take in the national 'sports'and give the 'juggins'tips from spirit land; we'll pitch our placards and bills about like snow-flakes and make the press-men our serfs by advertising; but, you must try to acquire the art of washing yourself and changing your

The Swampers

linen at least three times a week while the hot weather lasts, or it'll be all bunkum. Do you savy, my odoriferous psychometrist—don't you see what I mean? Plenty of water, Pears' soap, fresh linen, and a trifle of Jockey Club or Cherry Blossom for the sake of business, also a nail brush and a little attention to the nails, at present in deepest mourning for your rubbishy sins, which ain't worth so much respect; lemons are first-class articles for cleaning the hands and nails; and the Sydney waterworks are lavish with their supply."

"I ain't at all averse to washing in the warm weather," observed the Professor with an injured air. "I likewise like a frequent change of shirts and collars, and feel kindly drawn to clerical neck-cloths, if I had the articles to work on."

"You'll have them. Meantime, I want you to keep out your customers, or read their fortunes at your outside counter, this afternoon while my man of business is engaged with me, and we'll arrange all that afterwards. By Jove! you'd be a great man, Professor, if you had a fair chance, and I'm going to give you that chance."

"Will you have anything to drink now?" said the Professor respectfully, for Jack Milton had spoken to him in the lordly manner of one who has means at command, and the panderer reverenced him accordingly.

"Not at present, I have a lawyer to talk to and I bet he won't imbibe until he has finished this interview, and neither shall I. I say, do you know anything about my wife?" "I don't know exactly where she lives, of course, but I have seen her." "Lately?" "Yes, just recently, I may say." "Yes—yes; and is she looking well—my Rosa, my darling?"

A wonderful change took place in the disguised housebreaker as he asked these questions; he was no longer cynical nor supercilious, but eager and boyish, while by contrast the Professor seemed to become ill at ease and constrained. "You are proud of her yet, I see, Jack." "Of course, why should I not be?—my wife, the woman I love and have always kept as well as I could. She doesn't know what I have

The Swampers

had to do for a living and to keep her comfortable, unless my lawyer has proved a traitor; which I hope he hasn't for his own sake—tell me, what do you know about her?" "Did you see the young lady in white who went out of here as you entered?" "Yes." "That was your wife."

"I thought there was something familiar in her figure and walk, but what was she doing here?" "She came to have her fortune read."

"I know, the little stupid, she wanted to learn when her husband would be home again, eh?"

The Professor looked at the eager face before him as if he were making up his mind to say something difficult, and then he replied: "Yes, that was what she wanted to know."

"Of course, and you gave the little jade a lot of idle promises and sent her away happy?"

"Yes, in the usual fashion. I promised her a lot according to her desires, and sent her away fairly well pleased." "Good! I'll make you a true prophet this time, you old scoundrel, ha, ha, ha!" At this moment the hand-maid put in her head, and said: "There's a gent outside as have called by appointment."

"That's my man," cried Jack cheerily. "Show him in, Molly, my darling, and you," to the Professor, "clear out till I'm done with him."

As he spoke, there entered a well set-up man of about thirty-three, with a blonde moustache and close-cropped fair hair, blue eyes a trifle closely set together, and a vulture-like nose. He was a keen-looking, business-like man, well dressed and well groomed, and one who would not be likely to let scruples stand in the way of personal advantage.

At his watch chain he carried, as an appendage, a pair of compasses and square, his neck-tie pin was also adorned with the same quaint

The Swampers

design, while on the fourth finger of his left hand he wore a plain gold signet-ring with the same device; evidently showing to all the world that he was not at all ashamed of the society to which he belonged.

As he entered, he looked at the white wig and blue spectacles, with an air of perplexity for an instant, until the wearer of these gave him a quick sign, then he advanced smilingly, and said: "How do you do, Mr. Milton?" "All right, my friend, sit down." The Professor had cleared out of the sanctum by this time, dropping the heavy curtain behind him, and leaving the lawyer and his client together. "Well, Mr. Chester, have you carried out my instructions?"

"Yes, Milton, I have carried out your instructions to the letter, and, I need not tell you, at considerable risk to myself."

The lawyer, now that they were alone, spoke in a severe tone of voice, as one might use to a criminal whose case is in hand, but who has placed himself beyond the reach of ordinary courtesy, while the ticket-of-leave man listened meekly and without appearing to observe the curtness.

"I have invested your money, as you desired, in my own name. I do not ask you how it was made, I have no desire to know, and I am happy to say it is yielding fair returns, even in these depressed times. Your wife is under the impression that you are still in the South Seas, treasure-seeking, and I have delivered regularly to her the letters you forwarded to me." "You have been a true friend to me, Chester. Where is my wife now living?" "With her parents; they have removed lately to the Glebe; this is her address." He handed an envelope over as he spoke, and waited further enquiries. "Is—is Rosa well?"

"Yes; last time I saw my cousin, she was very well indeed. Do you intend to visit her at once? For candidly, I don't think it would be advisable if you desire to keep your past a secret from the poor girl."

"No; I have some business to do before I can see her, or let her know I am in Sydney. When I am ready I should like you still to act as my friend and break the tidings of my arrival to her gently, as I don't want to agitate her. We have been so long separated that it mightn't do to jump in on her all of a sudden."

The lawyer looked at the blue spectacles demurely for a moment, and then he said:

"That is only a right resolve on your part, and I will do all I can to help you, not to startle Rosa."

"I am dying to see the darling, but when I next come to her I hope to be beyond the necessity of leaving her any more. I have a little speculation on hand which, if it comes off successfully, will enable me to retire and live comfortably. Meantime——"

"Yes?"

"I require some ready money to enable me to carry out this speculation." "How much do you require?"

"Fifteen hundred pounds for a few weeks only, and with it I hope to clear fifty times that amount." "It is a large sum to get hold of at so short a notice, for your property is all tied up at present; still, if you can assure me that it is only for a few weeks and the return is sure, I think it might be managed."

"Within a fortnight from the time I get this advance I shall be able to place in your keeping perhaps a hundred times the amount."

"Very well; to-morrow night, I'll give you an open cheque, and an introduction to the bank. Have you any choice of banks?" "Yes, I should like to open an account at the 'Fiji Limited,' George Street." "Very good, I'll see to that—what name shall I make the cheque payable to?" "John Williams." "Any further instructions?"

The Swampers

"No—only, if you are near the Glebe at any time, you may say to Rosa that you expect me back soon."

"I shall make it a point to call upon my uncle and aunt to-night, and will deliver your message to my cousin at the same time."

"You are a good fellow, Chester, to befriend me, like this after what I've done, and believe me, whatever happens to me I trust to be able to keep the knowledge of it from your cousin."

"I hope so—indeed I expect so much from you, for that is only your duty towards your innocent wife and her relations."

"Don't fear for me, I'll be secretive and game enough, Does—does Rosa speak much about me?"

"Of course the poor child misses you dreadfully, but as I have paid her income regularly, she is comfortable enough and not under the same anxiety regarding ways and means as are some wives here. She looks forward to your return as a wealthy man, and she is anticipating a good time in England and the Continent, when that comes off."

"She'll have it too, the angel, whoever suffers, by George! That puts new blood into me, and my next diving operation will be a big success, you bet."

"Good-bye for the present," said the lawyer with a smile, as he rose briskly. "I'll come here with the cheque to-morrow night about nine o'clock—you'll be here?" "Yes—Good-bye."

Mr. Chester took up his slate tinted kid gloves with his stick and hat, and quitted his companion with a quick step, without shaking hands with him or looking back, while the disguised man watched his retreat with eyes that showed a little moisture behind his darkened spectacles.

The Swampers

"He is a fine fellow, if a bit cold and stiff with me; many a one in his position would have plundered me wholesale, with all that money at his discretion, while I'd only have had to grin and bear it; but Arthur Chester wouldn't do that. I expect he thinks one thief is enough in the family; besides, he is too fond of Rosa to do her a wrong."

His strong and resolute head drooped for a moment on his hand, as he thought on the Sydney girl, whose love he had won under false pretences, and away from this same cousin. True, the family had been poor enough when he first came amongst them as a man with an assured income, a fiction he had managed to keep up, with the aid of Arthur Chester, ever since. Arthur Chester, who had only been a subordinate until, with those ill-gotten gains, he was able to begin business for himself, for Jack Milton had been a daring and successful disciple of the late Charles Peace, except for that slight mistake of his in Victoria. He had been prudent enough to work alone as much as possible and confide a few of his secrets and what money he stole to this cousin of his wife, only when forced to do so.

"I wonder if it is principle that makes Chester so stand-offish with me; he was glad enough to borrow my money when he was a clerk, and the receiver isn't much better, if any, than the thief; I hadn't been in jail then though, at least he didn't know it if I had, and he pretends, rarely, not to know where my money comes from. Perhaps he is jealous of me with Rosa, and I cannot blame him if he is, for who could help being in love with that little angel?"

The Professor broke in here upon the cogitations of the housebreaker, and instantly his careless mocking manner returned.

"Well, you old scarecrow, I've settled matters with my lawyer and we are to have the supplies needful for taking those premises, so now I am off to arrange with the landlord about terms and occupation. You keep out of it for the present until I can make you look respectable, if that is possible, and brace up your tottering mind to be in possession and a fashionable soothsayer by the end of the week."

The Swampers

With these bantering remarks, he put on his soft hat and sauntered out to the blazing sunshine leaving the foolish psychometrist in a rapture of admiration and rosy visions.

Chapter III. The New Establishment.

IF the Professor had reason to be a proud man, four days afterwards, he could hardly be said to be a completely happy one. He was possessed of vanity and ignorance enough to have accepted any post, but the position wanted grappling with and getting accustomed to. These daily ablutions were decidedly irksome, and after being accustomed to limp linen, to be imprisoned in stiffly-starched shirts and collars was a trial, to say nothing about the soft carpets, and the flashy furniture, all on the hire system, which awed his silly soul. The habit of scratching was an ancient one and not easy to set aside, still he did his best to live up to his new surroundings and forego that luxury.

Jack Milton, in his character of John Williams, had engaged the servants and young ladies to wait upon expected clients. The Professor found them all on the spot when he arrived, with his bran new wardrobe, to take possession. Attractive and exceedingly sharp-looking girls, in sedate and well-fitting costumes, and a page-boy to open the door, with a face like a knife newly ground and eyes like a snake; not many page boys, even of the keenest colonial produce, would have had a chance with this remarkable boy, for activity, wide-awakeness and composure. He was a demon page, who could anticipate an order before it was half thought out, far less expressed.

The cook and housemaid were not beautiful, but they were agile and wonderfully constructed; quiet, freckled-faced women, who performed their duties deftly, and moved about the house like Malays or Chinamen. There was also a man kept on the premises to split wood in the cellar and look after the horse and dog-cart in the yard, for the Professor was stinted in nothing by his liberal patron; this man likewise had been chosen for his strength of muscles rather than his good looks, and he was very modest, for he seldom went out to the street. His duties lay solely in the back kitchen, cellars, and yard.

The Swampers

The sleeping partner and financier of the business took up his abode on the premises, and had his meals with the Professor, and generous meals they were, both as regards viands and liquors. The Professor for the first time in his chequered career had the delight of quaffing champagne and burgundy with his tucker, and like the hero he was, he went into those delights with heart-felt pleasure and thirsty energy when the daily duties were over. Each night after the hours of consultation, supper came on, and he never rose from that supper, but drank on, until he found the soft carpet sufficient as a couch for the night. Jack Milton had been correct in his estimate of the gullibility of the Sydney people when the bait is presented to them with a blaze and glitter. In his small and mean way the Professor had been able to keep himself going, with the low fees asked for his priceless services, but he was astonished now at the crowds who waited in his ante-rooms, and the golden offerings which poured in during the fashionable hours of consultation. As soon as the fashionables grasped the fact that such an establishment had opened in the locality, and columns of advertisements made them suppose that there must be money at the back of the concern, they at once patronized it. And because it looked genuine and like a success, the public made it so, with their generous fees. Psychometry became a theme of conversation from Potts' Point to Botany Bay, and the Psychometrist a decided boom. Of course this peculiarity of encouraging and bending down to apparent success is not altogether confined to Sydney, although in other places the public may not be quite so quickly got at by such shams, nor so candid in their contempt for failure or poverty.

"Make hay while your sun shines," Jack would say as he roused up the Professor from his hog-like repose each morning and superintended his bath and dressing. "Get as drunk as you like when business is over, but you must look capable to use the rake during the day."

Yet although he was so strict with Mortikali, the sleeping partner, after he had braced up and set the fraudulent machine going, would prove his position in the firm by going off to his own bed and sleeping for the best part of the day. It was astonishing what a quantity of sleep he could do with. He said that he did not sleep well at nights, and that was why he took so much of it during the day. Certainly in the mornings he did look worn and wearied enough to justify his assertion that he could not sleep well at nights.

"I'll have to put you under my magnetic treatment, my boy, if you don't get better. Let me give you a few passes now," remarked the Professor when he had picked himself up from the floor and cleared his muddled faculties somewhat with a shower-bath. "Them wines do pour the illectric force into a sensitive like me; I felt all of a tingle this morning, just see how my arms and hands are a-shaking; it's the healing power a-filling me to bursting point, that's what it is; my old mother, who was a rare mejum, used to tell me, I had the god-like gifts to make my fortune as a healer, and, by George! I begin to believe she was in the right."

He was engaged, while gabbling on, in making hypnotic passes round the recumbent head of his stalwart friend, who had pitched himself wearily upon one of the couches in their private dining room. "So your mother was a mejum, was she?" sleepily answered the drowsy Jack. "Ay, one of the right old school, and no gammon about her; she wouldn't give a séance for nothink, not she, like as some of them blooming fools do now. Her familiar spurruts only worked for the £ s. d."

"Good old party, and what about your wife and family—where have you left them? Eh?"

"Don't mention them," replied the Psychometrist with vicious emphasis. "I have cast them out of my heart for ever, leastways they chucked me out, the unnatural mob. That woman, my wife, fell to religion—the Methodists took her in hand and spoilt a first-rate trance mejum. She'd have nothink to do with me afterwards, and said that my gifts came from the devil, and what d'ye think my eldest son had the impudence to tell me?" "I give it up."

"That I was as ignorant as an unweaned pig—there, now, what d'ye think of that from a man's own son?"

The Swampers

Jack Milton, who had been gradually succumbing under his protégé's passes, or from his own fatigue, rallied a little at this, and burst into a hearty laugh, which however he qualified by saying: "It was cheek, and no mistake."

"What d'ye think, my boy, but that wasn't all, for he followed this nasty remark by taking me by the scruff of my neck and pitching me into the street, telling me never to darken the door or disgrace them again with my lousy presence. Ah! if they could see me now, though, wouldn't they feel ashamed."

"It's quite likely they would," murmured the patient, as he succumbed and fell asleep.

Barney, the stable hand and wood-chopper, was like his master during these hot mornings, and did a considerable amount of sleeping among the straw in the stable, after he had attended to the pony and split what wood was needed for the kitchen; however, as these were nearly all the duties yet asked of him, no one complained about his drowsy habits. The weather was too oppressively hot for anyone to work much, except the Professor, until the night came, and his work was not over-taxing either to the mind or muscles. He knew the formula of the cards, and how to prattle about the lines of life, girdle of Venus, and mount of Mars, with the breaks and crosses in between. His customers were also fairly credulous and not over critical either about the predictions or manners of the predictor. He was now well-dressed, his hair and beard were tidily trimmed, and his surroundings were flashy, and those completed the illusion. Each victim came to him desirous of listening, and with wishes to be gratified, and they gave him the key to those wishes quickly enough, therefore he sent them away happy, for he predicted exactly what they wanted to come to pass. His fees had been raised to suit his new surroundings, one guinea for the future, revealed either by card or palm; four guineas if the stars were consulted, and a chart drawn out. He generously threw in a little phrenology, palmistry, and card shuffling along with the astrology for the same fee. His massage and magnetic treatment was a ten-guinea per visit affair, and a course, or series, of visits were required before success could be promised.

The Swampers

As we have said, the Professor became an instant and pronounced success, for although the establishment had only been opened for six days, he had hardly time at this stage to bolt his lunch, through the flux of customers, while the sovereigns and shillings rolled into his coffers in a perpetual stream. It was better than a gold mine while it lasted.

"A pity these booms are so soon over," murmured Jack Milton regretfully to himself, as he took charge of the money each night, allowing the Professor just enough for his daily expenses. "I might have settled down comfortably in this business and dropped the other, but it can't go on."

Perhaps one cause of this rapid success was that this knavish and foolish fraud of a Futurist had as firm a belief in the spirits, the cards, palmistry and the stars as his customers had, or pretended to have. He had before now paid his half-sovereigns to get his own future divulged by other professors in his own craft, and they in return came to him, now that he was successful, to see how he did it, and learn a trick, or out of good faith, and it was his bona fide air of faith and credence which helped to impose on others. A man must be in earnest even in roguery, to become a success. Cynics are never successful money-makers.

The new branch which had been added to the business, the selling of certain "tips" for the coming races and sports, caused the Professor a good deal of uneasiness and feeble remonstrance before he would consent to take it up, for he knew nothing about horses, cricket adepts, or other gambling transactions, and he said "the spurruts" were not always to be depended on in such mundane matters. "They are tricky and play larks at times, and then where will we be?—busted!"

But Jack was confident about the success of this branch. He knew all the tricks of the turf and would not admit of failure. He could tell when the spirits were likely to give false information, he said, and put them on the right track, "so plunge, my sage, philosopher and friend, for plunging is our game now."

The Swampers

The Professor yielded, as he generally had to do when the daring Jack commanded. The first race would be over in eight more days, and this was Friday of their second week in possession, and that must either "bust" them up, or else draw the whole colony swarming into their net. The Psychometrist trembled, but accepted the position, and braced up his courage by sundry glasses of brandy and soda, while the sporting victims came in and paid lavishly for the "certain tips," promising him the fate of the welsher if he proved a false prophet. Each night also, while the wearied Futurist drank himself into a blissful state of unconsciousness with the generous juices of old France, Jack sat smoking hard, and concocting fresh advertisements for the newspapers in the name of "Mortikali the Great." Florid and humorous compositions, regardless of expense, these were of Jack's, which filled whole columns, and delighted both the readers and proprietors of the different papers, and the editors proved their gratitude by giving the Professor and his establishment constant pars. extra, and appreciative interviews.

"Won't all them advertisements swamp our profits, mate?" the Professor would feebly ask.

"Not a bit of it, our arrangement is to pay at the end of the month, as we do the furniture establishment, and we'll have lots of money by that time." "How did you manage it?"

"Easy enough; in these dull times people are only too pleased to give credit. I paid our landlord a month in advance, and got him down to the Marble Hall to speak about it and my bank account which I showed him. Free drinks at the same Marble den of Tattersall's and the 'Australian,' with a little discreet bounce, fluency of gab and display of jewellery, drew the blinders over the eyes of the Press. They can only see the road I lead them into now. Do you savy, old sage and psychometrist, eh?" "You're a big man, Jack, and ought to die a millionaire." "I ought, and I hope to live one also."

A short time afterwards, as soon as the Professor had found his customary couch on the carpet, Jack Milton, attired in his white wig and blue spectacles, took his usual prowl round the newspaper offices, handing in his copy, and shouting drinks; afterwards visiting the fashionable places of resort and paying his money like a man, amongst both dudes and capitalists; then, on his way back, he dropped a letter into a post pillar for Mr. Arthur Chester, solicitor.

On his return he put on an old suit and woke up the strong-armed Barney, and went with him for an hour or two of real hard labour in the cellar, for when they came from those underground regions, they were covered with dirt and sweating profusely, yet both appeared satisfied.

"That job's ready at last, Barney, my boy, and to-morrow night we'll all have to lend a hand."

"It'll be as clean a job as I ever was in, captain; when you take a thing in hand you does it neatly."

Jack smiled at the compliment from his henchman, and after a drink of brandy and soda, they both went like brothers into the bath-room, and, after a good wash, for the first time during those past six days sought their beds before daylight.

On Saturday forenoon Jack paid an early visit to the bank next door, paying in a good number of sovereigns, and enjoying a pleasant half hour's chat with the genial manager in his private den. The letter which Mr. Chester received ran as follows:

"Tell Rosa and her people that I have landed in Melbourne, and will be home on Sunday night.

"I shall also be at your house very early on Sunday morning, with the treasure I spoke about; leave your back yard and stable doors open for me, so that I needn't disturb the neighbours getting in, and be prepared for me.

"Jack."

The Swampers

"We shall all be prepared for you, Mr. Jack," murmured Mr. Chester, with a sinister smile, as he read and destroyed this interesting epistle.

The Swampers

Chapter IV. Treasure Trove.

ONE o'clock Sunday morning, and four resolute men are assembled in the dining-room discussing steaks underdone and strong tea, for they are different from the Professor, who lies in a hoggish state of stupor beneath them. They have much to do to-night that will make or mar them, and they require no wines nor spirits to brace their courage up to the sticking point for daring robbery, or cold-blooded murder. They are colonial born and the grandsons of convicts, inured to the sport of hunting from their earliest years, and astute as savages on the war-path; besides, they would rather gain their livelihood in this way, with its deadly risks, than live by any other means. They cannot help themselves, they are wild beasts, with a coating of craft and cunning, bred from convict fathers and mothers, and gifted with only the one ambition, to excel in this business.

There is not one of them who has not been state-school trained, and educated as highly as the standards can make them. They can all spell fairly, and can write with a flowing hand. They don't make any mistakes in grammar, they know their geography and some have even advanced in Euclid, but they are one and all hunters and sons of sportsmen. They like the excitements of the chase, and they will have it, even at the risk of their necks. Their present sports are a pawn-broker's shop and a colonial bank that has not yet failed.

Jack Milton is the only one amongst them who has no convict antecedents. He had become a master criminal, as Cromwell became a soldier, through the force of circumstances, but now he dominated them. They wanted fresh blood and a leader, for although they were wicked enough and false enough, yet the creative and inventive genius seemed to be destroyed. New South Wales seems always to want a leader, yet never to find one who does not swindle the country. There are no patriots amongst them. They cannot hit upon patriots, simply for the reason that patriots come plainly and simply costumed and without ostentation, whereas they want a flourish of trumpets, as the ancient Jews did when they looked towards a Messiah. Perhaps also it is the warmth or some other degenerating quality in the atmosphere that may be the cause of this deplorable decadence, but although the children of the second and third generation are wonderfully sharp, false, and crafty, they have not the quality to grasp greatness of soul, nor that grandeur of simplicity which stamps the hero. They can appreciate the smartness of a swindler after they are swindled, and indeed they seem to admire this sharpness, but they cannot comprehend an honest man. Jack Milton was a big fellow amongst them, he could plan and execute grand coups, and he had, what they could not exactly comprehend, a staunch interest in his friends, therefore they appreciated his talents to plot out schemes, and get them out of the scrapes, and they instinctively bent to the principle which they could not understand, his good faith. Each man of that small gang would have sold Jack Milton if it had been made worth his while, yet each man knew that he could trust Jack Milton to a pennyweight. It takes a lot of personality to persuade state-school trained savages to trust in anyone.

The women were there, the smart handmaids whom Jack had chosen. They were the keenest criminals in Sydney, who had managed to escape, for six full days, the supervision of the colonial detectives. The page boy was a young imp who had served him on former occasions, and who could be trusted as a setter. The cook and housemaid had discarded their petticoats and now appeared daring young, callous cornstalks, and sun-freckled demons who would pause at nothing.

"Girls," observed Jack when supper was finished, "you know your duty while we work. Cecil, my son, every three minutes, when you see the policeman approach, give us the hint, he passes and looks into the open pawnshop every three minutes, six minutes will do our business there if all goes well. The bank is guarded by a watchman, a housekeeper and a confidential clerk; a dog was also there an hour ago, but Barney has silenced him. I'll undertake to silence the watchman, the housekeeper and the clerk. Do you require any more grub or liquor?" "No, boss, we have had enough. We are ready."

The Swampers

"Come along then, get to your posts, Cecil and you girls: three quarters of an hour are all I need to do the whole business in, the biggest in my life."

"What about the Professor?" enquired Barney, looking down on that prostrate hero.

"Oh, he is all safe, I dosed his last glass of Burgundy," replied Jack. "Come on, boys, and brace yourselves up for work. The pawnshop first."

They all put crape masks over their features, by way of precaution, not that they expected to be seen, yet still it was best to be on the safe side.

Silently they followed one another downstairs and into the commodious cellars of the establishment, the Professor still sleeping the sleep of unconscious infancy, while the girls and the page boy crept outside. It was with some pride that Barney showed them the excavations he had made on the one side, from the cellar to the bank, and on the other from the cellar to the pawnshop. They had the game clear before them if they could escape the watchful gaze of the police on the one side and the inmates on the other. Jack and Barney were the mechanical engineers of the concern; they had bored the hole, and in a few seconds made the trap door to admit them to the premises of the pawnbroker, then they were all through and in the full glare of the gas light, and the open windows to whoever passed, for the pawnbroker had no shutters.

Jack and Barney waited a second and then they rushed forward, pulling down and piling up boxes and packages between them and the windows. In two minutes exactly, the barricades were raised in a natural fashion, and they could lie panting behind, while the policeman made his usual survey.

The next portion of the work was easy as far as detection went, although requiring immense presence of mind and personal strength.

The Swampers

Three great safes were standing by the walls filled with valuables and money; but Jack Milton had his plans arranged beforehand, therefore, getting all the clothing and soft pledges he could from the shelves, he pitched them on the floor and then, with their crow-bars and levers they overturned the safes, and rolling them one after the other, shot them down into their excavated shaft, where they could break them open and examine them at their leisure. It took the four burglars nine minutes to remove these iron safes, that would have taken expert workmen a couple of hours, such is the effect of sport or excitement on the spirits and muscles of men. The other business was simple after this exploit, to dart to the till and rifle it between the visits of the police and to take what else was of value, leaving the show-cases untouched in the windows. In fifteen minutes from the time they had entered the pawnbroker's premises, the deed was completed and the pledges were their property.

Jack Milton left Barney and the other two men to break open the safes in the cellars while he penetrated the bank.

It was not difficult to enter, for he had undermined the place and silenced the watchdog. He also knew where the confidential clerk and housekeeper slept, and where he was likely to find the watchman.

One of the young men who had acted as a servant went with him, and together they stole upon the watchman, who was fortunately nodding by his table in an ante-room, a chloroform-saturated handkerchief soon settled him, and then they proceeded upstairs.

Fate had gone well with Jack Milton up to now. The housekeeper was easily managed, for she was asleep when they entered her bedroom, so that she never knew what caused her to sink into a deeper and more peaceful slumber, but with the confidential clerk it was otherwise.

A toothache had kept him awake that Sunday morning, so that, as the crape-masked burglars entered the room, he leapt from his bed and confronted them with a loud cry. Then it was all over for the confidential clerk, for without a pause Jack rushed upon him and pinning him up against the wall, gave him the garrotter-grip, one grasp first on the shoulder and the elbow driven with sudden and savage force against the larynx, silencing his voice and breaking the apple. With a gurgling sound the poor man sank to the ground and all was quiet. Jack Milton was a murderer.

He looked at his victim for a second with horror in his eyes, then with a heavy groan he dragged his accomplice away and made towards the loot. It would be time enough to think of his crime afterwards, at present his blood was fired up for the sport.

* * * * *

The dying cry of the clerk had not reached the policeman outside, and all the streets were peaceful on this Sabbath morning. Only Jack Milton knew that one life had been sacrificed on this raid, and he kept that secret to himself, so as not to disturb the unholy glee of his confederates over their winnings.

It has been a rich loot, all in all, with the pawnbroker's pledges and the bank hoardings, and he may now retire and exist in love and comfort on his lion's share of the proceeds. He is a wealthy man now, with what he has made to-night and what he had before. But that poor confidential clerk's death has to be avenged.

It does not take long to win a battle, kill a stag, or break into a bank; by three o'clock in the morning the confederates had divided their loot and made all their arrangements to part company. Jack Milton has his share, all in coins, jewels, and ingots, in his dogcart ready to drive off, and the others are satisfied with theirs.

A boat at the wharf waits to take them off to a ship ready to sail, and a couple of cabs, already arranged for, hang about a side street. They are taking a parting cup, and Jack stands amongst them silently, and thinking of that dead clerk, whom the others know nothing about yet. The clerk who will hang him, if he is not careful. "Well, mates, you are satisfied, I hope?" says Jack, quietly.

"Thoroughly, boss. You have carried out the contract like a man. We may now leave old Sydney for a spell, but won't there be a blooming racket on Monday morning?"

"I expect there will be, but you'll be out of it, and I can cover my tracks. Mates, I have been a good pal to you, have I not?" "The best going!"

"Then do me a favour. Take this drunken sot, the Professor, with you, and land him somewhere, for it won't do to leave him here."

"You are right, mate, he might split on us," said Barney. "We'll land him in America, where he is sure to prosper in that business of his." "That will do, Barney, take him with you, and here, give him these five hundred quids. We couldn't have done without him, and it's only right we should look after a chum."

"Particularly if he is dangerous, as this one happens to be; here, boys, hoist the carcase along with the property."

They raised the intoxicated and drugged Psychometrist and dragged him off to the cabs at the corner along with the loot, while Jack watched them going with an abstracted air.

Half an hour afterwards the Psychometric establishment was minus servants, attendants and Professor, then Jack turned with a heavy sigh, and led the pony, with the laden dog-cart, into the street.

He locked up the back-yard gate and no one checked his course as he went along. The policeman at the corner touched his hat to him when he passed by. He thought nothing of the eccentric movements of the white-haired partner of the Fashionable Fortune-teller, for he had become used to his ways; often had that pony taken an early morning exercise during the past week.

As he drove along he looked at the stars and tried to console himself with the reflection that no one could foretell what might happen in a campaign. Warriors go out to battle and kill for their country, and no one thinks of blaming them.

A life had been taken that night accidentally. On Monday morning there would be wild excitement, and a big reward for the murderer, but he would be with his faithful and lovely Rosa then, with all his traces covered and an assured future before him; that surely was worth the candle he had burnt, the risks he had run.

Four o'clock and he was at Mr. Chester's house, the bachelor's establishment which this astute lawyer kept.

Jack Milton knew very well that the housekeeper would have a holiday on this morning, therefore he felt safe as he led his horse and trap inside the back gate, and when he had shut that, he knocked at the kitchen door softly. A moment, and then the door opened gently and a voice asked: "Who is there?" "Jack, with some baggage." "Bring it inside."

Mr. Chester did not help the housebreaker with his burden, and the packages were lifted from the dog-cart and carried indoors in the dark; then, when the door was closed and fastened, Mr. Chester struck a light and looked at his visitor with a scrutinizing gaze. "What is this you have brought in these bags?"

"Fifty thousand pounds in gold," replied Jack Milton quietly. "Put them away for me and invest them."

"All right, leave them there for the present."

"Have you told Rosa I'll be home to-night?"

"Yes, she expects you," replied the lawyer.

"Good, I'll go now."

"Good morning."

The Swampers

"Good morning."

They parted with these words and Jack led his pony and empty dog-cart out of the gate, which the lawyer closed and barred after him. After which he drove away into the country at a furious pace.

The Swampers

Chapter V. Jack Milton at Home.

THEY had a small tea-party at Trumpet Tree Cottage on the Sunday night when Jack Milton came back after his two years' absence.

It is only right and proper for a man to apprise his wife and friends of his home-coming, whether he has been absent for a short or long period—particularly if for a long period.

Surprises are seldom pleasant either to the receiver or the one who gives them; some men in Jack's position might have felt inclined to play the romantic and time-honoured joke of entering the Cottage suddenly and disguised in rags, just to see how darling Rosa and her parents would receive him. Jack could hardly do this, even if he had been disposed, since he had entrusted a considerable sum of money to Rosa's cousin before he went away. He was not disposed however to this sort of romance. He had always liked to pose as a rich man; he liked also to be entertained and made much of by his friends, and did not care how much he spent to gain this end.

He loved his wife Rosa with all the reasonless intensity of his lawless nature, and to have doubted her so far as to have tested her truth was beyond his strength. She had said she loved him, and she had married him, which seemed proof sufficient for his vanity and his desires. She seemed delighted with his presence. Therefore, like a good husband, he took it for granted that she mourned his absence as good wives ought to do. The lamps were lighted and all the stars were out when he drove up to the front gate, not this time in the dog-cart, or with his white wig on, but in a cab, with portmanteau and bag beside him, as if he had just come from a journey.

Rosa was on the look-out for his arrival, and ran eagerly from the verandah up the little walk to the gate, and here she flung herself into his arms, regardless of the grinning driver. "At last, you old darling Jack."

The Swampers

"At last, my fairy," replied her husband fondly, as he clasped her to his heart; and then they went indoors like true lovers.

Rosa Milton lived with her father and mother, or it would be more correct to say, since it was the money of Jack which had furnished and kept the home going, that the parents of Rosa lived with her.

Her father had been a draper's book-keeper, before his daughter's marriage enabled him to throw up his occupation and retire upon the bounty of his flash son-in-law. This he had promptly done, for few cornstalks of the second generation care for working if they can get out of it. The Sydney climate is too enervating for much exertion, and the example of other husbands and fathers is too infectious to be long resisted. It is almost the universal rule now for the women to keep their men, and this is what most of these young colonials enter the holy state of matrimony for.

The sire of Rosa was a genial, old, and gentlemanly loafer for all that, and looked quite a respectable father, as he sat in his arm-chair, with the Sunday papers before him, his spectacles on his well-shaped nose, and his silver-grey beard floating over his black vest. Mrs. Mulligan, his good lady, also bore out the appearance of a highly respectable matron as she sat beside the tea-pot and dishes, and, altogether, there was a decided air of home-like comfort about the lamp-lighted and well-furnished front parlour.

Rosa was like the generality of her Sydney sisters, creamy-complexioned, with features almost classic in their regularity, strongly defined eyebrows and clear, grey-blue eyes, with a plentiful supply of golden-brown hair. She appeared small alongside of her tall husband, yet she was above the average height of women, and possessed a figure which for symmetry would have won the approval of the most exacting lover of the beautiful. Clearly the road to Jack's heart had been by the eye.

They were a magnificent couple, and most people would have agreed that they were well matched. Jack with his strong, dark face, square jaw and powerful frame, and Rosa with the seductive wiles and graces of a Helen. A disciple of Lavater might have found characteristics in both these attractive faces to make him pause and ponder, as indeed he could have done in the other faces gathered round this festive board, Mr. and Mrs. Mulligan and Mr. Arthur Chester. But Cupid's glamour had blinded Jack, and what the others thought did not interfere with the warmth of their welcome to the new arrival.

The viands were lavish and well enough cooked, for most colonial women are adepts at home work. A couple of fowls, with a ham, and a prime joint of beef, flanked by roasted Kiameres, pumpkins mashed, and mounds of tempting tea-cakes. Mr. Chester carved the fowls and ham, while the gentlemanly father cut the joint, and the mother poured out the tea, thus leaving Jack and Rosa with nothing to do except eat, drink, and look tenderly at each other.

After tea was cleared away, at Jack's request, Rosa and her cousin went to the piano and sang duets. Jack was fond of singing, though he could not sing himself, and Rosa had a clear, if somewhat metallic voice; she did not play, but Arthur Chester managed to accompany her and himself with a creditable "vamp," therefore that part of the evening passed away very well.

Then, when the whisky decanter had been put upon the table and pipes were lighted, Jack began to tell his adventures of the past two years, in the South Seas, and in this he proved himself a perfect master of fiction. Othello could not have done better, nor could Desdemona have listened with more rapt admiration and devotion than did Rosa as she sat on a low stool at his feet, her pretty teagown falling in graceful folds about her, and her white arms bare to the elbows as the wide sleeves dropped back. She rested these white and shapely arms on his knee, with her chin on her ring-covered hands, and those steadfast, clear, blue-grey orbs fixed on his black eyes. Occasionally, however, she shifted her head slightly to glance with a kind of wonder at her attentive parents, or the quietly observant cousin. When she glanced at Arthur Chester and caught his eye, a slight flush tinted her creamy cheeks, and a tiny curl lifted her upper lip, revealing her white teeth and the redness of her full and moist

The Swampers

lower lip. At these times only a gleam shot between the eyes of the two cousins, and then she turned her face once more with touching admiration towards the fertile-minded Jack.

"I shall call round to-morrow evening after office hours and have a business talk with you, Milton," said the lawyer as he rose to his feet about nine o'clock and prepared to take his departure.

"Do," answered Jack, also getting up, "I intend to spend to-morrow at home and take it easy."

"I expect you'll be interested in the newspapers, after being so long without them."

"Yes, I'll put in my time that way—you get the papers, I suppose, Mr. Mulligan?"

"Yes, the Herald. I'll bring it up to your bedroom," replied the father-in-law.

Rosa now proposed, as the night was warm, that they should see her cousin a little way towards his house, and as Mr. and Mrs. Mulligan were not inclined for the exercise, the three young people went out together, Rosa in the centre, with a hand through the arms next to her of each companion. In this fashion they went, linked together, into the night.

* * * * *

Jack Milton did not venture out of doors the next day, but Rosa like a dutiful wife brought him all the newspapers. The Town and Country, the Australasian, the Guillotine, and the dailies, to amuse himself with, while she went about her household duties. Rosa liked to work in the kitchen with her mother and the servant, and had some favourite dishes to cook for Jack, therefore he had to yield, and do without more than a flying visit now and again from her, and a fugitive kiss, while he helped his father-in-law to "loaf."

The Swampers

The papers interested both men very greatly, for they were filled with the account of the great robberies which had been discovered on Sunday morning. Jack groaned inwardly as he read about the dead body of the confidential clerk being discovered. It was the first man's taking-off which could be laid to his charge, and it made him feel uncomfortable, even although he tried to persuade himself that it was an accident. He had, however, great command over his features and feelings, and read the account quite calmly out to his wife and his father-in-law.

Mr. Mulligan listened with the interest such a sensation raises in one, while Rosa, with a slight shiver of horror, hurriedly left the room for a moment, and then as quickly returned.

"I expect there will be a big reward offered for the murderer, Jack," she said, fixing her clear blue-grey eyes on him.

"I expect so, little woman," replied Jack with his glance still on the paper.

Mr. Chester came after the lamps were lit, with the evening papers in his pocket. "Have you seen the account of that big robbery and murder in George Street?" he asked as he entered.

"Yes," replied Jack and Rosa together, "any more about it?"

"The Bank people have offered a reward of five hundred pounds for any information that may lead to the capture of the principals."

As he spoke he turned for a moment from Jack and cast a straight glance at Rosa, who looked down at the table-cloth and began to smooth it out.

"The police head-quarters will receive the information and pay the reward," continued Mr. Chester, and then they all sat down to the usual high, or dinner, tea, and began talking about other topics. After tea Rosa said to her husband:

The Swampers

"I am going out to-night, dear, to see a girl friend in town, Mrs. Grey, you remember; and as Arthur has come to discuss business with you, I'll leave you alone for an hour or so. I won't be late, darling; will you stay till I come back, Arthur?"

"No, Rosa, I must be going soon, as I have a host of letters to get through to-night."

He did not look at her this time, but she looked at him, a lingering look, in which blended a little con tempt with some other emotion.

"Very well, I shall say good night. Now I'll leave you gentlemen alone to discuss business. Depend upon me, dear Jack, I'll not be late."

She rose and left them with these words, Jack smiling fondly on her as she quitted the room, then the two men sat down squarely to business, for Mr. and Mrs. Mulligan had gone early to their own apartments.

When the business was gone through Mr. Chester rose to leave.

"This is a serious affair, this murder as well as robbery, isn't it, Milton?" "Yes, very serious, and to be regretted," replied Jack.

"I can depend on your promise made to me, I suppose?"

"Yes, no one shall ever say that Jack Milton did not keep his promise."

"Good! and good-night."

After Chester had departed and until Rosa returned, Jack experienced a singular fit of dejection. Everything had gone right with his schemes. The horse and dog-cart were over the cliffs and his wig and spectacles and clothes were destroyed. He had left no traces that he could think about. His companions were clear away, for they had arranged that beforehand, and yet the spirit of that confidential clerk seemed to be haunting him.

He went to the sideboard and took as many whiskies as he dared to take, to brace up his courage, and give him some of his lost pluck. He dare not take much drink, in case he might talk and get reckless. He looked at his revolver and found that in good order, and then, before he got quite too desperate with himself, darling Rosa came back, beautiful and tender.

His wife took him straight away to bed and said she would shut up the place after she had seen him comfortable; she even went the length of going to the kitchen and brewing him a glass of whisky hot, as a night-cap, but although he felt he had taken enough, he did not like to refuse the dear girl, therefore he made some excuse to get her out of the room long enough to enable him to throw the stuff out of the open window, and pretend he had taken it.

She laid her creamy soft cheek against his for a moment when she had brought him what he wanted, and gently kissing him on the lips, said:

"Now, dearest, let me go and see that all is safe in the house, and then I'll come to bed."

She left him with these loving words, and stole gently down the stairs in her stockings, taking the lamp with her and leaving him in darkness.

For a moment he lay thinking fondly about her and planning out the future, then his acute and trained ears heard sounds outside, which banished sleep and woke up his faculties.

He stole softly to the open window and peered out, to see forms of men surrounding the house. He knew what that meant to him.

The Swampers

Down the stairs he crept like a phantom, with his revolver in his hand. Whispering voices in the dining parlour lured him on, and he turned in that direction and listened by the open door.

"You must be patient yet a little while, for he is a strong man, but in a few minutes he must be asleep, for I have given him a strong dose of chloral." This was the voice of his darling Rosa, and another replied:

"I'll wait, missis; hadn't you better go and stay beside him till he drops over?" "Yes, I'll go and see him now." He did not wait for the lovely traitress to come out of the parlour, the revulsion was too great for his wild, untrained and passionate nature. Without a pause, he planted the revolver to his brow and pulled the trigger.

The Swampers

Chapter VI. Jack Milton's Escape.

"CALL no man happy until he is dead," said Solon, that wise man of Salamis.

There is an instinct of insatiable discontent planted in the heart of every human being, which ever urges us towards the consummation of our desires, and this only more or less strong in its attraction than the horror of death in its repelling powers, according to the lives we live and the passions we indulge in.

Those who, like Socrates, or such saints as Thomas à Kempis, accustom themselves to self-denial, have fewer promptings towards suicide and less horror of death. Their unambitious and eventless lives satisfy their modest cravings. They have learnt to find enjoyment in the passing phases of the seasons, and, living outside their passions, they are drawn into the all-satisfying heart of Nature and exist for the moment that is with them. This is the nearest approach to happiness on the earth side of death, yet even that is not complete. Death is the only panacea for humanity.

As Hans Andersen says in one of his fairy tales, each human being hides under his cloak a beast of some kind. It may be a ruthless tiger, a poisonous snake or scorpion, a fox, or even only a timid hare, or peacock. I fancy, however, that most of us hide more than one beast under our jerkins, indeed that we are animated Noah's Arks, and while we parade the lambs and doves on our upper decks, the swine, snakes and other wild animals are all there under the hatches, only waiting their opportunity to show themselves.

The beasts that Jack Milton had encouraged mostly were of the scorpion and prey-like species. It had been his occupation to prey upon Society for many years, and gratify the passion of the moment without reflection. Yet the one passion, which, if it did not ennoble him very much, had been the nearest approach to devotion and simplicity that he could feel, had been his affection for this female Judas.

The Swampers

As with many criminals, who do not recognise the laws made by Society or Morality, fidelity to his own kind was the one point of honour which chained his wild and lawless nature. He could not "peach upon a pal," no matter what he suffered in consequence, so long as that pal acted right towards him, yet if the "pal" turned traitor, then his next natural craving was for revenge.

His wife Rosa had been more to him than all the pals in the world, for up to the last few seconds of time his trust in her love had been infinite. Had any other tongue told him that she was false, he would have killed the traducer and brushed the slander aside like a fly. He was not an Othello in his love, possibly because having youth and strength as well as full consciousness of his own powers of pleasing, he could not have believed that the woman lived, who was so loved, that could resist responding.

But the only tongue which could shatter his faith had spoken, and it had the paralysing effect of a lightning stroke.

When roused, he was like a tiger in his rapidity; he only meditated when he was planning out a robbery or an escape from prison, and he acted now on the scorpion's instinct of despair.

Six almost noiseless clicks, almost like one sound, broke the silence as the betrayed man sent the chambers of his revolver spinning round, and in that second of time his heart stood still and his mind was a blank. The weapon was in such perfect condition and so finely made, that the clicks were no louder than the ticks of a watch, so that only he could hear them.

Then, as he realized that the cartridges had been extracted by the traitress, the temptation for self-destruction passed like a flash, and the animal instinct of life preservation woke and braced him up. He even laughed silently and grimly as he thought almost admiringly of the adroitness and quickness Rosa had displayed in emptying the revolver. "What a pickpocket the jade would make with a little training," was the quaint fancy that crossed his mind, as he clutched his revolver by the barrel and crept close to the wall, for he had heard the rustle of her dress as she moved to the door, leaving the detective inside.

Five minutes before, that quaint fancy would have seemed sacrilege in the mind of this robber and murderer, if applied to his wife, but now it was the most appropriate idea he could think of respecting her. She was still beautiful and had proved her cleverness, but never again would she be a thing to respect and adore. If a bullet had dashed out his brains, his love could not have been more surely slain than it was at this moment of recovered life. He was now the trapped wild beast, with all his craft and resolution in full force.

He felt her glide past him as he crouched by the wall of the lobby leading to the kitchen, she touching the other side of the wall to guide herself towards the staircase. He heard her soft breathing as he held his own, and he grinned again, thinking how easily he could have strangled her at that moment, but for the man inside that parlour, with the necessity that he should himself escape. No, not for these cogent reasons only would he let her go by in safety. A dull pain crushed on his heart and made him pity her for what she had lost. He would not hurt her for her perfidy. He would only quit her for ever, but he must escape and punish her that way. She reached the top step before he moved, then noiselessly and rapidly he glided through the kitchen into the wash-house at the rear, where there was a door leading to the yard, and a window on the shingle roof. The door was barred, but the window had been left open, and it was large enough for him to get through.

He planned it all as he ran along, with the lightness of a cat, for he was a man of as rapid mind as he was swift of action.

The police were in the yard, and Rosa would give the alarm in another moment; then lamps and pistols would flash out simultaneously and he would be seen.

In the yard grew a large almond tree, that spread its branches over the shed roof and overlooked the narrow lane which divided them from their neighbour's back yard. In his mind's eye he saw Rosa pause at the bedroom door to recover herself before entering, for she wasn't yet hardened enough to be able to face her victim without some little preparation.

She would listen for a little time to hear if he slept, to still the beatings of her excited heart, and to call up to her pretty face that false and tender smile, and he laughed again bitterly as he calculated his chances.

With his soft touch he cleared away the pans from the top of the wash-boiler, then gripping up a billet of wood, with a light spring on the boiler, he was through the window and on to the thickest limb of the almond tree, with a thick covering of leaves between him and the watchers below.

He had studied that almond tree during the day-time as a mode of escape, for he never neglected any details in his surroundings, wherever he was. A housebreaker of his experience and acumen, resembles a great general, who regards every landscape as a probable battlefield and each corner or building as a spot to be utilized for his own particular business of war.

Jack Milton had now all his wits about him and was too cool to spoil his chances by undue haste. A snake could not have glided along that branch more noiselessly than he did, or with less disturbance of the leaves and twigs. He felt each inch of the way and moved as if he had the whole night before him, while under him the policemen stood watching the lighted bedroom and waiting on the signal, all the while his ears were also on the alert for that signal.

He reached the trunk and swung himself up to another thick limb which led from it and rested on the high fence. He could not see those below, but in front of him, that portion of the fence and branch came within the radius of light from the bedroom window, while, as the leaves grew thinly here, he knew he could be seen if any one chanced to be looking in that direction.

The Swampers

This was the point of danger, yet he got just behind the verge of light, and then raising himself, he stood clearing the leaves in front of him, while he waited to take the leap. If his wife had been his best friend, he could not have waited more anxiously on her coming cry of alarm. He calculated exactly how she would act when she found the room empty; she would rush to the open window with a shriek, and the police would look in that direction in their first surprise, and that would be his chance to leap along the line of light, then if he managed to get hold of the branch beyond without attracting notice, he could laugh at them for the time.

He seemed to see her turning the handle, with that false smile on her lips, then — —

Yes, there was the expected scream sent out to the night from the window above, with a sudden darkening of the light on the branch which he knew to be the shadow of her figure, and that made his path much easier.

He had been prepared to leap, but he changed his intention and walked easily along the branch to the fence, then over that again to the fence on the other side of the lane, after which he looked back before taking the drop.

"What a racket they are making, the stupid owls, waking all the dogs in the neighbourhood," he muttered, as he saw the flashing of the lanterns on every side but the one where he was. He saw the darkened form of his wife, with the detective beside her looking out, while their voices rose in a loud chorus. With a muttered curse he dropped quietly into his neighbour's yard, still grasping that heavy billet of wood.

A large dog rushed at him barking loudly, and letting him know by the sound where to strike. Waiting till it was almost on him he brought down the billet with his full force, and that antagonist was settled for the time.

The Swampers

Across the yard he sprang, through the little gate that led to the front garden and verandah; the people here were as yet asleep; so that he had no trouble in getting to the other side, which was only protected by a low fence, yet covered by tendrils and bushes. When he crossed this he was a couple of lanes from his own house with the road clear as yet in front of him.

The lane he was now in led to two different streets and he paused for a moment to think which was best for him to take, then, having decided, he walked quietly away, leaving the din behind him.

He was at present an object of suspicion if any one had seen him, for he was hatless, and clad only in his nightshirt and trousers, these he had hurriedly drawn on before leaving the bedroom. Yet that could not be helped, the one thought that now engrossed him was where he was to turn to find shelter.

Mr. Chester—yes, yet if Rosa was false her cousin was likely in the plot also. No matter, courage had freed him so far, and courage must do the rest. He would walk to Chester's house and bluff him for what he wanted. It was a warm starlight night and the street he was in was deserted, so that he did not find much inconvenience walking along bare-foot and hatless. He moved swiftly along keeping his keen eyes about him so as to avoid chance policemen and inquisitive pedestrians. He was also examining the houses he passed, wondering if he could not do a little business and rehabilitate himself on the way, only that he did not wish to waste valuable time.

Chance, assisted by the god Bacchus, served him before he had got very far, for, as he was passing a gate he almost stumbled over a man who evidently had been overcome by the Sydney whisky, and now lay on the foot-path in that deep and dreamless slumber which even good whisky will produce when too freely indulged in.

This chance benefactor to the hunted man was well-dressed, and near enough his own size to serve his purpose. With the gentleness of an expert valet, Jack Milton drew the drunkard through the gate into the garden, finding him more comfortable quarters under some shrubs, and there he made his toilet, leaving the other as he had been himself, in shirt and trousers.

The boots were a little too large, and the soft felt hat a degree too small, but the coat and vest fitted him fairly well, the gold watch which he likewise borrowed served to show him the time at the first lamp-post he came to, and the loose change he found scattered about the different pockets came in handy.

"A regular boozer that," Jack muttered as he counted about ten shillings in threepenny bits, mixed with copper pieces, other silver and several gold coins. "He has been visiting many pubs on the way and will need the half-crown I left him, in the morning, I guess."

He looked at the watch and found that the time was ten minutes to one o'clock, also that the watch which gave him this information was a good one. "Fortune favours the bold—now for my noble Chester."

This little adventure raised his spirits wonderfully, for it seemed a prognostic of good fortune in the future, so that he walked along with a light heart, and in about half an hour afterwards reached his destination.

The Swampers

Chapter VII. The Interview.

MR. CHESTER had either a great deal of work to get through on this early morning, or else expecting tidings of some importance, he was sitting up to receive them, for the light still burned in his office when Jack reached the house.

Jack stood outside looking at the illumined blind, with folded arms and a sinister smile on his dark features; he guessed why Mr. Chester was not yet in bed.

"So, my friend, you expect to have me trapped in my sleep or perhaps kindly knocked on the head, while you and your precious cousin play the surprised innocents. Dead I could tell no tales, alone and a prisoner, yet believing in your good faith, I'd have gone to the scaffold in silence. Ay, so I would, had I fallen asleep and not known what I do, therefore you only did me justice, but now that the blinders are off I'll make you serve me, whether you like or not, you infernal hypocrite; you were my master yesterday with your accursed cant, but I'll be boss this morning."

He muttered these words bitterly, with savage hatred in his heart, then stepping forward resolutely, he tapped smartly on the lower pane. In a moment he heard the lawyer rise from his chair, and drawing the blind back he opened the window. "Who is it?"

"I, Jack Milton," answered the housebreaker harshly, as he sprang to the window and entered that way with a sudden leap and force that made Mr. Chester stagger back, then quickly closing the window and readjusting the blind so that no one could see them from the outside, he faced round, his revolver in his hand pointed at the confused and astonished lawyer. "Hands up, Chester! I know your little game right to the core." "What do you mean, Mr. Milton?"

"That I was to be sold to the traps last night, so that you and that artful jade, my wife, might enjoy my loot without me—don't deny it,

The Swampers

or I'll blow out your brains. I heard it all with my own ears." "I assure you — —"

"Hang your assurances, the time is past for words of that sort. Listen to mine instead, for I must be quick. I have managed to get out of that net, Trumpet Tree Cottage, and now you must help me to get safe out of Sydney, or I'll make a clean breast of it and give you away — damme if I'll be the only one to suffer in this business."

"What of your promises?" said the lawyer, who not yet understanding what Jack knew, thought to play on his generosity. "I don't keep promises made to traitors." "I did not betray you."

"Didn't you? — well, the woman whom I robbed and murdered for, did, and you hold the stakes. I want money enough to take me out of the country and shelter while you get me a disguise." "How much do you require?" asked the lawyer sullenly.

"Three hundred pounds in gold will be as much as I can carry until I reach a place of safety, then you can send me more. I won't be too hard on you nor require any strict account of your stewardship, and I think, now that you know my intentions, I can trust you for your own sake. The bargain between us now is faith for faith, you be my banker as I require coin. There, decide quickly, for the police may be here at any moment."

Mr. Chester stood gnawing his sandy moustache and looking very much like Brer Fox when he was caught; however, he now recovered himself, and pointing to a chair, he took one himself while he said:

"I don't suppose the police will be likely to come here after you unless they followed you."

"Neither do I, since I took due care not to be followed, yet they may come to report progress to you, eh?" Mr. Chester looked at his boots and shook his head a little sadly.

The Swampers

"Then it wasn't the traps you were expecting so early this morning? Was it Rosa?" His black eyes looked searchingly at the other's, who replied quickly, yet without looking up: "I was expecting no one. It was work kept me up so late. These briefs."

He waved his hand with the masonic ring upon it towards the table covered with papers, and resumed:

"Besides, I cannot understand, since you have told me nothing yet. I am sure my cousin—your wife, Rosa, could have no hand in the police surprising you; indeed, such a thing must have been a terrible shock to her, poor girl."

"Still harping on the affectionate and trusting wife fiction, Chester," said Jack weariedly. "Haven't I told you that I heard the poor girl bargaining for my life with the detective, Billy Jackson? She wanted the reward to put to her other stores, sweet innocent that she is. No, I forgot to tell you that she prepared a dose for me to send me off to sleep, and that she——did another thing, which made doubt out of the question."

He had almost mentioned the extraction of the cartridges from his revolver, when he remembered that Chester had likewise a weapon of the same sort in his possession—one that he had presented to him—and he thought he had better omit that piece of evidence of his wife's perfidy. "What else did she do, Milton?"

"Something I don't mean to tell you, Chester—at least, not now. Some other time perhaps I will. Well, have you decided to help Justice as represented by Law, and know what transportation, if not hanging, is like—or at the least have to give up that fortune you hold of mine, for of course you can't expect to keep that if you turn Queen's evidence—or do you decide to stick to the plunder, give me a small whack out of it and help me to get clear?"

"Of course I'll help you all I can, Milton, if you show me how. By this time I daresay the telegraph has been at work and all the ports closed. You cannot take ship from the colony, for every man going

The Swampers

away, unless he is well known, will be subject to the strictest scrutiny, so that no disguise will serve you. The trains likewise are impossible, for at every station the same scrutiny will take place; how then do you think to escape?"

"I'll tell you, Chester; first, because I cannot do it without your help, and second, because it is to your interest to get me out of this. I mean to ride overland to Westralia, and lose myself on the gold fields there."

"What! Go over that infernal track where so many have perished? Milton, my boy, plucky as you are, you'll never do it."

"Yet I mean to try. See here, Chester, I'll speak fair to you, although I believe you have been an accursed beast to me—there, don't protest. I gave Rosa up last night between eleven and twelve—she is no more to me now than the commonest street-walker, and I want nothing to do with her in future. I don't know what she is to you, and cuss me if I care, now that I have whistled her down the wind. In old times men risked their lives over a woman of this kind. I'm not that sort. I'm the product of the new Era." He grinned a ghastly grin and continued:

"I guess she'll have a divorce from Judge Jeffreys. He is a sympathetic cuss with grass widows of her description, and then you two will marry for the sake of the plunder, for you will be both too much skeared to let each other go in single harness, therefore you need not care much what comes of a coon like me. I'll go on the Wallaby track across the continent. If you hear no more of me, you'll know that my bones are bleaching on the plains. If I get across I shan't trouble you more than I can help, for, by the Lord! I don't like the scent of you, and, robber and murderer as I now am, I'd rather the crows picked my bones out yonder than know anything more of your family—I'll have a drain of your whisky all the same, though!"

He rose, and lifting the decanter, poured himself out a stiff glass, then, tossing it off, he returned quietly to his seat. "You can stay here till I get what you want," said the lawyer coldly.

The Swampers

"Three hundred quid in gold—a good, serviceable horse—a wig, and some other articles I may want to start with." "Yes, I'll get you these," said Mr. Chester, still stiffly.

"That is all I want; say, where are your cartridges, I have only what my weapon holds at present?" "You'll find them in that table drawer." "Thanks."

Jack went over to the drawer and found there not only the cartridges but the revolver of his host. "I'll borrow this weapon for to-day," he said quietly. "All right." At that moment a key was heard inserted in the front door.

As Mr. Chester heard the sound he started to his feet to go out, when Jack stopped him with a frightful contortion of his face.

"God Almighty! don't go from this room, or I shall be tempted to blow both your brains out. Be open with me now that I know so much—I'll not harm either of you. Let me get behind this screen and see the last of the farce."

He grinned like a devil, as he passed behind a Japanese screen, leaving his host standing in the centre of the room.

Another moment the door opened and Rosa darted inside. She was in a wild state of agitation, and without pausing she rushed forward, and flinging her arms round the lawyer's neck she kissed him loudly on the mouth before he could prevent her. "Ah, Arthur, darling, what are we to do? The villain has escaped."

Brer Fox Chester fell limply in his chair, while she, thinking that her news had overcome him, went on in a feminine torrent:

"Yes, my pet, it is all true. I gave him the dose you got for me, and saw him drink it. I removed the cartridges from his revolver as you directed—everything seemed right—yet he made his escape." "Good God!" gasped Chester. "Don't mention that name," said Jack Milton coming from his retreat. "He must have left you both long ago, and the Devil, our master, looks after his own." As Chester sank down Rosa had gone with him, still embracing him, but at the sight of her husband, she started up with a savage cry.

"What are you mooning there for, Arthur Chester? That revolver he holds is harmless—shoot him like the dog he is." Chester's head sank down on his breast helplessly while he moaned feebly: "He has got my weapon and my ammunition."

"Sit down, Rosa, and compose yourself; I like grit, and if you are not the woman I thought you were, at least you are consistent in your own way," said Jack Milton quietly as he came forward. "Don't mind me in the least. If you prefer his knee to the couch, then take it by all means, for I won't object. You settled that as far as I am concerned two hours ago—sit where you please and let us talk over our concerns."

The young woman rose with a scowl on her brows and sat on a chair; she was now facing Jack, yet she looked at him remorselessly and defiantly.

"Well, Jack Milton, you know the truth at last, and I don't care what more you know." Jack shrugged his shoulders as he replied gently:

"There's no more for me to know, Rosa. I made a mistake, or you did, so what is the good of talking about that? It is past now, and I am not such a cur as to cry over spilt milk. The only thing now to consider is what is best for us three. Chester there will explain to you my proposition. I fancy it will be more to your interest than if you gave me away to the hangman."

Jack went once more over to the spirit decanter and helped himself to another glass, while Rosa looked at Chester as he lay limply in his arm-chair. It was one of these positions where the cuckold comes out the best.

The Swampers

A pause ensued while Jack lifted the glass to his lips and drank, then suddenly, before he had quite finished, he pitched the glass from him with disgust.

"Oh, dash it, Chester, take her out of this and explain matters to her outside. You know my ultimatum. Sell me if you like, but for pity's sake leave me to myself now."

Arthur Chester rose to his feet, and giving his cousin his arm led her from the room, leaving the housebreaker behind.

The Swampers

Chapter VIII. Cousins.

"GOODNESS gracious, Arthur, why couldn't you have given me a hint that the monster was with you?" asked Rosa angrily, when they reached the street, "and not let me blurt everything out like that?"

She was not ashamed of herself, such women seldom are when discovered. The sneakish sensation gets over the men now and again, when they meditate upon their actions, or a nasty wind blows the flaps of their cloaks aside, for they know the animal they are carrying. The woman is different, however, for she makes a pet of her beast and decks it up with so many ribbons, that she is rather glad when her mantle falls off and reveals the ape she is carrying. To her it always looks a beauty and well worth the carrying.

She does not like her mantle to be rudely plucked away from her shoulders, however—rudeness always wounds her feelings. Neither does she like to dwell upon the idea that it was through her own clumsiness and want of tact that she has lost her cloak. This makes her angry, and when a woman is enraged she has little enough to do with conscience or self-reproach, some one else has to bear the blame of that fault.

As this wretched pair left the study while Jack Milton watched them depart, his glittering black eyes fixed upon them, and Chester's loaded revolver held loosely in the hand that lay passively on the legal documents, the lawyer felt his position keenly. There was no nobility or assertion of manhood in his walk, but with bent back and weak legs he led out his guilty partner, as spiritless and dejected a cur as one could have met anywhere. Deceit and falsehood, when discovered, generally have this effect even upon the most degraded of men. Add to this that he felt like a mouse creeping out of the den of an infuriated lion, who seems all the more dangerous because he crouches quietly, and the reader may somewhat realize the sensations of Arthur Chester. Until he had closed the door of that study the nerves of his back had been quivering with the anticipation of a bullet being sent after him, and that feeling is not nerve-bracing as a rule.

Rosa Milton, however, had none of these sensations, as she had no consciousness of shame. Her husband had always been gentle and indulgent to her whims, therefore she had learnt to despise him as a "softy." That he had yielded his claims so quietly did not at all astonish her, yet somehow it angered her, for it stung her vanity and she was now writhing under this seeming lack of appreciation. Jack had never been so much an object of interest to her as he was at this moment of renunciation.

"I did my best to stop you, Rosa," replied her cousin dejectedly. "But it was no use, you were in on me like a tornado, and the complete tale exposed with a brevity and graphic force worthy of that Scottish poet, Robert Burns. The embrace would have done it to the watching eyes without words, knowing what he did—in fact the latch-key was revelation enough without even the greeting that followed, but when those terse sentences fell upon my ears, I morally and physically collapsed. The play was over with a bang. Only one thing surprised, while it robbed me of the few remaining atoms of brains that I had left, knowing Jack Milton as I do—and as you don't, sweet cousin."
"What was that?"

"That we two are walking along the street this balmy early morning instead of weltering in our mutual gore on the floor of my study."
"He would never have dared to do that, surely?"

"It isn't too flattering to either of us that he hasn't done so," replied her companion quietly. "However, here we both are, safe and sound, with our fiasco on our hands, and the present master of the position to manage." "What do you mean?"

"Only that we shall have to do our best to put the detectives off the scent and get Jack safely away. We cannot afford to let him be caught now, for he has sworn that he will speak up and give me away, if he is taken, and you know what that spells?"

The Swampers

"The mean, spiteful wretch," cried inconsistent Rosa savagely. "As if it could matter to him after he was hanged who had the money."

"That is just it, Rosa; and as he considers that he is no longer bound to provide for us, he makes this condition—his liberty or the giving up of his savings." "But haven't you secured them where they cannot be touched?"

"That is impossible if he tells his story. We shall both be as poor as we were before he crossed our lives, and worse, for if we escape transportation, I shall be degraded and under suspicion all the rest of my life, while you will be lost utterly. No, he must get away, or we are both ruined beyond redemption." "But Arthur, what of us, if he gets away?"

"Oh, he is reasonable enough. He only wants three hundred pounds for the present, and meditates taking the overland journey to Westralia, and that ought to finish him as surely as the hangman could do. As the wife of a condemned outlaw, you'll get a divorce easily enough, and a lot of sympathy besides, as no one will suspect that you know anything about his plunder, then we can marry and clear out of the Colonies, so that even if he reaches his destination, which isn't at all likely, he can never trace us out." "But the reward for his capture?" "You'll have to lose that five hundred, since he was not caught."

"Eight hundred pounds clear lost. Ah, that is too bad. Could you not poison or shoot him, and then deliver up his body?"

They were passing a lamp-post as Rosa made this suggestion, and she looked up in his face with the anxious expression of a prudent wife who wanted to avert a business loss to her husband. Her pretty features were puckered with this anxiety, and her blue eyes looked troubled as she peered into those of her cousin.

Arthur Chester, like Rosa, belonged to the fourth generation of cornstalks—those weeds who have grown up with white corpuscles in their blood, instead of red; lustful, yet lacking stamina; malignant, and sceptical of all that tends to raise humanity; devoted to pleasure, and regardless of the responsibilities of morality. Intrigue and wickedness were to them the necessities of existence. Jibing mockery and cold-blooded jests at all which the older generations reverenced were the ordinary subjects of their conversation. Such papers as the Guillotine served them as the springs from which they drew their wit; crude, indecent and viperish, without a spark of true humour or kindly instinct.

They were both on a slightly more elevated stratum than the hyena Larrikin, but their appetites and instincts were no better.

It has been stated that the absinthe drinking in France is reducing the coming race to the condition of beastdom. The coming race of cornstalks as represented in Sydney do not drink absinthe. They are even a fairly temperate race in intoxicants, and yet poetry, principles, affection and morality are almost dead amongst them; they only aspire to be smart.

Arthur Chester was not at all horrified at this suggestion from the milky-skinned Rosa; indeed, had it been at all possible he might have taken it up and discussed it, for it appealed to his acquisitiveness, the predominant passion of a cornstalk, as it likewise did to the depravity of his taste. But he was not altogether devoid of common sense, and he knew that the man who had planned and carried out successfully so many robberies, now that his eyes were opened, was not at all likely to be made an easy victim either to poison or any other form of treachery, so that he shook his head gravely while he thought, with the cunning of an Asiatic or a Sydneyite, "Ho! ho! Rosa, my girl, you would fain polish off your husband because he is your husband, would you, to save these dimes? I am of value now because we are not yet linked, since I hold the cash, but after that you'd serve me out the same. Not for this juggins, if I know it." He thought this, but said aloud in his tender and caressing way:

The Swampers

"It won't do, cousin, we must make up our minds to act on the square or we may lose it all. Let us get him away, and then we can plan out our future."

"If you think that the best way, I am agreeable, yet as long as he lives, I'll be in such dread of him betraying us and getting us into trouble."

"Oh, I think that he is safe enough in that respect so long as we humour him now. He has some strange notions for a thief—at least as far as my experience of our Sydney thieves go, as they would give away their own mother for a cigarette, but Jack Milton is quite a maniac about keeping his word—that is one of his cracks."

"He is cracked in more parts than one, the fool. He was downright daft to think that a girl like me would stick to a housebreaker," said Rosa, disdainfully.

"Ah! I think he has got over that mania by this time," replied her cousin reflectively.

"Don't be nasty, Arthur. I bet you I could make him as dead gone on me as ever he was," said Rosa daringly.

"Well, perhaps you might, Cousin. Samson was deluded by Delilah three times, therefore I'll not take up the bet, yet I think you had best not try to make it up, or he might drag you through the interior with him, and I don't fancy that would suit your books."

"God forbid!" ejaculated Rosa, with a shudder of dread. "I want to see no more of him."

"Well, cousin, you stay at home till I get him out of the road and call upon you, and I'll manage all the disagreeable business for you meantime." "What about the police, though?"

"You know nothing about him, so that they must scent about for themselves. You have done your duty as a respectable citizeness in giving them the word, therefore you'll be exonerated—and of course you kept my name strictly out of the business."

"Ah, yes, Arthur, I always look after your interests," she answered with a fine accent of scorn in her tones.

"Our mutual interest you mean," he said quietly. "As long as I am kept in the back-ground, I can work for you as I have done."

"I know—I know, dear," she replied hastily, and putting her arm round his neck, she drew down his head and kissed him. "You are cold, to-night, Arthur; here we have been walking and talking like a blasé married couple and never a fond word."

"Forgive me, dearest, this contretemps has worried me, and by Jove! that reminds me, how foolish you were to come to my place this morning." "You knew I was coming, Arthur?"

"Yes, if all had gone right it would have been perfectly safe, but now—suppose you have been followed?" "I don't think so," she replied hesitatingly. He glanced round quickly and was just in time to see the figure of a man on the opposite side, yet some distance behind, dart back into the shadow of a trumpet-tree overhanging a fence.

"Ah, don't you think so?" he whispered mockingly. "But you have been shadowed for all that, so let us hurry on. I must go with you to the Cottage, and put them off the scent if possible. We must now be open with our love affairs, and that will serve as the best motive for selling Milton." "Oh, Arthur, what shall we do?"

"Keep cool. Our shadower is too far away to have heard what we were speaking about; let us go on as we are doing, and when we reach the gate do a little spoon there. He will likely get close to us then, so that what I say to you will be for his benefit. Remember you only came to tell me of the escape and nothing else." "I drop," she replied, in the slang which ladies of her class love to indulge in. After this they looked no more behind, but kept on until they reached the gate.

Here the farce of sweethearts saying good-night was gone through elaborately, while the spy crept up to hear what they said in this supposed unguarded moment.

It was a farce to both of them by this time, this lingering at the gate. When a woman possesses the latch-key of her lover's house, the necessity for gate-lingering has gone past, yet with some the folly is still kept up for the sentiment of the thing. So thought the watcher as he saw the embracing and heard the good-night uttered several times over before they finally went inside together, and he chuckled even while feeling disappointed that his shadowing had only brought out this result. He thought he knew now why the false wife had betrayed her husband, and felt it much more natural in a Sydney girl than any flimsy sentiment about horror of the murderer or Spartan desire for justice.

"Keep up your pluck, my girl," said Arthur, as they stood at the gate. "It isn't possible for him to get away."

"But suppose he should be about and return now that the police are away. He'll murder me, Arthur, for what I have done."

"Don't be afraid, Rosa, he won't return here. He cannot possibly make his escape, so be easy, you'll be a widow soon enough now."

"I hope so, but I'm desperately afraid. Come inside, Arthur, and see father and mother."

They went indoors and had not been long there before the man knocked, and when he was admitted and saw the family up, he told them that he had called to say that they need not be alarmed, for the house was still watched on all sides, so that they might retire with perfect security. "This is my cousin, Mr. Chester, the solicitor. I went to his house to get his advice," said Rosa, introducing her cousin to the detective, who shook hands and said calmly:

The Swampers

"Quite natural on your part, ma'am, under the circumstances, only he need be under no fear of your safety, as you are well guarded."

Arthur Chester took his leave soon after this, and went out with the detective, while those inside locked up the door. "Miserable affair this. I was the last man to have suspected Jack Milton."

"He is a cute card, but he has reached the end of his tender this time, I guess. She is a fine woman that wife of his, poor girl; how did she find him out?"

"Well, from what I can gather, he got talking in his sleep about the murdered bank clerk on Sunday night, and then he was so anxious for the papers next day, that she worked it all out in her own mind and was horrified. She'd have forgiven him anything short of murder. That did for her."

"It mostly does with the women, although they are not all so game as she is. They are more apt to act like the mother of Barnaby Rudge. Does she know anything about the plunder, do you think?"

"No, he has doubtless planted that. He was always reticent about his income, but he has left his traps at the Cottage, so something may be discovered amongst them. This is a devilish unfortunate affair for all of us, to be connected with such a scoundrel. It will make such a scandal, you know."

"Yes, but the prompt behaviour of Mrs. Milton must counteract a good deal of the scandal." "I hope so. Good-night." "Good-night, sir."

The detective looked after him, placidly satisfied in his own mind that Jack Milton had not much chance of escape if Arthur Chester could spoil it, after what he had seen.

The lawyer, however, went along the victim to a thousand fears for his own safety, and cursing the imprudence of his cousin, whereas he ought to have been more grateful.

The Swampers

As for Rosa, now that the way seemed clear, she went to bed strangely discontented and dissatisfied with her cousin. The charm of secrecy was over, and with it had departed the only romance that her vicious heart had pulse to thrill over.

The Swampers

Chapter IX. Jack Milton Waits.

JACK MILTON watched the guilty pair pass from the study with a sardonic grin on his lips that drew them back and bared the strong white teeth, so firmly locked together. A grim humour possessed him at the moment, and held his hand, which was toying with the revolver, and forced him to laugh as he heard the outer door close.

Was that white-faced traitress the witch who had beguiled his thoughts in jail, and made him feel almost religious? "Oh, Lord! oh, Lord!" he uttered, while he laughed softly; "what a miserable fool a man can be, and all for a fancy."

He thought on a past fancy—a female pick-pocket, who would have gone through fire and water for him. She was a handsomer woman by a long chalk than this flimsy chit who had only brains enough to sell him, and the other woman had both grit to the backbone and talents that this sham was utterly devoid of. He had thought her possessed of the one quality which the poor pickpocket couldn't boast about.

Ah, ye gods! Was there a woman in the world who possessed that charm who wasn't ready to fling it away at the first chance? And yet, for this imaginary virtue he had hitherto staked his happiness.

He somehow felt no anger against Arthur Chester, who, indeed, was now in his estimation too poor a tool for any man to be angry about. If it hadn't been Chester, it would have been someone else. Possibly Chester was only one of a crowd of hounds who ran baying after this Sydney beauty.

When a man has worn a bit of paste in his breast-pin, under the impression that it was a diamond of the first water, he does not care much who wears it after he has discovered its real value and cast it from him. The price it has cost him may give him a slight twinge, but that will only be momentary, unless he is a weak fool who mourns over things lost.

The Swampers

Jack Milton was no fool, although under the influence of a mad impulse he had nearly consummated the most idiotic act any man can be guilty of, but for his betrayer's prudence in removing the cartridges from his revolver, but he was cool now, and ready to look at his difficulties all round and take full advantage of every trick that Fortune gave him.

His love for his wife had been a blending of respect and remorse which flavoured and refined his passion. He had discovered what he supposed to be a pure-minded, artless, and affectionate girl, different from all his other companions, and these supposed inner qualities made him value the casket at a much higher figure than it was worth. No sacrifices on his part were reckoned hardships which could keep that unopened casket and supposed sacred treasure as it had been given to him. The aim of his life since he had won her, had been to keep her ignorant of his transactions and abandon them as soon as possible for her sake.

He had accomplished what he had set himself to do, and was now rich enough to retire from his risky business and lead a respectable life, and but for her treason might have got safely out of the colonies and continued to adore and reverence her while he lived, denying her nothing, and as easily deluded as the most unsophisticated of simpletons.

Well, she had opened his eyes and saved his life with about the same expedition as the hangman opens the eyes of his patients, and he ought to be grateful to her for these favours. He knew now that there was nothing better inside that casket than what was inside the one given up for her—the Melbourne pickpocket, indeed Rosa was a more miserable compound of deceit and heartlessness, without a single virtue of qualify her baseness. The pickpocket was the victim of circumstances as he was, and made no pretence to be better than she was, yet she had fidelity to her friends. This one was a wanton by choice, and rotten to the core.

With a laugh of contempt he shook the nasty reflections from his mind, saying as he rose and stretched his arms:

The Swampers

"She and Chester have put me in a bad hole that'll want some kicking to get out of, but they've done me one service; they have rid me of a mighty bad bargain, and now I can think of myself without any cursed sentimental nonsense."

It certainly would have been more flattering to Rosa Milton and her cousin if her husband had offered to do them violence instead of treating them with this contemptuous toleration. To kill the adulterer seems to throw a certain glamour of romance over his sordid and sneaking treachery. It is a much better punishment to pitch the object to him as we might make the thievish boy a present of the cake he has been nibbling at in secret. This reduces things to their proper value. The divorce court has done away with all the glory of seduction, and the betrayed husband is now the party who has the best of the laugh, if any one can laugh at such miserable complications of life.

As Jack rose and stretched himself with a yawn, his glance fell upon a large map of Australia which filled up one side of the wall. He stepped over to this, and with the barrel of his revolver traced an imaginary line to the Merchiston River on the western coast.

"It is a tidy stretch for a man to take by himself, but it has been done before for the sake of science, to say nothing of the stockmen who are not mentioned in colonial history. Yes, that must be my game; I'll play the stock driver out of a job while I traverse New South Wales. The veteran stockman will do. Once I get over the borders there isn't much fear of pursuit, although I guess my likeness and description will be in every station and township throughout the country. Well, I must be extra particular in my get-up, I suppose.

"Chester will get me what I want to start with, I guess, after that I must sacrifice the plunder, for that alone will keep his mouth closed. Ho! ho! what a comfortable legacy that will turn out for him with Rosa along with it. I wonder how dearly they will love each other in six months from now? He'll have to splice her to keep her mouth shut, and mind his p's and q's afterwards not to get her dander up, with me in the background to keep their nerves steady. It's a fine thing he has got on hand, I must say. Let's have a squint round his diggings."

He gave only a passing and regretful thought to the bank-clerk. It was an accident, for he had had no intention or desire to hurt the poor fellow, therefore that crime did not represent murder to him any more than the killing of a sentinel to a soldier. Yet this accident would be the means of hanging him if taken, so that he could no longer afford to be captured alive, otherwise perhaps he would not have cared to face that terrible overland journey.

"I wonder if there is anything of interest to me in these documents," he muttered, stooping over the table, and turning over the papers that Chester had been forced to leave behind him. "No, only cases. The Fox has plenty of business, it appears."

He next opened the table drawers, but found nothing there of any consequence or interest to him except some cigars and cartridges which were lying together. He pocketed the cartridges, and selecting a cigar, he cut and lit it.

"Safe open—oh, yes, safes are always easy to get into when there is nothing inside. He keeps his business books here, but carries his bank and private books about with him—no fear of Chester leaving anything here likely to incriminate him."

He glanced at his borrowed watch and found the time half-past three. As he did so he chuckled.

"Chester must get me a 'Waterbury' to take with me, and I'll make him a present of this ticker and toggery. Won't he be in a pickle when he discovers them to be stolen property, as he very soon will if he tries to sell them, as he did me?"

The sound of footsteps on the front verandah at this moment startled him. At first he thought it might be Chester returning, but when the door was not tried, he became alarmed.

The Swampers

"Surely he is not fool enough to betray me a second time—surely not. I'd let them take me if I thought so for the pleasure of rounding on the cur!" He softly pulled off his boots, and opening the door noiselessly, crept along the lobby and into the front room; here he found the blinds up and the morning outside intensely dark.

Stealing to the window he stooped down and listened with his senses on the stretch. He could not make anything out, and for the moment all was still, but soon again he heard a sound.

A boot striking against the boards almost in front of him?—another step—then all at once a wild clattering accompanied by a rush of pattering hoofs and a wild barking. It was some prowling goats, who had taken to the verandah and been hunted out again by the ownerless dogs of Sydney. Jack Milton rose to his feet with a gasp of relief.

Yet he still stood at the window and watched the only objects visible. The lustrous stars, more brilliant now than at any other hour. How bright the morning star glowed from that dusky space, while higher up flashed the Southern Cross. As he watched, a great sadness fell over this outlaw robber.

The sense of his isolation pressed upon him with a dreary pain. All his life had been a struggle against destiny, and he never had an intimate. What he had gathered he could not hold. Like the Flying Dutchman, he only got so far, to be driven back again.

He thought upon his youth and childhood, and there were no joys in these reflections. He never had a childhood, and his boyhood had passed without a gleam of sunshine to remember. He had been loved by women—at least women had offered him what they called love, but while they wanted him he had revolted against them.

He had loved, or would have loved, only that where his affections went there were no respondings, and this last one had proved wanting, as did the others, yet he did not blame her; as Professor Mortikali told him, he was born under the conjunction of Venus and

The Swampers

Mars, and those who are born under this fatal conjunction are bound to be unlucky in all their efforts, whether with love or war—particularly with love.

He had been gifted with a sturdy determination and dogged will-force, which had torn open the hands of Fate in spite of its clenching; but not for long, for the fingers of Fate are steel-clad and resistless in their gripping. He was able to plan out and execute a bold scheme, but he could not keep the results.

Alone he had passed through his life so far. Those with whom he worked used his brains and may have owned his abilities, but they had no union with him. They trusted him, but they did not fraternise; when the work was over for which they had joined company the partnership was dissolved, with mutual relief to both sides. He was their leader in danger, but in their pleasures he had no part. Ah! how the watching of stars makes the most realistic of us sentimental—of course no really realistic man ever looks at the stars unless it is to find out their position astronomically, and that kind of gazing does not awaken sentiment.

Jack Milton looked at the stars raptly and thought of himself—for that is what star-gazing produces. He had been as a piece of driftwood all his life. Cast off in early youth by those who might have made something of him. Drifting out to the colonies. Taken up and petted for his handsome face for a brief space, and taught during this period of petting how to discriminate between a good and a bad cigar, and how to appreciate a glass of wine, cognac or liqueur—how to comport himself in a drawing-room or take a hand at cards—to treat a sovereign as if it were a shilling and chuck coppers to the crowd. He had matriculated in an expensive college during those few months between eighteen and nineteen.

Cast on the world without a friend, when the patron had tired of him and left him to shift for himself. He had tried then to be honest, and starved—until the Melbourne girl had picked him up and taught him how to utilize his talents, then he became as he might have been on more reputable lines—a leader of men.

The Swampers

This female outlaw had devoted herself to him and taught him how dimes were to be made by a bold man. She was a heroic woman, but she had loved him, whereas he could not then love her, therefore this dark hour before the breaking of day, he stood and looked at the stars with that vague longing that the eagle may have as he sits on his lonely perch waiting for the dawn. Jack Milton had not yet found either his mission or his mate. How many solitary souls spend their lives on a lonely perch, waiting and watching, as he was doing, for what never comes?

The Swampers

Chapter X. An Unpleasant Dream.

"WELL, Chester, you reckon I'd take in my mother, supposing I had one, with this disguise?" "Yes, Milton. Your make-up is perfect and you are a born actor."

"Ah, yes, I am a man of many parts I allow. I fancy I'll be able to dodge the traps; now let us come to some personal business before we say adieu. Rosa is your cousin. You know her, I daresay, better than I do—you mean to act square with her, now don't you?"

Arthur Chester did not answer at once, perhaps he was too ashamed. It is an awkward business to arrange with a husband, who is about to relinquish wife and fortune together—a kind of death-bed arrangement without the corpse.

Jack Milton sat before him, dressed in corduroy pants, top boots, red flannel shirt and riding jacket. To an outsider, he was a rough bushman with matted grey beard and straggling tresses. As he opened his mouth to speak, two gaps showed where the front teeth were absent. He had knocked these out that afternoon, which makes a wonderful alteration in a man. He was no longer the youthful and trim swell, but a sun-tanned and full-bearded bushman of fifty.

"You mean I shall marry her, and share your money with her?" said Chester. "Yes, I reckon we can say that is settled."

"I'm a romantic cove, Chester, you will say. Yet I wouldn't like Rosa to drift too far down for her mistake. You are low enough for any revengeful fellow's desires." Chester winced at this, but said nothing.

"I reverenced that girl once, as men who know the world sometimes make saints of women. I think all men are Roman Catholics or heathens when they are in love, and afterwards, even when they wake up, they don't like their images to be battered—therefore keep Rosa as straight as you can. I'd like to think she died in what the world calls the odour of respectability." "She is my cousin, you need not be afraid of her future, Jack Milton."

"No, you accursed scoundrel, I can trust you as far as I see you. You marry Rosa and treat her square, and I'll ask no more than those three hundred quid you have given me. I'm going away, but I won't lose sight of you for all that. Leave her in the lurch, and, by Saul! I'll make you wish you were dead every day of your life for five years before I kill you, as John Chinaman promises his pet criminals."

"You seem mighty anxious about Rosa's future," said Chester with a slight sneer; "she hasn't treated you so well." "Chester, I loved your cousin, and had she been grit would have laid down my life for her. She wasn't grit to me. Perhaps I got her from you because I had the spondulux at the time and you hadn't; yet I don't want her to know the world as I have found it. You have the chink now; make her life easy and I'll forgive you all you have done to me." "Don't be afraid, my cousin is all right." Jack Milton touched the pendant on the watch-guard of Arthur Chester. "On the square, Chester?" "Yes, on the square." "Enough, and now good-bye. I hope you'll hear no more of Jack Milton."

Mr. Chester accompanied him to the door and saw him ride away in the starlight. He had done his part, and for the first time felt relieved. The world was now before him, so long as that incubus could get out of the ken of man in safety.

They had made no arrangements for communicating with each other. If Jack got clear of the colony, the lawyer would not likely hear from him again, that is, unless he was very hard pressed for money. If he was caught en route, then the papers would soon inform Chester of the disaster, for a disaster it would be to him, since he could no longer depend upon the silence of the refugee.

Jack Milton need not have been at all fearful concerning the future of Rosa, for that young person was quite able to paddle her own canoe. Some men have a habit of regarding the female sex as timid and harmless idiots, where ways and means are concerned; as poor, soft,

The Swampers

supersensitive innocents, who are victims of man's brutality and selfishness unless hedged about and protected. Jack Milton was one of this kind, and even although he had so recently an experience of his wife's capability of looking after her own interests, still he could not divest himself of the idea that she might starve, or drift to the bad, if not provided for; as if either man or woman could possibly sink lower than this young woman had already sunk. When a page is blotted past writing upon or reading, what does it matter how soiled it becomes before it is sent to the pulp-house?

If Cousin Chester felt disposed to play her false, as was but natural with such a shifty cornstalk, she very soon showed him how futile would be his efforts, for Jack had hardly galloped out of hearing before she made her appearance and brought her recreant lover to his senses. A speedy divorce and marriage were the only means of securing his safety. The divorce proceedings she placed in his hands to push on for her with all expedition, so that, whatever he had intended to do, he discovered that it was much easier to drop into an intrigue than to slip out of it, once in the toils. Rosa was mistress of the position, now that all necessity for concealment was past, as far as her husband was concerned, also with that other secret still at her discretion.

Double harness was the only safe mode of making life's journey now, therefore the lawyer accepted his destiny.

A week went past and no word of Jack, although the papers, particularly the Sunday Verity and the Guillotine, rubbed it in warmly for the detectives. Puffadder, the editor of the Guillotine, was always rubbing it in venomously somewhere or other, for this was how he showed his sense of humour and wit.

"Give them cayenne-pepper all round," was his war-cry, and his contributors obeyed the order with zest, and spared no one whom they thought their poisoned blow-pipe needles could prick on the raw; this being the sort of new-humour that the readers of the Guillotine best understood; subtlety or playful satire would have been lost upon them.

The Swampers

Singular to say, however, this same Puffadder, although such a callous and malign beast with respect to other people's feelings, was one of the most super-sensitive and easily wounded of reptiles where his own feelings were concerned. At one time a respectable paper had so far forgotten its dignity as to criticise his shameless, vicious, and asinine tramplings, which just, if too lenient, remarks so wounded his vanity that he immediately fixed upon a well-known contributor, who chanced to have been in the colony at the time, as the author of the criticism.

To suspect the man was enough for Puffadder, and to make him lose all the little mental balance he possessed. He writhed and brayed out his rage and distress, making a laughing-stock of himself. He drank himself into delirium, and besides airing his grievance to all his acquaintances, he took to writing the most scurrilous and senseless letters to this suspected critic at the rate of three or four per day, which he first read to his friends and then posted on to the unconscious journalist, and although years had passed, that wound to his vanity still remained open and as raw as when first inflicted, while the mere mention of the critic's name would send this editorial humourist into a fit. This was the kind of philosophic censor who controlled and directed the popular and mirthful Guillotine. A worm, that the heel of an infant could torture and crush, was permitted to fling his venom broadcast and make good and strong men tremble, all because to outsiders he appeared to be triple-armoured.

While the police were at fault and the Guillotine was showing them how their work ought to have been done, the divorce case was carried through the court, and Rosa Milton made a free woman, amidst the general approval of all right-minded people. She had only done her duty as a good citizeness to repudiate such a villain, and Judge Jeffreys wept over the wrongs of one so fair and young, he being one of those sentimental holders of the scales of Justice who had done much to render divorces fashionable in the Colony of New South Wales.

The Swampers

After this signal triumph of virtue, the fair Rosa went home, to receive the congratulations of her friends, and prepare for her coming wedding with her cousin.

The police, seeing her act so promptly, relinquished any trace of suspicion they might have had of her as being an accomplice of the escaped criminal. Judge Jeffreys also went home in a virtuous mood.

He had endured a trying day in the divorce court, for where women were concerned he was the most sentimental of men, and would weep almost as copiously as the wronged wives, while he listened to their evidence and summed up the case, pointing out to the jury their clear duty, and making the unfaithful male monster squirm under his scorching remarks. The wronged wives adored Judge Jeffreys as much as the shivering husbands feared him. He would roughly interrupt all evidence in favour of these male desecrators of the domestic hearth, and in spite of weakness of proofs, would shake his fore-finger in the direction of the culprit, and tell him that he was as positive of his guilt, as if he had accompanied him all through the shameful affair. He would blow his nose and wipe his lachrymose eyes as he turned towards the fair victim, to bestow upon her and the jury the flowing tide of his sympathy, then after the verdict had been found, he gave thumping damages, regretting it was not in his power to transport the scoundrels as well.

He liked to transport male criminals when he could not sentence them to death—he always sent men to the gallows when he could possibly stretch his power, and according to the penal laws of this favoured land, it required a very slight offence for a man to be hanged, for the implied intention was punished with equal severity as the actual deed.

Judge Jeffreys was not an eloquent speaker; he drawled out his words with painful effort, and connected each word with a long-drawn "Ah—hum" but these ominous "Ah—hums," although laughed at by the uninterested audience, created small mirth in the heart of the trembling culprit, for he knew well that, innocent or guilty, once he was before this merciless judge, he had no prospect of justice or escape. Also, as this judge possessed the prescience of infidelity, so likewise had he the gift of being present at the commission of crime, with the infallible power to read the intentions of the frustrated criminal. When he summed up and delivered his address to the jury, he would tell them that the evidence which they had listened to was nothing, but that from his own knowledge they must return a verdict of guilty, for he was as positive of the guilt of the prisoner as if he had seen him commit the deed. With this assurance, these enlightened thirteen citizens found "guilty" with hardly a pause, and the victim was led out to his doom. The secret of this prescience, which controlled justice and biassed the minds of the thirteen good and true men, was an open one. Judge Jeffreys was a firm believer in Spiritualism, and had for his guides in all matters relating to law and the discovery of vice and crime, the spirits of two ladies, who had long since freed themselves from the bondage of earth. "Katie," the daughter of the grim old pirate, Morgan, and "Clara," who had in her day been known as Mrs. Manning, the murderess. With such experienced familiars in the intricate ways of crime at his beck and call, when he required advice in obscure cases, Judge Jeffreys considered himself superior to the evidence likely to be got out of such perjured witnesses as this head centre of military laws could produce.

On this day, he had dismissed the suits of three husbands who had sought liberty at his hands from their maligned and angelic spouses—declining, according to his usual arbitrary custom, to hear the witnesses who were ready to give evidence against the sweet innocents. He had liberated six other tearful innocents from the hateful bondage of matrimony, with withering condemnation on the husbands for their vileness and brutality. He had granted separation, with handsome maintenance, to a number of other female applicants, committing the wretches who could not pay the demands to prison, until they could, and through the day's hard work, he had wept almost enough to have watered some of the most arid districts of this sun-dried land; therefore it was no wonder that he found his usual allowance of sherry, claret and port insufficient to quench his thirst, and was forced to take a few extra glasses of whisky and water, after dinner, the night being a hot one.

The Swampers

In the prison a criminal lay waiting his execution whom this righteous judge had sentenced to death, for resisting a policeman, who had taken him in charge for sleeping in an empty house; unfortunately for the homeless "dosser" a revolver had been found in his pocket, and the policeman (the only witness) swore he had been threatened with it.

Three boys had been strung up together the previous day for being concerned in an outrage, although the evidence was so contradictory and flimsy against them that even Judge Jeffreys might have paused, had he not been privately convinced by those infallible criminal investigators, "Katie" and "Clara."

He lay back in his comfortable arm-chair, wearied as well as thirsty after his fatigue and tears, and as he puffed his fragrant cigar, felt his eyes fill again with moisture as he thought upon those martyred women whom he had made happy that morning.

He felt intensely emotional and full of sentiment. A feeling was upon him that Katie and Clara were close at hand and about to communicate with him. Knockings began to sound over the room, while curious twitchings ran through his joints, all unmistakable spiritual signs. "Is that you, friend Katie?" he murmured from his chair. "No," sounded a single knock from the back. "Clara?" "Yes." Three knocks now sounded from the table. The late Mrs. Manning was his visitor. "Can you manifest yourself to-night, Clara?" "Yes." "Then do so, like a dear," said the sentimental judge drowsily.

Instantly the lamp began to grow dim, and burn blue, until the apartment was almost in darkness; then about a couple of yards in front of him a pale star-like spot loomed up. This luminous spot became enlarged, rapidly taking on, first, the shape of a smoky pillar, and next human proportions; then, as he watched, the dim cloud grow brighter, and all at once there stood revealed a fearful-looking Chinaman with an ugly gash on his forehead. "Who are you?" cried the judge wildly. "One of your victims unavenged," replied the ghost sombrely. "I haven't hanged a Chinaman yet," muttered the watcher. "No, but you set my murderers at liberty."

The Swampers

"You surely don't expect a colonial judge to condemn a citizen for merely killing a Chinaman, do you?—why, that would be downright murder."

The Chinese ghost grinned horribly, and stood aside to let a crowd of other ghosts come forward. They were of all ages, the three boys just hanged gibbered at him while they kicked up their heels in a strange fashion, others denounced him as their remorseless murderer, while the worst was, that he knew them all and remembered the words he had used when he sentenced them to be hanged. He was a dogged old man, yet he did not like these ghostly reminders of his justice.

"Get out with you—you gang of criminals, or I'll sentence you all over again," he cried wrathfully, his patience at last worn completely threadbare.

"You can't; we defy you, Judge Jeffreys," the ghosts yelled in a chorus, "and as for hanging, it's your turn now."

"Bah!" replied he scornfully, "you are only—ah—hum—spirits—and they can't hurt, ah—hum—a strong man like me."

"That's all you know about your religion; wait and we'll show you what materialized spirits can do."

The three murdered boys leapt on him as they yelled the words and pinned him to his chair in an instant; then the Chinaman, who had been busily materializing a rope, vaulted upon the table and unshipping the heavy lamp from the hook in the ceiling, slid the rope through that, and there it was, noose and all complete, and ready for him.

"Where is Clara?" cried the judge, thoroughly frightened at last by these adroit preparations. "Here, my sweet judge," answered that lady promptly, at his elbow. "Save me, dear Clara."

The Swampers

"Nonsense, Jeffreys, hanging is nothing, when you have a good drop. I wonder at your bad taste, refusing to join such loving friends as Katie and me, after all your professions of affection, particularly since you are so lavish in ordering the rope for other people. Up with him quick, lads, and I'll draw the table from under him, then it will be over in no time, and we'll be all so happy in the spirit world."

It was useless to struggle in the hands of that materialized crowd. In a moment they had him on the table and the noose round his neck, then, with an exultant shout from his executioners, he had dropped the four-feet-six and dislocated his neck. "Did you call for coffee, sir?" "Eh?"

Judge Jeffreys sprang up from his seat and regarded the servant with a maniacal glare; then, feeling the back of his neck ruefully and tenderly, he answered shortly: "Yes, Jane, you had better bring in the coffee."

The Swampers

Chapter XI. On the Wallaby Track.

JACK MILTON made his exit from Sydney by the side streets, going at an easy canter until he reached the suburbs, then he put spurs to his horse and through the long night only rested long enough to breathe the animal.

He skirted the town of Penrith soon after midnight, and crossing the Emu Plains, when morning dawned, was able to seek a shelter for the day amongst the sheltered and secluded gullies of the Blue Mountains. Here amongst the ferns, wild flowers, rocks and overhanging gum trees, he led his tired horse to the banks of a clear stream, where it could spend the daylight feeding to its heart's content, while he likewise lit a fire and boiled his billy, after which he lay on his back and enjoyed the rest he needed.

He had hobbled the horse, which was a good one, so that it could not wander far, nor was it likely to do so with herbage and water so close at hand. Here also he could sleep with security, for although he was not far from the team road, a wayfarer asleep was too ordinary an event for any one who might penetrate this seclusion to pay any heed to. The police, as he calculated, would be still hunting after him about Sydney, or watching the roads between Queensland and Victoria.

He had the advantage of being able to take time by the forelock, for the police could hardly expect, after his betrayal, that he would be aided by his betrayers. They knew that he had been run to earth, and would be searching for him amongst the criminal quarters in Sydney, and this must occupy them for some days, after which the search would be extended.

Once, however, over the Blue Mountains he did not reckon on having much trouble in eluding the country police. West Australia was drawing many towards its gold fields, and he would as likely as not meet many adventurers taking the same route as he was doing. If

The Swampers

he fell upon any of these explorers he would join them and so be able to escape scrutiny.

Thousands were rushing from all quarters to the golden West. Those who could afford it going by steamer round the coast, others trecking across the country.

In the days of the early explorers such a journey as he was taking was looked upon as well-nigh hopeless. The want of water generally stopped them, while the desert claimed its countless victims.

But the conundrum of penetrating the interior had been solved by the most ordinary of bushmen, while the scientific and learned explorers had failed, through depending too entirely upon what ought to be, and failing to take advantage of what actually was.

Jack Milton in his varied past experiences had known all sorts of men, while he invariably kept his eyes and ears open. He knew the water-tree by sight, and had been told that even in the driest and most arid tracks it grew and flourished for the benefit of the initiated. Where the water-tree grew no man need suffer thirst, for its roots were unfailing taps. If therefore he succeeded in getting past the surveillance of the police, he was not afraid of the desert.

When night once again fell upon him, he remounted his horse and pursued his way, and at the end of the second evening had reached Forbes, on the Lachlan River.

He had passed many people on that second day, for, relying upon his disguise, he considered that he would be less likely to be stopped and questioned if he travelled by daylight.

He rested that night in one of the small outlying shanties of Forbes, and laying in a fresh stock of provisions, pushed rapidly forward to Booligal, which he reached on the eighth day after his departure from Sydney.

The Swampers

He had now covered over four hundred miles of his long journey, going at the rate of nearly sixty miles per day with one horse and without a relay, which for endurance equalled, if it did not eclipse, Turpin's famous ride to York.

English owners of horses might well think this to be an impossible feat for either horse or man, even on the well-ordered highways of delightful old England, with cool green lanes and refreshing breezes wafting over the grassy downs, but here in hot and parching Australia, with powdered dust instead of grass blades and fiery sunbeams shooting down like heated darts, it would have raised no special remarks. It was a good pace, certainly, to keep up over these rough and dust-choked roads during such a dry and hot season, and not over merciful to the beast that carried him so enduringly and pluckily. Yet men so circumstanced as Jack Milton was, do not generally study the bridge that carries them over the stream, more than to consider whether it is sound enough for their purpose.

Yet I defy any man, no matter how unimpassioned his temperament may be, who is forced by fate to have a dumb companion and no other, to remain selfishly indifferent to the feelings of that companion. It may be a cat or a dog, or any other specimen of that life which we call the lower world. When the man is cut off from higher companionship he will cling to and consider that.

Jack Milton had been with his horse for eight days, and although he had urged him on, and on, yet after the second day he had cast from him his spurs and whip. When a good rider gets a horse that he knows understands him, and the horse gets a rider who can manage him, there is no need for spur or whip. The pressure of a knee, the touch of a hand and the single word are enough; for the horse and rider are en rapport.

They were chums, these two, by this time—the horse and the man. Jack had reached forward often on the ride to brush the flies from the face of his mate, and the horse knew enough of men to appreciate that kindness. He had mind enough to feel that such a friend would not urge him on, unless there was a good cause for sweltering under these blistering sun-rays—trust any sensible horse who feels the clasp of an experienced pair of legs to know that. He will exert himself cheerfully for such a rider, yet he knows that the entire game depends upon him not over-exerting himself, but reserving his strength for the emergency; therefore he will keep steadily on, resting when he requires to rest, yet doing his best to please his rider, that is unless he is a cynical and man-hating quadruped, which few horses are.

It is as natural for a good, young, healthy horse to want to gallop as it is for a boy to run, and, like Sancho Panza, so long as he has a good master to serve he is quite content with what is going, good hay or juicy grass when he can get it, or gum leaves and grass roots to fill up the vacuum when the luxuries of life are not to be had.

What he likes are friendship and experience, and Jack had both of these qualities to bind his horse to him. The first night's canter had made them chums, and nothing in the world could ever alter that. Both animals and horses will exert themselves and count the effort as nothing if they have sympathy to carry them along. Bad luck, scorching sun-rays, choking dust, and short commons are easy to endure so long as harmony prevails.

Jack rubbed down his chum Billy each night when the day's work was over, and gave him the best he could to make him comfortable. Billy reached round his velvety if dusty nose and touched the human cheek to show that he understood those attentions and would do his best to deserve them. The lustrous brown eyes of Billy looked affectionately and trustfully into the black eyes of Jack whenever they stood face to face, so that no words were needed to cement that mutual bond. Jack wanted to get away and Billy was ready to serve him with his life, for this is ever the compact between man and beast. The beast offers his life to the man he has learnt to trust and the man accepts the sacrifice—sometimes selfishly and sometimes sentimentally, yet always unreservedly, for this is the way of man and his slave.

The Swampers

It was a hot and trying journey, for the summer season was at its height and no rain had fallen for months, so that everything was parched and withered.

They passed through a landscape arid and bare as ploughed fields, with furnace-like wafts of burning air and gaseous, quivering heat-fumes that raised mirages on every side of them. The cloudless bleached sky arched overhead with that fierce and relentless orb moving from east to west, without a change, and beating down upon them heavy beams of white fire. The grey dust went with them constantly and enveloped them from morn till night, filling their nostrils with that impalpable powder and making them like flour-coated millers, yet westward they rushed with hardly a pause.

Jack thought sometimes about his wife, Rosa, yet no longer with bitterness. She had become a vague and misty shadow of the past, something like a game of cards that he had lost and which he need not mourn about. Chester was the winner, and he did not grudge him his luck. He did not think much about the money he had relinquished. The world was before him with its chances of good and evil.

The man whom he had done to death no longer troubled him. No ghost followed in his tracks. It had been an accident which he was now paying for, and the fiercer the sun rays beat and the thirstier the dust made him, the more lightly throbbed his heart. The man had left no one behind him whom his death was likely to hurt. Jack had read this from the papers, therefore that remorse was spared him. It would have been different if he had killed Rosa in his rage, whom he had kissed and fondled in his love. This man's death woke no memories, and it is only memory that raises ghosts. Cain would never have felt accursed if he had not grown up with Abel, and as Jack felt now, he would be more likely to mourn over the death of his horse, Billy, than he was likely to do about that defunct bank clerk.

He stayed two days at Booligal, purchasing a pack horse and some other articles that he required, also making enquiries about his route.

The Swampers

He fixed upon the Hanson county from the map he had provided himself with, and gave that out as his ultimate destination to the residents of Booligal.

They were a kindly, simple and hospitable lot of settlers in this little township of Booligal, to whom the advent of a stranger was a welcome sight. News were pretty stale before they reached them, and fashions were not greatly considered, lying as they did out of the line of railway traffic.

Money, of course, was at a discount, as the depression of the market for the past several years gave them, but small inducement for exertion or competition, yet they were able to jog along fairly comfortable, in a primitive sort of way. They had plenty of cattle and good grazing land, and grew what they required in garden produce and cereals.

The account of the Bank robbery had not yet reached them, and Jack Milton was not likely to relate that bit of news, yet he was able to satisfy their curiosity by informing them what had occurred for a few days after their last batch of weekly papers, therefore he was made much of by these pioneers of civilization. He paid for what he had honestly, yet was careful to keep up his character by not being lavish, parting with his coins prudently and behaving himself discreetly, so that when he said good-bye he left behind him quite a number of hearty friends and well-wishers.

It was a long and not very interesting ride after this until he reached Tacnall, and after that Pooncaria, on the River Darling.

He was now seven hundred and eighty miles west from Sydney, and about to enter upon the most trying part of his journey.

Hitherto he had avoided railway tracks as far as possible, striking from small township to township. He was now little more than a hundred miles from Silverton on the New South Wales border land, where possibly the police were already on the lookout, therefore if he wanted to escape their scrutiny, he must turn his course now due

The Swampers

north towards Cooper's Creek, avoiding the Broken Hill district, and depending entirely upon his own exertions after this.

Six hundred miles to Cooper's Creek, and after that two thousand five hundred miles before he could hope again to touch civilization.

He made his calculations with great care, and reckoning that it would take him two good months, he provided himself with two more pack-horses, which he loaded with flour, tea, sugar and matches.

He had a good fowling-piece with him and a Winchester, also enough ammunition to carry him along besides his revolver; and as his pocket compass was in correct condition, and his map of the latest date, he had little fear of losing his road.

Water might be scarce, until the rains came on, but as soon as he got over the borders, he meant to take it easy, so that his own beard and hair might grow to a proper length before he showed himself to his fellow-men. He would live as the aboriginals do, and make his way from water-hole to water-hole and risk it, as so many had done before him.

Therefore, congratulating himself that hitherto he had escaped detection, he started on his arduous journey with a light heart.

The Swampers

Chapter XII. Anthony Vandyke Jenkins.

"OH, sanctimonious, centuries behind the times Sydney. Ah, city of Sadducees and—Jenkinses."

"Here, I say, you Wallace, what the Dickens do you mean by Sadducees, and coupling my name with such a lot?"

"By Sadducees, Anthony Vandyke, I mean people who do their utmost to ignore the traditions of the past, yet slavishly adhere to the written word, and by Jenkinses I mean touchy little mining experts like you."

The scene where this playful badinage took place was in a Hessian drinking shanty in Canvas Town, Kalgourlie. Outside the moon was shining almost as bright as sunlight in England, while on the roads crouched the camels, making night hideous with their demoniac shrieks. Between the tents stalked the majestic Afghan drivers of the camels, giving the Australian landscape a strangely picturesque appearance, in spite of its familiar bareness, dust and heat.

Inside the canvas shanty, men clad in flannel shirts, dilapidated trousers and battered hats, sat playing cards or drinking champagne, for this was one of the crack shanties of the place, and these were all successful speculators and mine proprietors, many of them gentlemen accustomed to the West End clubs of London, others a mingling of all nationalities gathered here on the one common game, gold hunting.

Bob Wallace, a tall, jovial man of about thirty-five, had floated his mine and made his pile already, yet he could not keep long from the field, as few gold-seekers can who have once tasted of the excitement. He was at present on a flying visit, looking the place up a bit, in the interests of his shareholders and extending his speculations.

The Swampers

He was known to all there present as one of the sure and lucky ones, also for some other social qualities which made him always welcome. He was the Bret Harte, or story-teller of the diggings, and had likewise made a reputation for his sincere and candid abhorrence of everything that smacked of Sydney. He had been there as he had been over the greater portion of the colonies, and while he extolled Victoria, Queensland, South and West Australia, he never veiled his utter contempt for the institutions of New South Wales.

Anthony Vandyke Jenkins was a little withered man who hailed from the obnoxious city, so that whenever the two came together there was sure to be some diversion.

On the present occasion Anthony looked ready for war. He was the only dressy man in the shanty, and as he passed his well-ringed hand through his long tresses he looked wrathfully at the giant before him, and with pretended coolness took a fresh cigar from his silver case, which he lit carelessly with the half of a bank-note, the other half he pitched on to the floor.

"Well, I see nothing wrong either in the one or the other. Only a fool would boast about traditions, while as for booming, I fancy we all know that business; but what's got your dander up this evening, Wallace, to make you abuse the city of my birth, eh?"

"I told you some time ago, about that asinine piece of legislature which had been passed respecting expectorating in the streets?"

"And I said then that I didn't believe it," replied Jenkins hotly. "It is all a made-up gag by some enemy. I have not been many months away from Sydney, and you bet no one dared to stop me from spitting when and where I liked."

"Oh, no, you couldn't, Anthony, my son," observed Bob Wallace sadly. "You forget Mrs. Jenkins." "Oh, dash you and Mrs. Jenkins. Here give us a fresh bottle of pop."

The Swampers

"What is this you are talking about?" asked another member of the company. "I have only just arrived and haven't heard anything about this singular regulation."

"The law I could have forgiven, only that it has been the death of an old friend of mine, by name Soapy Sam."

"Spin us the yarn, Wallace," shouted out several, as they closed round the speaker, leaving Jenkins in a high state of disgust in the background. Bob Wallace cleared his throat and began: "The law I refer to was announced in this fashion:

"'The City of Sydney has imposed a fine of one pound upon any person convicted of spitting upon the street, or on floors of public buildings.'"

This most admirable bye-law was not carried through the House of Representatives without a considerable deal of angry and personal dispute amongst the opposition, and even amongst the friends of the Government, for many of them were heavy smokers or chewers, and it did appear to be the last straw in the matter of curtailing liberty, which had been laid on the back of that already loaded animal, the public.

But as old Spikehead, the framer of the law, wisely pointed out—supported, as he was, by medical authority—that besides the objectionable sight presented to the sensitive eyes of the refined citizenesses on their fair and sunny streets, the danger of infectious diseases being spread broadcast by this filthy habit, he silenced all opposition and carried his point.

Now Spikehead did not waste tobacco by burning or chewing it, besides, as he pointedly remarked: "Pocket handkerchiefs are cheap enough, and gentlemen are expected to carry them."

That clenched the business with the "House," for Sydney members of Parliament pride themselves on their gentlemanly instincts and behaviour, as all can testify who have listened to or read their

The Swampers

debates. Bob Wallace was evidently reciting from some newspaper article.

It caused wild excitement as well as consternation in the city and suburbs, however, for everyone did not use handkerchiefs, while many who did indulge in this extravagance, often forgot them when changing their coats in a hurry to go into town. There were epidemics of influenza and whooping-cough in the air at the time, which artful Spikehead was aware of, asthma was quite a common complaint during that damp season, while chewing tobacco was almost universal. People also, who had never acquired the habit of spitting, no sooner read the announcement than pure nervous dread at once gave them a plethora of saliva, with the almost irresistible desire to get rid of it in the very way which was prohibited.

Spikehead was a wily old politician, who had turned over a good deal of profit by several of his former Parliamentary dodges, and here he saw the chance of making another pile, therefore he promptly took time by the forelock.

He knew, of course, that it was impossible to restrain people from spitting, by fines or imprisonment, and he had up his sleeve a nice little patent of his own in the way of public spittoons. When the people could stand no more, and rose in their fury, then he would present his model and get carte blanche from the Government to put the patent up at every corner, on every lamp-post, at the end of every church pew, in theatre seats—in fact the city would be forced to use spittoons both indoors and out in unlimited numbers.

His idea was to force the public to the verge of rebellion first, and then introduce his remedy; therefore, in order to keep the interest up, he employed an old pal of his and mine called Soapy Sam, who had fallen in the world and become a confirmed and homeless loafer. He concocted with Soapy to go about and spit right and left.

He could depend upon the secrecy of Soapy Sam, and as that aged loafer was supplied freely with his favourite negro-head, and was an

The Swampers

inveterate chewer, besides caring no more for prison than he did for boots, he took to the job in the kindest manner possible.

His first offence against the law happened within half an hour of his engagement, and having no money to pay the fine, he got off with fourteen days and a caution.

"Wot's a man to do as han't got a wiper?" he asked the magistrate, and that worthy told him to spit in his pocket for want of a better place. Now Soapy didn't own a pocket free enough from holes to carry this kind of luggage, but the kindly hint gave him an idea, the humour of which tickled him so highly that he spent his fortnight of prison in alternative fits of uproarious laughter.

No sooner was he set at liberty than he hastened to put his idea into practice. He marched into one of the principal streets, and going up to a policeman, said: "See yer, mate, I want to spit; where can I do it?"

The policeman looked at the tatterdemalion with contempt, and while he was doing so, Soapy deliberately seized the coat tails and shifted his masticated quid into the policeman's pocket.

He got a broken head for that feat and two months' hard, but he was no sooner out than he repeated the offence. Sometimes, he would take out a gentleman's handkerchief, and after using it, return it to the owner with an ironical bow, sometimes he would favour a lady's reticule.

At last in the wantonness of his humour, he committed a capital offence, according to the law of this enlightened land. He rang at the frontdoor bell of the offices of Judge Jeffreys, that terror of all evildoers.

When his summons was answered, Soapy Sam informed the attendant that he had some particular information to give to the judge, and on being introduced to that gentleman, he deliberately expectorated on his white vest. That did for the humorist, for this

The Swampers

gentleman had no appreciation of this kind of new humour. Soapy was arrested, tried for treason and outrage against the sacred majesty of the State, and sentenced to be hanged.

And, gentlemen, poor Soapy has died game to his principles, for he spat on the scaffold into the clergyman's hat. He also remained faithful to his employer, which was more, I daresay, than old Spikehead would have done by him.

The latest news I have to give you all is that the free and happy city of Sydney is blessed with compulsory spittoons with Government officials to empty them; let us drop, therefore, a tear over the martyrdom of Soapy Sam.

"Bah! as if any one could swallow that beastly tommy-rot," shouted Anthony, as he crammed his hat over his eyes and prepared to leave the tent.

"It's a quotation from your favourite periodical—the last edition of the Guillotine, Anthony. Of course I cannot therefore vouch for its accuracy, but you have it as I read it," answered Wallace gently to the departing visitor.

"It's much too washy for Puffadder. I don't believe a word of it," and the little man disappeared. "Who is this Jenkins?" asked the new arrival.

"Oh, one of our successes here," answered Wallace. "He has had a wonderful career of his own." "Oh, give us the 'Rise and Fall of Jenkins, Wallace." "That is a historical tale, therefore a long one, for with Jenkins, the whole land boom of Australia is inseparably linked. In fact Jenkins is the Land Boom." "Let us have it, old fellow, the night is young, and we have nothing else to do."

"Well, boys, you have seen how Jenkins comes out in the way of costume here—ah, that is nothing to what he was five years ago. I'll spin you the yarn, but to do so properly, I must describe Jenkins before his first rise, next when, like King Solomon, he was in all his glory, and afterwards, before he came out west." "Drive ahead in your own way," shouted the company.

It is difficult to trace the exact and original causes of the great and disastrous Australian land boom, which ruined so many, and plunged the colonies into such a depth of despair, from which they are now only beginning to emerge. It may have been a wave of contagion spreading from the Liberator building fever in England, that touched the brains, and made men go mad on this other side, or the passion for gambling engendered by the turfite and predestinating proclivities of the colonials. Whatever the original causes were, the Australians went as furiously demented over the buying and selling of land as did the people of England, during the reign of Queen Anne, over the South Sea Bubble, and with as disastrous effect.

There are as level-headed and shrewd men in the colonies as in any other part of the world, that is, outside the excitements attending horse-racing, for when the great national sports are on, there is but small chance of getting calm reason or common sense from either man, woman or child. In the ordinary course of business, however, if the colonial is swindled at all, it must be either by an impostor sporting a bogus title, or making a display of wealth on expectation, or else the Australian is taken advantage of by his own fancied cleverness, or desire for speedy gain. He is seldom fleeced through an appeal to his benevolence or generosity, as English gulls so frequently are.

This is more particularly observable in New South Wales than throughout any of the sister colonies, for here they support such peculiar institutions, are so positive about their own superior wisdom, knowledge and shrewdness, and devote themselves so exclusively to the worship of the great god Ego, and yet withal are so easily led by the nose if adroitly managed, that this portion of the colonies has always been regarded as a kind of paradise for the genteel rogue and swindler.

The Swampers

The land boom had been fairly set afloat, and legitimate business was looked upon with contempt by all except a few of the oldest colonists, and those who had neither property to sell, nor credit to trade upon. The others who could command even the most limited trust, became speculators and went stark, staring mad.

They rushed to the original owners of the land, purchasing, with bills, when they had not cash enough, the most swampy, unprofitable and unlikely plots of ground. They formed companies, subdivided the ground, put it up to auction, and sold it over and over again at exorbitant prices. They raised what cash they could, at compound interest, from the banks, to pay the preliminary expenses, and realised fortunes on paper, as fast as they could sign, purchase and sell. As long as a man had enough to pay for the stamp, his bond was taken, and he became the owner, without a consideration being given to title deeds. Within half an hour he had sold his bargain to some other speculator at twenty times his purchase price, who again transferred it to some one else, at the same rate of profit.

So the ball kept rolling from hand to hand, getting bigger as it went on, while the excited speculators flourished their paper fortunes in the faces of those friends who were inclined to stick quietly to what they had earned by honest toil, until they also caught the infection and rushed blindly into the market. Talk of kite-flying in China or Japan, the whole of the azure atmosphere of Australia was so crammed with kites that it was impossible to see blue sky or daylight anywhere.

Our friend, Anthony Vandyke Jenkins, was a sign writer and grainer by profession at this time, and he practised his art in the historic city of Sydney. Now, as I suppose everyone here may have noticed, house painters and paperhangers are great dandies as a rule, and aim at being very genteel and artistic in their habits. They like to curl and anoint their long tresses, and are careful about the cut of their moustaches and beards. They wear very tight and dressy boots, with high heels, and are generally a swaggering and cavalier set of beings, who are apt to fill the policemen's hearts with envy and despair when they take possession of the kitchens and maid-servants of big

The Swampers

houses. At such times the policeman has to keep to his own beat, or transfer his guardianship to some other house, where the family are still at home, and leave those fascinators a clear field.

The grainer and sign-painter is a kind of superior officer of this gallant army of invaders, and gives himself accordingly greater airs, but if he chances also to dabble in pictures at his leisure times, then the largest mansion built is hardly grand or large enough to hold his proud and lofty spirit.

A. V. Jenkins had a fair reputation as a grainer and writer, that is, he passed muster in his own town, and as did the other natives of this delectable city, he considered that what he did not know, no other man in the wide world need attempt to learn. He painted pictures also, or what he called pictures, and therefore was the most condescending and insufferably affable of artistic prigs.

He was then a thin, little, withered man of about thirty, with a pot-hook nose, wearied-looking, crow-blue eyes, long auburn tresses and a highly-cultivated moustache which curled over his wan cheeks like a pair of corkscrews. He always wore elastic-sided and exceedingly high-heeled boots, a size, if not more, too tight for his small feet, a Byronic shirt and collar, with a flowing necktie, brown velveteen jacket with light tweed trousers, a crimson or blue sash round his waist instead of a vest, and a broad-brimmed Alpine felt hat with puggerie attached, cocked jauntily on the side of his frizzled hair. If the weather chanced to be cool enough, he added to this picturesque costume a Spanish-shaped cloak, which, dangling carelessly from his narrow shoulders by a chain and hook, gave him, in his own estimation, that distinguished appearance which characterized the Dutch painter after whom he has condescended to name himself.

As might be supposed from this description, he was not a married man at this date; wives generally soon take this kind of vanity out of a man, although while sweethearts, the class of girls which dashing gentlemen of this sort patronize, are captivated with it. In principles, he shared the atheistic ideas of a vast number of the rising race of cornstalks, took in the Sydney Guillotine and the Sunday Verity, and retailed the enlightened and refined opinions and delicate humour of these journalistic Titans. In his amours he was a disciple of Rochester and the cavaliers of Charles the Second's period, yet being prudent, as well as somewhat weak in his digestive organs, he saved his wages and sipped moderately from the bowl, enjoying himself, when he could do so, gratis.

Being of an economical nature, he had managed to bank a little money, as well as invest in some leasehold land about the suburbs, before the boom came to upset his equilibrium, as it did most other people's. He also had entertained serious thoughts about ranging himself and marrying a dressmaker, who carried on a paying business in the city.

But this was in the industrious and steady period of his life, before he became the director of several land companies and realized the foundation of a colossal fortune on paper; then, of course, he broke promptly with the dressmaker, discarded legitimate art, and laid himself out to capture something infinitely more substantial.

His two or three plots of ground, which, by the way, he had been purchasing by instalments, gave him a position of influence at once. By subdividing these into minute portions, and aided by a number of experienced gentlemen and flaming prospectuses, the shares were rushed at, and with the first instalments, an army of builders began operations and flung up houses almost like magic. As I have said, a little money went a long way in those flourishing fever-days. The builders were paid by shares and bills. The materials were paid for by the builders also with notes of hand. The banks advanced cash on the buildings to cover current expenses and wages that had to be paid. The company sold the leaseholds and buildings to other speculators, who paid so much down and the rest in bills at three, six, and twelve months' date. The speculators transferred at enormous profits their purchases to other speculators, and then, when the property reached the extreme limit, it was sold to people who wished to hold on, and who borrowed and cheated to get money to meet their liabilities as they fell due.

The Swampers

There was no limit to the game, while it was being played by the reasonless or swindling mob. A man would buy an estate at auction, without a shilling in his pocket to settle the discount of the auctioneer, put it up again without leaving the Mart and sell it for five times its price, to some other adventurer who had just enough to pay for the transfer, then the needy speculator settled his first claim and gave bills for the remainder, and went out to enjoy himself with the surplus cash won in that gamble.

Trust was unbounded and money poured into the tills of hotel-keepers and bookmakers, for there were men, who had money, so infatuated, that they paid on the nail in order to get a discount. These were generally the last purchasers, or if they sold again for a large profit, they got paper promises for what they had paid cash, and also went their way happy and confident that they had done a splendid stroke of business.

As pure love of lucre was the order of the day, our pity must be qualified for these victims when the crash came. The speculator who for a thousand pounds expects to get twenty thousand, merely by signing a cheque and taking a bill, cannot expect much sympathy if he loses his thousand.

The needy kite-fliers were the men who flourished during this period like green bay trees. Substantial bank depositors rushed into the nets, and hungrily snapped up the shares, thereby making themselves responsible for the rotten companies. There was hardly a man who was not bitten by the land-boom Tarantula, who did not spin round recklessly and consider himself a millionaire. It was splendid, a hundred times better than gold-digging. Fathers who had been saving and prudent in the old days, now frantically wrote home to England, where their sons were, imploring them to throw up their businesses there, borrow all they could, and come out at once and make their fortunes. It was the wildest stampede after spoil that had ever been witnessed by humanity, and although the feeblest intelligence might easily have foreseen the end, the goddess of Reason had departed from Australia, and blind and deaf Chance alone guided these besotted victims.

The Swampers

Chapter XIII. The Prosperity and Fall of Jenkins.

ANTHONY VANDYKE JENKINS was in clover. He lived in the most sumptuous of apartments, and dined as a lord is supposed to do, all the days of the week. He drove about the city in the handsomest of carriages, and dressed himself in a fresh suit twice and thrice daily. His pockets were filled with sovereigns, while he got pretty well all he desired on credit.

All day long it was a case of buying and selling, his profits were enormous, so also were his liabilities, but these he did not consider; when a bill fell due, he raised money from the banks to meet part of it, while he renewed the rest, and to meet the needful expenses and careless extravagances, he and his brother directors made calls on the shareholders who could pay, and gave those who could not, credit—as they were getting themselves on all sides.

It seemed so easy to rake in money now, that he wondered he had ever been so spiritless as to work for his living. The companies that he had floated were of course responsible for all liabilities, that is, the shareholders and those brother directors who were solid enough to be responsible for anything. Anthony, and those brother sharks who had taught him the lucrative business of the stock exchange, having no household gods to risk, sailed along gaily and plunged with giddy recklessness into the rapids, pledging themselves and their shareholders as if they had the exhaustless coffers of Monte Christo in the cellars of their city offices. They were using the milk of their cows for themselves, and buying the grass to feed them with the money which their customers were foolish enough to pay beforehand.

Of course it became a strict necessity for the swindlers to be dressy and flash in their personal adornments, for this display imparted confidence to the flock who came to be shorn. The love of finery and ostentation which had been the weakness of Anthony in his sign-writing days, became his strength now that he was a board director and company promoter. His passion for airing his opinions made him valuable to his less eloquent partners. Public dinners could not be dispensed with, and the oftener he showed himself at race-courses, theatres, fashionable drinking bars, and clubs, the more he was respected and run after, by the moneyed gulls who were needful for the continuance of this lively existence.

He became an honoured member of the Athenaeum and other clubs. At Tattersall's, the Marble Hall and the "Australian" bar, most of his richest fish were caught, for he had won the reputation of being a lucky guide to follow, and that was everything in his new business. Educated men and gentlemen forgave his palpable ignorance and objectionable manners, and eagerly invited the inflated little cad to their private houses, introducing him to their wives, sons and daughters, all to have a slice of the fortune that seemed to be following him.

On his part, being a native of the city, he knew where to look for the victims who would be able to give solidity to his floating concerns, and so he cultivated their friendship assiduously, and being now amongst the set he had aspired to, he cast his conquering glances round for a suitable wife, and at last fixed upon one whom he considered would do credit to his position and artistic taste.

Sir Timothy Gumsucker, K.C.M.G., was one of the most notable veterans in the colony, having served Parliament and his country in many capacities. He was a strong protectionist, and had been extremely popular with the democratic section before he had weakly consented to receive the honour of knighthood. He owned a good deal of property and had accumulated a considerable fortune by extensive jobbery during his different terms of office. However, neither this nor his bare-faced swindling of tradesmen interfered with his being respected by his constituents and party, for he had only done what every other public character did in this colony, and the people would have regarded him as a fool, if he had not improved his opportunities.

He had been married five times and was blessed with eight daughters, three of whom were as yet unmarried. It was the youngest of these charming damsels that Antony Vandyke Jenkins fixed his ambitious fancy upon, a fair girl of about twenty-three, and as the honourable and venerable K.C.M.G. regarded the little cad as a person of influence and fortune, he gave every encouragement to his pretensions. The young lady also received her suitor with amiability and accepted his presents, so that it looked as if he was going to be as successful in love as he appeared to be in financial matters.

His impudence and overweening colonial conceit as I have already shown, were unbounded, and it is amazing how some foolish girls are impressed and attracted by these qualities in a man. He had been smart enough to draw the father into the boom, or rather the unscrupulous politician's own insatiable rapacity had driven him into the web, so that it was not so wonderful that Anthony's flashy impudence and bold confidence should have caught the maiden.

To calm and dispassionate people like us, it will appear a foolish action on the part of Anthony to inveigle his intended father-in-law into the vortex in which himself and so many were madly whirling. A little forethought and common sense might have suggested the reserving of that fortune for the bursting of the whirlwind, as something to soften the tumble. But common sense and forethought were the two qualities that were utterly wanting in every colonial during that period. Sir Timothy Gumsucker was as infatuated and reasonless as his neighbours, and no persuasion on earth could have kept him out of the gang. Anthony also never had a doubt about the reality of his fabulous paper fortune. How it was to be realised never troubled him for a second. The shares were rising by bounds every day. The public confidence and enthusiasm were increasing. The Auction Marts were thronged, while land and property every day rose in value. Earth, sand, stones and mortar were already more precious than gold-dust, and everyone considered the limit was a long way ahead.

Sir Timothy, like an old spider, was waiting and still buying in, and during his long career of state duplicity he had acquired a confidence in his own wisdom that nothing could shake. Of course he knew that the moment to sell out would arrive sooner or later, for he had been too long in the colonies not to know the real value of property and land; but with Anthony in his hands, he considered that he had his finger on the pulse of the market, and therefore was content to wait and watch.

Anthony likewise had a profound faith in the astuteness of the great Gumsucker. While he held on, everything was safe, so the knaves blindly trusted each other, and no man dared to sell out entirely.

As a proof of the confidence of Anthony in the soundness of his position, he presented, as a salve for the wounded affections of his former flame, Mary the dressmaker, a number of shares, for her to keep or dispose of as she liked.

True, Mary had not suffered her wrongs silently, for of late she troubled the young man a good deal, threatening him with a breach of promise suit, and to drag him before that sympathetic judge of the divorce court, Jeffreys, who, although merciless enough where men were concerned, had a most indulgent and weak side for the ladies. It was, therefore, not altogether regret or generous shame for his ungallant conduct that made the little man yield his former sweetheart those shares, but rather from the laudable desire to purchase her silence.

Mary took the shares and gave Anthony his liberty and love-letters, but, being a woman of more common sense than imagination, she promptly placed her shares on the market, and sold them without difficulty to Sir Timothy for cash down. This money she locked up in her desk, and continued her dressmaking business quietly, considering a thousand pounds in gold to be more satisfactory than a verdict in her favour, and even the thousand pounds damages paid for in the famous bills of Anthony Vandyke Jenkins. Whether she was wise in her generation will be seen presently.

Meantime the love affairs of Anthony went on prosperously. Maud Blanche Gumsucker, who was a tall and finely-formed young lady, with a wealth of golden hair and china-blue eyes, liked her impudent

The Swampers

little cavalier amazingly, and considered him quite a remarkable genius. He had bestowed upon her, with other more costly presents, a few of his past copies, from the Illustrated London News prints, in oil and water colours, magnificently framed, to decorate her bedroom; and although she could not but perceive that his education had been somewhat neglected, and that his manners were not all that might be expected at Government House, still he was not much worse than many of the other young sons of colonial grandees, while his easy pertness and caddish insolence eclipsed even the most audacious. When he uttered his opinion about any matter they were glad to side with him, for he had a pretty turn for delicate repartee, acquired from the Guillotine, that generally silenced opposition or dissent.

As a sign-writer, of course, the lady-like Maud Blanche would never have looked at him, or treated him otherwise than with the most supreme contempt, but as a prodigiously wealthy speculator and director, as well as an authority on Art, she considered him to be an adorable little darling.

Anthony, when Maud and he were standing together, only reached up to the young lady's shoulder, yet this did not interfere with her respect for him, for she was one of those tall girls who are rather ashamed of their own size; while as for him, he was perfectly satisfied with his stature, and disposed to jeer at those great awkward fellows who fill up rooms and knock down china; yet he liked to look at a fine-built woman so long as she had the good taste to admire his own graceful perfections. The conditions being favourable, in the present instance, the course of true love ran smoothly with this well-assorted couple.

His long and extensive experience with the fair sex, as far as servants and dressmakers were concerned, had made him a master in the art of treating the tender lore. "Flattery, Fervour and Familiarity" were his policy and motto. Flattery to commence with, in plentiful and constant doses. Flattery with fervour combined, when the subject had grown interested in the operator, and, to use his own words,

"The three F's without stint as quickly as possible. Don't give them time for consideration, and the victory is sure."

And the little conqueror was right with Maud Blanche, as he had been with the housemaids. He kept at her without a pause, and gave her no time for thought, jibing at other suitors to their faces, and jeering at them after he had chased them from the field. He made her laugh at his rivals at the same time that he filled her ears with the most florid compliments about her own undoubted attractions. Being above all sense of the ridiculous and indifferent to being charged with plagiarism, he quoted the high-flown language of that favourite with colonials, Lord Lytton, and talked to her as the romantic hero Claude Melnotte did to Pauline, using the free actions that he had seen with actors on the stage, while she, who also had seen the drama personated and knew it well, "As the bee upon the flower, hung upon the eloquence of his tongue."

She was wooed and won easily, and after he had knelt before her, amongst the exotics in the conservatory, in the orthodox style, and she had stooped over him and leaned her fair head upon his breast, he sought her father, and they discussed business together and arranged terms, and then the marriage was fixed to take place at an early date.

"Will you realize before or after the wedding?" enquired Sir Timothy blandly, as he gave his consent.

"Oh, hang it, no, the time isn't nearly ripe yet," replied the bold and confident young financier. "I've got cash enough for all our expenses, and if more is required, we can have another call, or borrow from the bank on our securities."

"I think you are right, Anthony; your mansion is almost ready, and will be quite in order before you get over the honeymoon. Where do you intend to enjoy that?"

The Swampers

"Oh, Coogee Bay, or the Blue Mountains," answered the younger man. "I must be within touch of the market." "Right again, my boy. You will have to go into Parliament, after you are settled."

The catastrophe came with the suddenness of a thunderbolt. Speculators and shareholders went to sleep, filled with confidence and security, and woke up next morning, dishonoured paupers.

It happened just two days before the day which had been fixed for the wedding. Maud Blanche was ready with her trousseau. Sir Timothy had made elaborate preparations for a gorgeous breakfast, and Anthony was feasting his host of bachelor friends like a Sardanapalus.

I fancy the crash occurred first in Victoria, but if so, the telegraphic wires spread the thunderclap almost immediately over the colonies.

Anthony had read somewhere that it was the correct thing for an accepted lover to make a clean breast of all his former weakness and frailties to his chosen one before marriage, and, as this was an agreeable task to him, he went through the programme like a man, making Maud think what a treasure she had stolen from her despairing sex.

"You are done with all that now though, aren't you—you won't break any more hearts, will you, Anthony?" she said, with tearful eyes.

"I am done with my free, wild days, Maud, my beloved, and will be faithful till death," answered Anthony nobly, while he kissed and comforted his betrothed.

He had spent nearly all his ready money on his preparations, and went with confidence to his bank to borrow more, and was astonished when the manager informed him that there was no cash to spare. From the bank he proceeded to a board meeting, and it was while they were discussing matters that the appalling tidings reached them. Three of the needy directors promptly took their

The Swampers

departure, but were captured and brought back with the loot they were carrying off, and put in prison as defaulters. Another director shot himself, and after this the trouble commenced.

The banks suspended payment one after the other in rapid succession. Builders and tradesmen failed right and left, and the workmen were thrown out of employment and left to starve. Men who had bought the houses to live in, were turned out without the slightest possibility of getting the instalments they had paid back again. Shareholders who had money were held responsible for those who had not, and stripped bare.

No one escaped, except those who had nothing, for the paper transactions were so complicated that no satisfactions could be got out of them.

The original owners claimed the houses and land; but as many of these owners were also involved, these rights became a curse to them. The country was in a state of bankruptcy and not a shilling could be raised. It was a total collapse and a ruined people. Consternation, despair and death, reigned supreme. The pluck was completely taken out of the Australians.

Sir Timothy Gumsucker was worse off than he had been when he came to the colony fifty years before, for besides losing all that he possessed, he had made himself responsible for such sums that he could never raise his head again. There was no inducement for any one to struggle, they were all hopelessly submerged.

Anthony Vandyke Jenkins escaped prison only by his insignificance. The wardrobe which he had bought on credit was seized, as was the trousseau of his intended bride, and both were left with what they had on their persons in the shape of clothing. Of course, beggars, as they were, could not think about marriage, therefore the engagement was ended by mutual consent.

Jenkins' high spirits had left him for the time, yet his luck did not quite desert him, for Mary, the dressmaker, came to his rescue in his hour of need, forgave him so far for his lapse of fidelity as to marry him and make him her servant. She kept the business open, although there was little trade doing, yet the thousand pounds carried them over the crisis. She looked strictly after it and him, while he settled down contentedly with his subordinate position, doing what most of the other married men do in Sydney, that is, running errands, looking after the house and garden, with an occasional saunter in the domain, which is called seeking for work, and living like tame tom-cats on what their wives have, or are able to make.

His jauntiness was gone, his Alpine hat and velveteen coat had grown rusty and frayed, his trousers were patched and baggy, his boots heelless, and all that was left to him of his former pride were his moustache, long hair, and atheistic opinions. Mrs. Jenkins permitted him to retain those, so long as he did not bounce about them, for being mistress of the position, she put her foot firmly down and meant to remain mistress.

"Such, gentlemen, is the edifying history of Jenkins in the past. What he may become in the future I am not clairvoyant enough to prognosticate, yet, at the present, he is piling up the dimes and making cigar lights of five-pound notes."

The Swampers

Chapter XIV. Jack Milton Makes for the West.

TO the mind poetic, artistic, romantic or retrospective, Australia is not the land for the development of these imaginative faculties, and I much fear will not be for ages, or at least generations, to come. Yet if ever Apollo condescends to honour this vast continent of gold with his presence or those of his handmaids, I fancy that they will avoid those latitudes between 30° and 35°, for it is there that Pluto holds his empire.

Opals and other precious gems, gold, silver, copper, iron, coal, and all the other hard gifts which the god of the nether world offers to his serfs, are to be found here to those who can wrest them from the Genii of the fiery and waterless desert, yet the streams and woodlands so necessary for the existence of the gentler deities are wanting.

Truth may perchance be found at the bottom of an artesian well, as trusting people will persist in believing that she dwells with the mining expert, but the Naiads are not be found beside the condensed water tanks. The skies are too metallic in the hardness of their lustre for Poesy to soar through, the gum trees too shadeless and avaricious in their thirst, for Dryads to disport under.

And yet, who knows? Perchance in the far and distant future an Australian race may come into existence who will in some sense resemble the Greeks in their art instincts, as now they do in their vices. It may yet come to pass that suitable and fair cities may fringe those sapphire seas, instead of shapeless blocks and arid streets.

When they have dug gold enough out of the flinty soil to satisfy even their eucalyptine souls, they may begin to patronise native-bred sculptors, painters and architects. The art instinct seems already dawning in Victoria, albeit the pioneers of art there are likely to be martyrs. In New South Wales it is as yet darkest night.

The Swampers

But, if the great ideas and noble aspirations which have made the Greeks the admired of nations, and those tender and pretty fancies which render England and Germany such haunted lands, are absent from this dry-as-dust and materialistic continent, no one who has visited its sadly uninteresting shores can deny that, as far as worldly prosperity and rude vitality go, it is stupendously great. The present possessors may be girded inches thick with callous selfishness, and totally devoid of originality and ideality, but they are undoubtedly robust and go-ahead in their blundering and heartless manner. Ready to endure untold hardships and discomforts to gain their aims and win a position. Existing only for lucre in its most sordid sense, they force nutriment even from the most arid sand-desert. For this strength of purpose and indomitable will-force, they must be admired, if they fail to win affection. Their country also, to those who can exist without traditions or sympathy, is great, and must yet be greater as it is developed and its resources fostered. Sensitive and poetic hearts may be broken, but Australia must advance as she desires to advance, in worldly prosperity, aggressive materialism and ostentatious parade. Every Australian, male or female, is born with the one great desire, which bears down every other passion, to become rich in worldly goods. He or she can only respect wealth, therefore they have no room in that land for a Socrates, a Buddha, or a Jesus Christ. They are plutocrats to the inmost recesses of their souls.

When a man is hard up in Australia, there are but three courses open to him, for the fourth, that of trading upon the sympathy or benevolence of his fellow creatures, is an utter impossibility. If hope still clings to his heart, he turns his face towards the wilderness, and with his pick and shovel, attempts to force from Mother Nature her gifts. He knows as he steps out, that he will probably die of starvation by the way, yet that fate is as certain in the city, if he lingers after he has lost the only thing that can win him a smile or a hand-shake from his fellowman; there is no disinterested friendship in Australia, which is the cause why so many turn criminals there. He may join the school of Jack Milton in whatever branch his talents lie. House-breaking, pocket-picking in its simple or more elaborate methods, that is, he may dip his fingers directly into the pockets of his fellows and get a trifle now and again dangerously, or he may become the speculative adventurer, start offices or enter Parliament. There are a hundred different openings for the inventive thief, who is reduced to trade on his talents, but not one for the honest man who has become destitute.

The third course is suicide if he has not courage to face starvation and the Wallaby track, and too much sentiment to go in for robbery. One thing he may be sure of, neither his relations, his so-called friends, nor Society at large, care one iota what becomes of him.

Thus he learns to live for himself, as his wife, children, and other relations are doing. When he is rich he buys his pleasures with callous disregard. When he is poor he has to learn to do without, so this knowledge braces him up in the hour of his adversity, and he goes forth with a hard laugh, and renders him impervious to pity in the hour of his prosperity. It is not the philosophy of Socrates I will admit, nor does it tend to make humanity a lovely contemplation, yet it is a philosophy of its kind. The philosophy that comforted that ancient band of refugees who left their wives and children to the mercy of the foe, satisfied that there would be no difficulty in finding women and raising children wherever they chanced to settle.

Jack Milton was too much experienced in colonial city life, as well as colonial prisons, to play the folly of Lot's wife and look behind him as he went on his journey. What the future held for him was alone the subject to speculate upon. He had committed the mistake of giving way once to sentiment, possibly he would do so again, for that he had chosen housebreaking instead of the more lucrative and respectable game of swindling, proved that he had a weak strain of sentiment about his composition, which was decidedly anti-colonial. Yet the past, as far as this weakness, Rosa, was concerned, was as much beyond recall as last week's dinner.

At Euriouie, a small township fifty miles from Silverton, which was the first place at which he ventured to rest after leaving Pooncaria, he got a glance at some of the late Sydney papers, and read an account of the divorce and knew that he was now once again free from the noose of Hymen, although still within the reach of the more speedy noose of Ketch.

He had still his false beard and wig on, but they were getting sadly worn and would soon be useless as disguises; however, the small population of this township being mostly rough-and-ready miners, they were not too inquisitive. Indeed, their main desire appeared to be to induce him to move on as quickly as possible, being fearful that he had come to look for work.

They told him they were on half-time themselves, and even that at reduced wages, so that there was no use his applying if that was his intention.

"The mines all round here are over-crowded, the work is killing, not one man in a hundred can stand these mines longer than nine months, so take our square tip and clear out while you can."

Jack thought this advice wholesome in more ways than one, although he sneered a little at the narrowness of these New South Welshmen. No, strangers are not made welcome where there is any work likely to be had, in any portion of that colony.

He enquired his way north and was directed to Milperinka, the township of the Albert Gold Field near Mount Brown, and after a good night's rest and with a fresh stock of provisions, he shook the dust of Euriouie from him and set off on the coach track for another hundred and fifty miles.

From Milperinka he passed through Tibbooburra, twenty miles' distance, only waiting at each of these gold centres long enough to refresh himself and his horses, and then, crossing the borders, he found himself at Wompah in Queensland; at last he was out of the dreaded colony, although still too near it to be able to breathe safely.

He had now shaken the blood-hounds off his scent, and need go no farther north. By making careful enquiries at Wompah, he learnt that due west a hundred and fifty miles, he would reach a small

The Swampers

squatters' settlement called Tinga-Tinga in South Australia, with outlying stations for another couple of hundred miles north-west beyond the top of Lake Eyre. He announced to the residents of Wompah that he was on an exploring expedition, therefore he was received with great kindness and furnished not only with every information, but presented with another good horse and as much provisions as they could carry.

"You have a roughish bit of country to cross before you reach West Australia, but this isn't a bad time of year to take it. The rains may be on any day now and fill the creeks, and there are water-holes on the way if you keep well to the southward. Look out for the natives, that's all, for they are a bad lot about these quarters."

He had now four pack horses, two laden with food and sleeping blankets, and two with water kegs. These were all in first-rate condition, and as the route to be taken was pretty clearly mapped out, he resolved to get on to Giles' lower track as soon as he could make it. Once out of the reach of the telegraph posts and out of sight of men who studied newspapers and public descriptions, he could afford to cast aside his disguise and be himself.

Of course the natives were to be reckoned as one of the formidable dangers in crossing that vast track alone, but Jack had before now been amongst natives, and he had a theory of his own respecting them. It was well known that whereas they often fell upon parties, yet they had been known to extend their patronage to the solitary traveller. With the probable risks of death from hunger and thirst, the risks of a spear-given quietus must be also taken.

Therefore, thanking his kindly friends for the hospitality and gifts they had so freely bestowed upon him, he bade them adieu and rode into the wilderness.

He had no intention of touching upon Tinga-Tinga if he could get past it without being observed, for he had now provisions enough to last him a couple of months, and a fortnight's supply of water, as he meant to use them. For the past fortnight he had been training to do

The Swampers

with as little food as could carry him along, and had succeeded wonderfully in restraining from liquids. He now resolved to limit himself still more and only boil his billy once every two days. He had read that the Arabs who have to cross the deserts make a rule to eat and drink only once every-twentyfour hours, and what an Arab could do, he meant to try.

The temperature was hot and dry, but the atmosphere was clear and exhilarating, in the latitude in which he was. The ground also well covered with grass, so that he had no trouble in finding his horses.

He was still within the belt of civilization, and might at any time come upon a party of outlying police, for there was a large reward offered for his capture, therefore he kept as much as he could within the cover of the bush, avoiding such open tracks as were used by the sheep.

He made a long journey each day, starting at daybreak and only resting when night came on. At times the sky would be filled with heavy clouds as if rain was coming, but as yet none came. In six days' time he came to what he guessed was Cooper's Creek, which, although pretty dry, had yet some well-filled water-holes along its channel. Here he rested for a full day to refresh his horses, then, filling his kegs, he went on, keeping north-west as he had been told.

During those seven days he had met no one and seen no signs of habitations, although he could tell from the ground that flocks of sheep had been feeding there; therefore he still wore his disguise, although longing to cast it aside.

On the tenth day he saw in the distance a shepherd's hut, and at the sight his desire for companionship grew too strong to resist. He had been feeling the depression of isolation like a nightmare for the past two days, and could have parted with half the gold he carried to hear the sound of a human voice; therefore he made for the hut and about sundown came up to it and was hailed by the shepherd with as much eagerness and pleasure as he himself felt. These shepherds lead terribly lonely and monotonous lives in such isolated back

The Swampers

stations as this was, often seeing no one from year's end to year's end.

After supper the shepherd, who was a man of about sixty, and appeared stupid with his dreadful existence, informed him that his was the last white face he would see this side of Western Australia. In another day Jack could with all safety cast aside his disguise.

The hut he was in was built of rough slabs, yet the owner had papered the walls with prints cut from old illustrated papers and such cuttings of poetry and specimens of humour as these papers give.

As Jack was looking over these listlessly his attention was suddenly attracted to a wood-cut of himself, and under it a full description with the reward offered for his apprehension. It was a police sheet, and had only recently been stuck up. "What have you got there, mate?" he asked carelessly.

"That," answered the man, looking at it stupidly for a moment, then brightening up somewhat. "It was left me the day before yesterday by a party of traps who came here with the trackers. A big bank robbery and murder at Sydney by a fellow called Milton."

"Have they tracked him this way?" asked Jack quietly, yet with the perspiration breaking out on him.

"No, they are merely patrolling this district and leaving the description at all the stations, in case he may try this road out of the colony—have you not heard about that business?" "No, I haven't been near a newspaper this two months past."

"He's not likely to come this way," said the shepherd. "With all that loot, I reckon he's been smuggled away in some vessel that was ready prepared for him." The shepherd as he said this flung himself on his bunk and fell asleep, while Jack still sat smoking and thinking.

The Swampers

Chapter XV. The Dream Mine.

"GIVE us that yarn about your mine, Wallace!" cried the boys as they sat inside the Hotel at Kalgourlie, on the next night. "By George! it was a lucky dream, and no mistake."

"It was," replied Wallace serenely. "Well, as you seem in want of conversation to-night, it may enliven you, so here goes."

There were three of us on that prospecting job. Coolgardie Joseph, Forky Ben, and myself.

Forky Ben was a singular customer, of about fifty years of age, not bad as a mate, for he could cook well, and did not shirk his work, and was besides an entertaining companion, having seen a great deal of the shady side of the colonies, done various times for misdeeds in the past, and yet was about as honest as one can expect to find on the gold fields nowadays.

He had started his colonial experiences as a convict, and, having served his time, had likewise served his adopted country as a policeman, and won considerable reputation in the force. His bane had been his wife, who represented his evil genius in all his undertakings, until she left him, ruined, yet with a chance of doing better himself. We fell across Forky Ben when on the "Wallaby track" (the tramp), and as he showed up gamely then, we had stuck together ever since, through good and bad luck.

Not much good luck hitherto, I must say, for although Westralia has gold enough, it is the rich man's country, and you know what that means, the men who can afford to fix up machinery will make the coin all right, but as for nuggets and alluvial mining our show was not up to much, and we could not afford to play about the quartz.

I can tell you, though, I have seen that same quartz with the ore thick enough through it to make one's mouth water and wish that quartz-crushing machines didn't cost such a pile of money. I could lay my

The Swampers

finger on spots of the map of Westralia where I am positive that fortunes lie pocketed, and I can tell you the boom isn't big enough. Westralia won't disappoint its backers, so far as the ore is concerned at least.

For all that, it isn't quite the place to bring a young, blushing and delicately-nurtured bride to yet, who may not have grown up to live on tinned sardines, condensed water, and such like luxuries exclusively. No, the bride mightn't like it much; besides, if she was a cleanly-inclined girl she would be apt to pine after a bit of soap, which would ruin her husband, as water is too expensive to waste that way.

Yes, you all know the truth about this land, boys, as I know it. The water is about as expensive as the whisky, sometimes more so. The tinned meat isn't always to be depended upon, and there are a hundred other inconveniences to be endured that I needn't mention at present, only the gold is here all right, also other natural means of wealth yet to be utilized.

My mate, Forky Ben, was an old colonial, he had seen three generations growing up, and as he said, each one seemed to be going back; "in fact, if the colonial goes on growing much more legs, and don't develop a little more body, the country will be to let in another twenty years."

Forky was great on this point as to the decadence of the colonials. "I've watched 'em," he would say, striking his pannikin on the log, "I've watched them a-growing up, and gradually losing all principle and humanity; the first lot as comes out for their country's good, may be a bit vicious at times, but they have hearts in them and stick to a friend, the second breed ain't so dusty, still they don't care much for their friends, nor do they think a man's word is worth considering, but the good Lord help us from the third generation; they'll sit on a fence all the blessed day planning out a mean robbery on a benefactor: they don't know what truth means, and as for faith or trust, they are sounds to laugh at with the young bred Australian; he knows how to bet on a horse or a cricket or a football match. Oh,

The Swampers

yes. The youngest baby is up to that as soon as he can toddle, but as for work, or sticking to a pal, they couldn't see it and don't know what it means, they don't believe in a God, they have no country to believe in, and no traditions to uphold. They only credit the one who can get the better of them. All legs, conceit and bounce, without belly or brains, they are like stag-hounds, inveterate and sneaking biters."

Forky Ben was a philosopher in his crude way, and he knew the people he talked about particularly well. He was a Sydney side colonial in the adopted sense, yet he did admit that the Victorian had not gone back quite so rapidly as the New South Welshers.

"They are rotten," he would shout wildly sometimes. "What they want now, is to be conquered and wiped out."

I was merely a trifler in the gold-finding business. I had left London for a time for my health's sake, and was merely waiting on a disputed legacy. The House of Lords would, in good time, settle my affairs; meanwhile, I thought I'd look round me a little and gain experience; therefore, as Westralia was on the table when I left, I thought I might as well take that portion of the globe. Africa tempted me for a time, but I finally decided to take it afterwards. I picked up my chum on the road. I was riding along when I fell first upon Coolgardie Joseph, as we always called him. The country was arid. I was hot and thirsty, and my knacker ditto, when, as I passed a portion of the gulley, I heard a human voice, husky and doleful as despair and pain could make the voice human; it was a moan—a groan and a curse combined—the sound men utter when God seems to forsake them, and they repudiate the Forsaker.

I went over to where he lay and lifted him up to my saddle beside me, and then, when I had carried him to where I could give him some succour, he told me his yarn, which somehow endeared him to me.

He had left England in a fit of spleen—had grown sick of his club-friends, likewise those who tried to get nearer to him, to use his own words:

The Swampers

"I loved a woman, but she didn't seem to care much for me, so I left. When love gets hold of a man, it seems to blot out all the rest of life's interests. I didn't care much for anything else after that woman, she seemed to comprise my all. My friends—yes, I liked them, but I didn't want to see them just then, I wanted to be by myself with my special wounds to doctor, therefore, I came away from England. The boys knew my woman and knew me, therefore that was enough; they knew that I didn't want to say good-bye to them, and so they let me go quietly.

"I had a mighty craving on me just at that time. I had relations in Australia, in Sydney—a brother and two sisters, to whom, as a boy, I had felt tender, therefore I thought, like the prodigal of old, I'll go to my father's house, and peradventure they will receive me.

"I was no prodigal in the sense of the husks, for I had done work enough to make people who owned me, as I fondly thought, proud enough of me. Well! at Albany I got a letter from this brother, repudiating me utterly—he thought I was coming out to ask help from him, and he told me, in language forcible and terse, to go to the Devil.

"I went to Sydney and interviewed him, and the rest of the domestic crew; he repeated in language what he had written, and with an effort I plucked him out of my heart. My other relations were kind after a style, yet I had not represented the family dignity, so they also gave me the cold shoulder, with their middle-class parvenus relations; they were rich so far, and they politely ignored me; in fact, I was a pariah amongst these wretched provincials.

"I studied the vile crew, I had grown accustomed to aristocrats as my friends, and as I saw the paltry tricks of these wretched menials, I gave the game up and said to myself—let me out to the wilds once more, where I can see men and women as God made them and meant them to be. I cut all that by blood belonged to me straight out of my heart, and, mounting my horse, rode off free and so far happy." This was the tale of Coolgardie Joseph, my mate. He was personally to me a more interesting character than Forky Ben,

The Swampers

because he felt a strain of poetry, and had experienced a touch of heart bitterness, which, as I have also felt it, always appeals to me.

In this fashion we got together, the three of us. Forky Ben, Coolgardie Joseph and myself; we never quarrelled, and we always worked for the common end. The making of money enough to get home and enjoy ourselves—for, after all, England is the place for Englishmen.

The story of Coolgardie Joseph, however, was not much more edifying than that of Forky Ben, and considerably less amusing, for while some humour may be extracted out of the wily ways of a tricky spouse, with the hundred and one dodges that a man has to take to in order to live in the side paths of colonial commerce—the quarrelling between uncongenial and unfeeling relatives is too commonplace and sordid to get anything like a grin out of.

I did not of course endorse this wholesale condemnation of Forky Ben respecting the third generation of New South Welshers; there must be good, bad and indifferent specimens in this section of humanity, as there are in other communities. What I have studied of their politicians, hasn't greatly impressed me as to their probity. The shopkeepers' notions of fair dealing may, to put it mildly, be just a little vague, and there are certainly an overwhelming proportion of bounders and larrikins amongst them, yet, for all that, the parent colony of New South Wales has its points, and many a warm dispute we had about these, Forky Ben and Coolgardie Joseph siding against me, while I stuck up for the condemned section as well as an impartial man could do.

Forky Ben had a face, old and seamed as a piece of crackle ware, with crow-blue eyes and a neck like an English terrier; his figure also was thin and spare, but wiry.

Coolgardie Joseph was a tall, good-looking fellow of about thirty-three, without much flesh to his bones, and mostly serious in his demeanour. Possibly this habit of regarding things too earnestly was

The Swampers

the cause of his taking so much to heart the paltry meanness of his own kindred.

Where I had found him on the point of giving up the game, was as lonely a gully as one could well imagine. Desolate and bare, with an odd patch here and there of dried-up scrub, and nothing but stretches of hot dust and sand on either side of it.

He had been on the tramp with two other colonials whose acquaintance he had made on board the steamer coming round, and they were all pushing on to get to the gold-fields, forty-six miles distant from where he caved in. His feet had given way, and after one or two rough remonstrances, his mates had left him to die and be done with it, which was the only course they could have taken, unless they desired to share his doom likewise. There are no almshouses or pauper establishments in the colonies, so that when men and women get played out there, they are at liberty to hang or drown themselves, get into jail or the infirmary, and die as soon as possible, no one else cares how soon, for each is fighting for his own hand. The soil of Australia is more productive of cynics than philanthropists, and humanity is not quite so highly valued as sheep and cattle.

He had dropped to earth and there they left him, without more than a backward glance to see if he was not following. Two days afterwards they reached the goldfields and got a job at four pounds a week each. Joseph also might have got a job on the same terms, only that we decided to do a bit of prospecting on our own account, for Forky Ben was an experienced miner, and when he spoke hopefully, we believed in his prophecies.

We prowled about here and there as far away from the general camp as we could get, and with varying luck; sometimes we picked up enough to keep us in grub, sometimes we worked to a dead loss, and at odd times we made enough in one or two hours to keep us going for a fortnight or three weeks.

The Swampers

We were working on the dry system, yet Forky Ben had a keen touch and slight, and seldom allowed many specks to slip through his hand. During the day the heat was intense, while the nights were cold and bone-piercing; the water also which we had to purchase was bad, and, as I have said, the provisions were worse even than the water; so that there was only hard work and little comfort to be got out of the life we were leading, and I, for one, had almost made up my mind to give it best and return to civilization.

One night we were lying in front of our tent, trying to extract what comfort we could glean out of our pipes, after a supper of damper and tinned salmon, which was not conspicuous for its freshness. None of us had washed for a week past, and then it was only the end of a damp towel passed over the eyes to clear the sand out, which we dignified by the title of a wash.

Coolgardie Joseph, who was always of a sentimental turn, had been telling us about that young lady of his in the old country whom he yet hoped to marry, if ever he was rich enough, and some other fellow didn't get before him, and then, his yarn over, he turned round with a yawn and fell asleep.

Forky Ben lay on his back and dilated on the delights a small and snug country inn would be to a man at his time of life, and with his vast experiences. He was content to talk, and did not ask too much attention from his hearers, so that I lay half dozing and looking at the moon which was just appearing over the distant range, when all at once my mind became concentrated on the gully where first I saw Coolgardie Joseph. The actual scenery seemed to vanish from my eyes and instead of the half moon a bright glare of daylight pervaded the scene. I saw the spot where Joseph had lain when I rode up, but where his body had covered was now a hole, and in it a man digging and throwing up the earth.

He had not got far down, but he was working with a purpose and as I strode over to the edge and looked in, I recognised Coolgardie Joseph himself pegging away. I picked up a handful of the earth that

The Swampers

he was shovelling out and as I filtered it through my fingers, the sun-rays glistened on the yellow specks—it was thick with gold-dust.

Next instant the fancy picture vanished, leaving me lying in front of the tent with Forky Ben still gabbling about that old English inn where he meant to end his days, and Coolgardie Joseph grunting in his sleep like a pig after an extra feed.

A moment afterwards, and while I was still rubbing my eyes, he started up with an exclamation:

"By Jove! but I have had a dream, to be sure."

"What was it?" I asked curiously.

"You remember that gully—where you found me?"

"Yes—yes!"

"Could you find the spot where I was lying?"

"Easily—why?"

"I dreamt just now that I was back there and digging a hole from which half the dirt I flung out was gold dust."

"Ah," said Forky Ben, "dreams always are to be read contrary fashion, so that dream of yours means nothing."

"Well, Ben, just at the time Joseph was having his dream, I also saw him on the same spot digging away, and I specimened the earth to find it as he has described—crowded."

"Did you dream that, mate?" asked both Coolgardie Joseph and Forky Ben with eager interest, sitting up and looking at me open-mouthed.

The Swampers

"Well, boys, I don't know whether to call it a dream or a waking vision, but I saw it and handled the dirt."

"Then by the Lord Harry! dream or vision, that's the spot for us to fossick. Two men can't dream a lie at the same time. It's a revelation, that's what I call it," cried out Forky Ben, excitedly.

We did not sleep much that night you may depend, and when morning came we were off to the camp for a month's supply of stores, and then packing up, we went on the backward track, without mentioning the matter to anyone.

The gully was easy to find, and it did not take me long to peg out the place where I had found Joseph cursing the Providence that had brought him to his fortune, for the first two hours of digging showed us that our dreams had not been delusions, then each bucket came up, filled with earth, thickly impregnated with gold.

Curious how nasty bad tinned salmon and condensed water taste when luck is hanging back, and how little we are apt to consider such trifles when good fortune is with us. The camp lay forty-six miles from us, and our single horse had little enough to eat in that desert; every drop of water had to be carried from the camp, so that although we were most economical over it, still the water bags had to be replenished every third or fourth day, which meant a waste of time that we grudged, so eager were we to pile up the dust, before the rush came.

And we got it too, in minute specks at first, yet plentiful, then as we went deeper into the earth, the nuggets kept growing bigger — pennyweights, then half and whole ounces, with occasional lumps which were worth the lifting.

We knew the big nuggets were all right, but we were better pleased with the tiny specks and dust, for those meant a long bit of business. After we had satisfied ourselves with the one hole we struck out in other directions, to find that we had discovered a field. There were quartz ridges round us on every side, and doubtless they also were seamed as the soil was with the precious ore.

In two months we had made three thousand pounds apiece, which would be enough to carry us to England and float our company; therefore, like wise men, we sat down to consider our future plans. We must purchase the ground first and then seal it up, without raising suspicion, not an easy matter amongst gold seekers.

I was deputed to work the oracle while with Winchesters and Colts my mates mounted guard over our future property, and I fancy, for a new chum, I managed fairly well to pull the blinkers over the warden, so that cautiously we purchased the entire gully, after which we pitched aside all disguise and exhibited the field.

Gracious Heavens! what a magic power gold has to transform a man in the eyes of his friends. Coolgardie Joseph, who had been metaphorically vomited out of Sydney, returned to it before he sailed to England, a king. The narrow-minded provincials wallowed before him and literally worshipped him, without winning a spark of respect or regard from him in return. It is difficult to blind even a millionaire by flattery, who has had the reverse side of the picture presented to him in the days of his adversity. In England he found this young lady still waiting for him. Certain malicious persons told him that she had almost got married to the wrong man during his absence, only that the wrong man had gone away without committing himself, but that is the way of the malicious world, and Joseph had the good taste not to believe them, so that he married his own true love, and I think they are bound to be happy, for they are very wealthy, and wealthy people are always happy, are they not? His relations write every mail gushing letters to him and his bonnie bride, but Coolgardie Joseph does not answer these affectionate epistles.

Forky Ben has reached the height of his ambition—a cosy inn, situated in one of the most charming parts of dear old England, yet he is not quite happy because, singular to relate, after a twenty years' absence, his dear wife turned up to manage the bar for him. They

The Swampers

met, as spectres are supposed to meet on the shores of the Styx, both having been dead to each other for so many years. Forky Ben looked aghast, panted for a few moments, and recognised the good lady. Mrs. Forky likewise started back, at the sight of her dear and lamented one, but she had come upon him prepared, for a rich man cannot hide his light nor his name under a bushel. After her first start of surprise she asserted her rights, and Forky collapsed. She now manages the country inn, and her respected husband makes the best of the situation.

I have nothing personally to grumble at either, for we are garnering in the golden grain, and our field has a considerable boom in the market, with the shares steadily rising and eagerly sought after, as you all know.

The Swampers

Chapter XVI Rosa's Second Marriage.

"DASH it all, Arthur! You don't mean to say that you expect a girl of my colonial spirit to go on leading the same hum-drum existence after we are married that I have done so long."

Rosa and her cousin were sitting on a little rock on the Clontarf sands one afternoon a few days before the celebration of their wedding. They had come here for quiet and a chat over affairs, and the prudent Chester had raised her just ire by suggesting that it would be wise for them to lie low, like Brer Fox, for a time.

"With all the money we have I mean to cut a splash in Sydney," she said energetically and with flashing eyes. "Therefore you may as well drop those mean ideas, Arthur, as fast as you like. Nothing less than a house at Potts' Point will satisfy me, with a proper set-out in the way of horses and carriages, and all the rest of the flummery. We can easily afford it, therefore drop your preaching and let me boss that show, or your bed won't be rose leaves, I can tell you, my boy."

"As far as cash goes, yes, I daresay we could afford Potts' Point and the other etceteras if we were anywhere else than in our native city, but, Rosa, don't you forget this, if the police don't suspect us at present it is only because we are not making any extra splashing. If we do so, we shall have them down upon us with a hundred nasty inquisitive questions as to our means of keeping it up, which will be extremely difficult for us to answer to their satisfaction. You see, my dear, our townsmen all know us, and what we were before Milton came on the scene, while if my books are called for, I cannot show a bigger income than four hundred a year, and that won't run to Potts' Point by a long chalk."

Rosa beat the sands with her shapely feet while an angry glow burned on her cheeks. What tenderness she had felt towards her cousin, while he was forbidden fruit, seemed to have vanished now that the law was about to sanction their union.

The Swampers

"Well, what do you propose to do after we are married, Arthur?" she asked at length.

"Take a little house and furnish it modestly, if you are tired of Trumpet Tree Cottage, and live quietly on my income for a year or two until this affair is forgotten, then come out by degrees——"

"Goodness gracious—a year or two?" cried Rosa aghast. "Thank you kindly, but I have no intention to wait till I am hoary-headed before I partake of the sweets of life. No, I mean to enjoy it while I am young or not at all—give us another suggestion?" "To leave this and go to London or Paris where no one knows about us, then we may do as we like."

"This is as bad as the obscurity you first proposed. It is just because I am a Sydney native, that I want to show off in Sydney. There would be no fun showing off anywhere else, and I'd die amongst strangers. I'll tell you a much better idea, that ought to cover all your miserable and cowardly objections."

"What is that, Rosa?" he asked meekly, for he dared not resent her words, and was already tumbling into the proper condition of a Sydney husband.

"Let's take a wedding trip to the west instead of the Blue Mountains, and so kill two birds with one stone." "What do you mean, Rosa?"

"Go to the goldfields of West Australia where Jack is trying to reach, and stay there for a time. You can start a business as solicitor and mining expert and speculate a bit, and I'll open a hotel. We need not stay there long—only long enough to satisfy ourselves as to whether Jack gets through or not, and give our friends in Sydney a good reason for our fortune, d'ye twigavous, Arthur?"

"By George! Rosa, I believe you are a bit anxious about Jack, now you have chucked him," said Chester jealously, and with not a little dread in his voice. Rosa looked at him with twinkling eyes, and uttered a mocking laugh.

The Swampers

"Yes, I am anxious to learn the last of Jack Milton, for after all he wasn't white-livered, but not for the reason you suppose, Cousin Arthur. You are much better suited to me than he was. I don't feel mean with you as I did with him, and when a fellow makes a woman feel mean she is bound to hate him. That is why so many of us take up with Chinamen, and like them as we do; they don't expect too much from us. I want to see if Jack gets through safely and keep him under my eye if he does until he is past blabbing on us, then we need have no fear in the future—and if I take a hotel I'm sure to learn something about him if he turns up on the other side."

"And then, Rosa?"

"Oh, I'll manage that part of the business without bothering you, Arthur—the then—I'm good enough looking to get some man to do for him if he comes to hand on the diggings. You leave all that to me."

Arthur Chester dared not look at this creamfaced modern Lucretia, but kept his glances fixed on the point of his walking-stick. He was a craven to the core of his false and crafty soul, and for a moment again he meditated sneaking away with the loot before the wedding took place, but the next instant's reflection showed him the futility of such a plan with that telegraphic belt of Puck's round the habitable globe. No, he had as helplessly meshed himself as ever any of the subjects of the Borgia, and was as much dependent upon her caprice as were the suitors of that fair but fatal Italian dame.

An icy chill struck his heart as if already he felt the first symptoms of the aqua tofana, and a deadly abhorrence filled his whole being for the handsome wanton at his side; if he could only have been sure about hiding her corpse he would gladly have strangled her where they thus sat, but that also was not to be thought of. He must marry her and let her do as she liked, and look out for his own carcase. "Well, Arthur, what do you think of my plan?"

The Swampers

Arthur roused himself and replied smoothly: "It is good enough, Rosa—perhaps the best under the circumstances, if you are willing to rough it amongst the 'sand gropers.'"

"Ah, I'll rough it for the short time we are there. Besides, there is money to be made and good fun to be got out of the boys. We'll cart round my piano, and make our hotel the swagger canvas establishment on the fields, while the mining expert business will just suit you. You know little Tony Jenkins is doing well at Kalgourlie. He'll put you up to all the wrinkles, so we may consider that settled, I suppose?"

"Yes, since you wish it, Rosa."

"There now, you are once more the model husband I expected you to be, dear old boy. Set to work at once and sell your practice, also secure an agency or two for wines, etc., and we'll manage our honeymoon without any expense, and have a roaring time of it as well. You see what it is to have a practical girl at your elbow, you dear duffer."

They were alone on the shore, so she flung her arms round his neck and kissed him effusively, while he responded as best he could to that embrace. Her kisses no longer had the same flavour to him as they had when he was robbing another man of them, therefore there was all the more necessity for feigning, although as far as she was concerned he need not have done so, as she had long ago lost all verve for such lover-like demonstrations, if ever she had taken pleasure in them. Callous and utterly depraved by nature, deceit was the only caviare that could raise her appetite.

Arthur Chester had one strong hold over his cousin, and this he did not mean to relinquish if he could retain it by fair or foul means. He held the money, some of it invested and banked in his own name, and the bulk of the last haul concealed. He would not tell her where he kept it in spite of all her blandishments, but yet he knew that the possession would not be his long if she chose to give a hint to the police and a diligent professional search was conducted. Thus they

The Swampers

were held together by a more powerful bond than love or kinship would have proved to such natures, and that was mutual interest. Rosa trusted that he would take this money with him on their trip west, but, much as he hated to leave it behind, he was too wary to carry so much money about; therefore, after a good deal of agonized cogitation, he decided to bury it under his own house and shut the place up during their absence.

This he did at such times as he could get Rosa and his housekeeper out of the way, by lifting the flooring and digging into the earth under it. First he dismissed his housekeeper with an advance of her wages, then he locked the door so that Rosa might not surprise him, and before afternoon, had his treasure secured and all traces removed. As it chanced, that day Rosa was busy with her trousseau shopping, so that he was not disturbed.

He did not sell his practice, but handed it over instead to a solicitor to manage for him during his absence, still keeping his door-plate up and the offices open. The house only he fastened up and left untenanted.

Rosa's father and mother were mighty indignant at her idea of leaving them and going in for the hotel business in Western Australia. They did not, of course, know how she had been provided for, for Australian children do not make confidants of their parents as a rule, but look after their own business from a very early age. They might also have condoned the hotel business, although it seemed to be a drop, had their daughter been more generous with them, but Rosa gave them very plainly to understand that after her second marriage they would both have to look after themselves, as she had no intention of contributing any longer toward their support.

This behaviour almost broke the heart of the gentlemanly loafer. To have to set once more to seek for work was a bitter and a desolate outlook, which turned Trumpet Tree Cottage almost into a house of mourning.

The Swampers

The marriage was a very swagger affair altogether, and the lunch arranged by one of the most fashionable caterers. Rosa was allowed to take her full fling here, and she spared no expense to make the exhibition a complete success. Her costume was a dream of angelic purity, shimmering silk, satin, gauze and orange flowers. Her blushes were almost virginal as she softly murmured the necessary responses, a lovely, timid, yet trusting and beautiful bride she looked at the altar that any amorous husband might well be proud to possess.

The champagne was excellent that flowed afterwards, for Chester had secured the Kalgourlie agency of the best wholesale firm of wine and spirit importers in Sydney, and they stood the liquor for the marriage feast. Already a large consignment had been forwarded by rail to Adelaide en route for the west, and paid for by the lawyer. He could afford to pay on the nail for what he ordered without raising any suspicions, therefore there was nothing to do now except to follow the stores which he had sent in advance. The usual speech-making took place, and good wishes expressed from those who envied them their luck, while Rosa had the soul-satisfying delight of knowing that her female friends would be ill for days after viewing her trousseau, which is quite enough to make any bride cheerful during the early days of her honeymoon.

Her father and mother wept bitterly at parting from their dear child—real heartfelt tears these were on the parents' side, as they thought ruefully upon the ten sovereigns which she had given them as a farewell and final gift. After these were melted, the desolate couple would once again have to take up the weary burden of life.

"Ah," they sighed, wiping their eyes as they returned to their lonely cottage, "Arthur Chester may be more respectable as a son-in-law, but Jack Milton would never have cast us adrift like this in our old age." Those two hearts that ought to have beat proudly at the change in their daughter's life felt a pang of regret for the divorced and vanished housebreaker.

The Swampers

The happy couple went by train to Melbourne, halting for the first night at Goulburn, where they put up at the best hotel and enjoyed themselves thoroughly.

No one suspected them to be on their honeymoon, as they conducted themselves like a wellmarried couple. There was none of that maudlin gushing that usually denotes the freshly yoked, nor any attempts to get into empty compartments. Arthur Chester read the papers, while Rosa made herself agreeable to her fellow-travellers, and as she was stylishly dressed and sprightly, she had no lack of attentive admirers on the way.

They spent two days at Melbourne, going about and looking at everything with the prejudiced and disparaging feelings of all true-bred cornstalks towards things Victorian, and decided with gleesome alacrity that its days were over. The magnificent houses of parliament, the splendid buildings of Collins Street, the library and picture gallery in Swanston Street, the gardens and arcades, even that wonder of the world, "Coles" book arcade, failed to impress them with any other feelings save disgust, or at least jealousy seemed like disgust to them. They sneered openly at the post office, and boasted about their own ornate establishment with happy pride, asking scoffingly, according to the wont of Sydney visitors, what there was about this wretched mud flat to be compared with that glory of creation, "The Harbour."

The Melbourne people, being accustomed to this sort of ignorant and narrow cackle, laughed good-naturedly at the infantine criticism, and chaffed them genially, as grown-up people will chaff children, which made this gentle pair depart with rage in their hearts at these rivals who considered themselves big enough to laugh at the virulent passions which their superior qualities created in their narrow-minded neighbours. "I never saw such a rotten hole," remarked Arthur vindictively, as he stood with his wife on the deck of the Adelaide steamer, while she steamed from the Yarrayarra. "The buildings are perfect botches."

"And the women hideous frumps," echoed Rosa; then more reflectively she added, "the men, however, are not so bad."

The Swampers

Chapter XVII. Tracked.

JACK MILTON rose as soon as the loud snores announced that the shepherd was asleep, and moved from the hut to a stump outside, where he could have his meditation undisturbed.

What the man had told him was enough to give him subject for thought. He had already travelled hundreds of miles, and spent nearly two months on the journey, reaching without hindrance the extreme outskirts of civilization only to find that he had not yet got beyond the long-reaching arm of the law. Now, were his efforts to be rendered in vain through this accursed sentiment that made him long for the sound of a human voice, luring him to visit this miserable and half-witted outpost?

Would he have been any better off, however, if he had gone on unconsciously into the wilds with those human bloodhounds of black trackers hunting about? He knew his danger now, but had he gone on without this warning he might have been trapped at his next resting place.

These terrible trackers, whose keen eyes could read and trace any footprints, no matter over what ground they trod or how long a time elapsed unless they were erased by their own countrymen. They would come here again. Oh, yes. That was a moral certainty. Perhaps to-night, to-morrow, or the next week. It did not matter, though it was a month after, they would be able to see at a glance that strangers had been here since their last visit, question the man inside as to who had been with him, and follow on until they ran him to earth.

The dreary waste before him was not at present in his mind. The days he might have to wander, suffering the pangs of thirst, with the countless other risks and dangers, did not at present trouble him. It was the appalling thought that after this he could no longer find even a temporary rest in sleep with that uncertainty behind. Those dusky-skinned, eagle-eyed, and indefatigable trackers.

The Swampers

To kill that shepherd would be of no service to him, since he could not cover his tracks. It was equally useless to confide in him and ask him to make up a story; the man had not wit enough left, after his crazing occupation of counting sheep, to hoodwink those man-hunters. Only one hope was left, that they might not come before this incident passed from the man's dazed and figure-crammed mind.

These shepherds lead a terrible life. To count their myriads of sheep daily and hourly is the sole occupation and diversion of their miserable hermit existence. Kingdoms may rise and fall, disasters overwhelm nations, people come and go without leaving any impression upon them, so long as the numbers of their flocks are the same to-day as yesterday. They can remember the visits of the dingoes, or the hostile blacks, only by the decrease of their numbers, which they have to account for out of their wages. They have become numbering machines and nothing else.

Reasoning in this way, Jack felt sure that the police must have been there only very recently, otherwise even the proclamation would have failed to recall their visit to him. Perhaps that very morning, or at the farthest within the last two days.

If he stole away now, while the man was asleep, to-morrow morning when he woke up, if he thought at all, he would conclude that he had only dreamt that he had a visitor, that is, if Jack removed all traces of his visit, and the police might pass on without calling upon the services of their bloodhounds.

It was a delicious night, in the month of May, with a keen, frosty air, and the hoar lying whitely upon the plain. The moon was at her full, shining from a deep green sky upon the far-reaching landscape, thickly covered with root-grubbing sheep. Fantastic-shaped clouds clustered over the heavens, with silvered edges and darkly grey sides.

Bare and dead gum-trees stood up like twisted white stumps on the near plain, over which the sheep grubbed and looked like patches of

The Swampers

dirty snow, while far away in the distance spread the shadow of dense scrub-land.

One leafless tree, or rather the decayed trunk of a gum-tree, stood a little way from the hut, with a rude ladder reaching up to a sturdy lower branch; this was the post from which the shepherd overlooked and counted his flock.

The dogs were all out guarding the sheep, with the exception of one who now lay by his master's bed. He was a docile, well-trained animal, and Jack had no fear of disturbing him as he moved about, now that he had once been admitted. His horses were at some distance, near the water-hole, within which still lay a fair supply. A deep well also had been dug to serve as an emergency when this supply ran short; yet there had been some rain lately, so that the water-hole had been replenished.

Jack stood for a few moments looking over this solemn and weird-like picture, the last of the kind he would likely see for some time if he managed to get away. He was glad now that the shepherd had not been at all curious to know his destination; glad likewise that he had asked so few questions about the country beyond. It was better to ride forward and trust to destiny.

Would that destiny lead him to a lingering death in the desert, or the ignominious but speedy doom of the gallows, and which was the consummation most devoutly to be desired?

He lifted his eyes for a moment to the arching heavens with the impotent yearning for wings, so that he might fly and leave no trace behind him. The yearning which comes upon hunted beast and man when they are beset, and is the unuttered prayer which afflicted life sends up so constantly to God, through that space vibrating with those messages from earth to heaven; and then like the answering whisper from an unseen guardian came to his mind some lines he had once read, and these braced him up.

The Swampers

They were lines from a poem by Joaquin Miller, and he only now remembered the two last verses, although at one time he had learnt the complete poem. These, however, rushed upon him like the briny blast from an arctic ocean.

"They sailed, and sailed, as winds might blow, Until at last the blanched mate said: 'Why now, not even God would know Should I and all my men fall dead.' These very winds forget their way. For God from these dread seas is gone. Now speak, brave Adm'ral, speak and say— He said: 'Sail on! sail on! and on.'

They sailed! They sailed! Then spake the mate: 'This mad sea shows his teeth to-night, He curls his lips; he lies in wait With lifted teeth as if to bite. Brave Adm'ral, say but one good word— What shall we do when hope is gone?' The words leapt as a leaping sword: 'Sail on! Sail on! Sail on! and on.'"

The unseen admiral of his soul had said the word in answer to his unspoken prayer. It was "Sail on" with or without hope, for although the ship fell to pieces, there was no turning back for him.

All doubt and dread had now departed from his heart; with a light step he went into the hut and carried out load by load his packs and gear. These he took over to where his horses were feeding, then after placing the pannikin on the nail from which the shepherd had taken it for his use, he walked out again for the last time, without disturbing the inmate, and harnessed his horses.

The dog, however, rose quietly and followed him, watching him get ready for his journey; then, with a friendly wag of its tail, it put its moist nose into his hand as he was about to mount and thus mutely bade him god-speed; with a gentle pat on the head of this well-wisher he went off, the dog watching him as long as he was in sight. The touch of that kindly nose lingered in his memory and moistened his eyes for many a day afterwards. Jack Milton rode forward briskly for the first dozen miles, urging his beasts on as fast as they could travel with their burdens, until he had put a mile or so of scrub

The Swampers

between himself and the shepherd's hut, then he slackened pace and permitted his horses to crop a little now and again as they rested.

He had no desire to fag his horses at this early stage of the journey, indeed he meant to take things as leisurely as he could after he had covered sufficient ground to render a hunt so far unlikely. The horses were heavily loaded, for he had been particular to provide himself with a good supply of water bags, and had replenished those that required it from the water-hole, so that he had a sufficient supply to last him and his horses at least twelve days with care, and provisions enough to last the journey, provided he could find herbage for his animals.

It is marvellous to think on the kind of food that contents cattle in Australia, grass from which every particle of moisture has been burnt out by the sun, until it has become mere dust; they can grub and find food on ground as bare as a new-ploughed field, satisfying themselves with the roots when they can get nothing else. A good fall of rain will also transform a desert into a green country in a magical quickness of time.

Jack Milton was no novice at bush-travelling, and like most of these unchronicled explorers, he was not easily frightened by the accounts he had read of the horrors of the interior as related in travellers' books. Of course there were chances when a man might wander for days over arid ground, particularly after such a dry season as had just passed, but at the present time he was more frightened of being swamped in some watershed, than of being starved for want of water. Although the clouds had not yet dropped any rain in his locality, it was hard to say where it might not be raining even then, or when the flood might catch him.

Through the night he went in a south-westerly direction, pushing his way through the dense mallee scrub, and when morning broke, he was still surrounded by the bush land, yet he kept steadily on, going in as straight a line as he could by aid of his compass.

The Swampers

For four days he kept on, making a distance as he supposed of about forty miles between early dawn and sundown each day, without any variety in his surroundings; then on the fifth day the country became more open and undulating, so that he could see round him as he went along. As yet he had not come to any water, but on the sixth day he reached a spot where the grass was green, in the centre of several high and rocky ranges. Shortly after this he came to a creek with several water-holes in it, also the signs of natives. Here he decided to rest his horses for a day. In front of him and still in the south-westerly direction, this grass-covered valley stretched as far as he could see. There were also some red gum and native fig-trees, with pines on the ridges.

It was a place which, as a bushman, satisfied him in all respects except one, which was that he was not likely to possess it long without interruption, as he saw on the sides of the water-holes the footprints of natives in considerable numbers.

However, here he was and here he meant to remain until his horses were freshened up a bit. If the natives came, they would either kill him or act as friends and rob him, and better that than fall into the hands of the police.

Considering that his disguise was now past all service, he cast it aside and after a good wash, he boiled his billy of tea, and making things comfortable for the horses, he lay down and went to sleep.

In the morning when he woke up, he discovered that the wig and beard that he had cast aside were gone. He had intended to bury them when daylight came, but now he knew that during his sleep he had been visited by these native owners of the land. He looked anxiously round him, but could see no one, nor were his horses or packs in any way interfered with, at which he wondered greatly, yet with considerable relief, for he took this as a sign that these midnight visitors were not hostile in their intentions at present.

The Swampers

All that day he waited and watched, but no one came to disturb his vigils, and so trusting once more to luck, he again lay down, placing his packs in a little cavern, in front of which he took up his position.

He was anxious now to be gone and slept very little that second night, therefore as soon as daylight broke, he was up filling his water-bags. This done, he made a hasty breakfast of cold water and damper, and then proceeded to load his pack-horses.

He had finished this task, and was just about to mount his riding-horse, when some instinct made him glance towards the entrance of the gully, and he saw that which made him leap into the saddle and move off at double quick time.

Three white police and half-a-dozen trackers about a mile distant, and urging along their jaded horses as fast as they could get them to go.

To wait for their coming up was not to be thought about. To run away was to declare his guilt at once, for they had seen him and were cooeeing to him to stop.

Cursing his ill-luck, he caught at the leading bridle of his pack-horses, and pretending not to see those coming or hear their cries, he urged them along at their full speed, thinking how soon he would have to abandon his pack-horses and ride for his life.

Up the glen he rode, heedless of the wild shouts sent after him, heedless also of the shots which they sent to attract his notice. As he looked back cautiously, he could see that their horses were dead beat and could go no farther, therefore a slight ray of hope passed through him that he might distance them, for they had stopped at his old camp and were unpacking their horses. Now that they had sighted him, they were in no immediate hurry. It was to be a long and stern chase. With a groan of anguish he drove round the angle of the gully and looked ahead.

The Swampers

Chapter XVIII. The Old, Old Game.

ONE quality colonials have, which is highly commendable, albeit it sometimes leads to awkward results. They pick up acquaintances easily, and make themselves at home anywhere without much loss of time.

Mrs. Rosa Chester and her husband had hardly delivered themselves of those criticisms, prompted by patriotic pride for their own settlement, before a suave and modulated voice repeated in their ears:

"You are perfectly correct in your remarks, and I heartily endorse your sentiments. It is a rotten hole without doubt, and the women are vulgar frights—from the delightful city of Sydney, if I mistake not?"

Rosa looked at the speaker and flushed prettily, for he was young and handsome, although vulture-like about the nose. Arthur regarded him with a slight restraint.

"Yes," replied Rosa readily, "we have just come from dear old Sydney, and are going round to West Australia."

"How very nice, since that is my destination. Also, madam, nice for me to have such charming company."

He bowed to Rosa, who blushed again, and looked at him from under her eyelids, not that she felt at all shy, but that she considered this sort of affectation fetching.

"Do you smoke?" said the stranger, turning to Arthur, after a sweet smile or leer at Rosa.

"Yes," replied Chester gruffly; he thought this stranger a little too sweet and complimentary for his taste.

The Swampers

"Try one of these—I fancy you'll like them," continued their fellow-passenger, producing an elegant cigar case and holding it out, again turning to Rosa with his most fascinating air: "That is, if madam does not object."

Madam could hardly object, seeing that on every side the passengers were puffing away like engine funnels; however, she replied: "I simply adore tobacco."

At that instant a noseful of negro-head wafted her way, and caused her to choke for a moment.

"When it is tobacco, and not tar-barrel," she added, with an angry glare at the owner of the negro-head.

Chester looked at the open case and noted that the contents were choice; his glance also travelled to the hand that held the case, where he saw on the little finger a plain gold signet ring with the square and compasses stamped upon it, and his reserve instantly melted.

"How old are these?" he asked, looking at the polite stranger.

"A little over ten years."

"Ah, then they ought to be good enough, yes, I'll try one."

Both men laughed as if a joke had been uttered, but a little dried-up-looking man with a dark and sallow face, who was standing near, stepped forward and coolly also abstracted one of the cigars, saying:

"Excuse me, gentlemen, but I am in the cigar business, and if these cigars are ten years old, they are not worth—a match."

He looked at the cigar closely for a moment, then smelling it, he bit off the end and proceeded to light up.

"Cool rather," remarked the young stranger, glancing sarcastically at Rosa and Arthur, while the withered man said calmly:

The Swampers

"Not so dusty, only it's been forced in the drying, and has not yet passed the first anniversary of its birth. I'll give you both a respectable cigar after tiffin."

In this way an acquaintance was begun between these passengers that rapidly ripened into a close intimacy for the rest of the voyage. Bertrand Decrow was the name of the young man, with the vulture-like nose, and steely blue eyes. He had come from the Charters Towers gold fields, and was going round to investigate the West Australian mines in the interests of some financial capitalists and partners of his. "You are an M. E. then?" asked Chester with considerable interest.

"Not exactly, if you mean, is that my profession? I certainly know all about the geology of mines and gold finding—and am going to act as an expert just now, but it is merely for the selfish purpose of purchasing if I see a good chance."

He spoke with the careless dignity of a man who had money to spend, and Chester resolved to cultivate him and draw him out. Being a native of Sydney and a lawyer, he considered himself smart enough for that bit of by-play, therefore, with a meaning glance at Rosa, he allowed her to take the young capitalist in hand, while he turned to speak to the cigar merchant. "Delightful passage so far, isn't it?"

"Oh, we'll have it like this all the way," returned the little man. "I travel this route often."

They had got round Port Philip Head by this time, and the sea was still calm, almost as a mill pond. At tiffin there had been a full attendance, and no one showed the least symptoms of scorning dinner.

"The company won't make much out of their passengers this trip, I guess. They have cut down the fares very fine, and must lose on tucker when it is weather like this."

The Swampers

Certainly the coasting steamship companies have almost arrived at the extreme point of cheap fares in Australia, as passengers are able to travel now first-class at about the same rate that was charged for steerage a few years ago, and at considerably less than people can travel round the coasts of England.

The company on this present passage, with the exception of the four who had struck up this sudden friendship, were of the most ordinary and uncouth description that it was possible to fancy ill-using a well-furnished saloon. They rushed and jostled each other for the seats on deck, and at the first sound of the bell for dinner drove downstairs like a stampede of cattle, "jumping" the seats, and refusing to abdicate if told that they had taken the wrong places.

The captain sat at the head of the table in a most dejected attitude, as if ashamed of the male and female animals he was forced to preside over, while the stewards in a panic, vainly tried to keep order and attend to their duty.

These colonials had paid their money, and they meant to take as much for the sacrifice as they possibly could, so that dispatch was the order of the hour, and each emptied the dish nearest him as rapidly as possible, without the slightest regard to his neighbour.

The first night Rosa might have fared badly, for she had not yet got over her strangeness, but Bertrand Decrow took her under his wing, got her down rapidly, and placed her beside the captain, with himself on the other side. By good luck also, Chester and the cigar merchant secured the two opposite seats, and so kept the rabble at the lower end of the table.

Decrow also proved himself a man of resource, and seemed to know the people he had to deal with, for as the steward entered with the vegetables, he stopped them from going past him until he and his protégés were served, therefore, Rosa felt grateful to him and soon recovered her native courage.

The Swampers

"Now, steward," he said in a loud tone, after dinner was over, "please to recollect that these four seats are engaged by us, and if anyone attempts to 'jump'them during this passage, I'll teach them a Townsville trick that'll make them sorry for it."

The steward nodded knowingly and replied: "I know that trick, sir, and I think you may rest easy. I'll look after them." "All right, then we needn't break our necks after this over meal times."

Decrow was a strong young man, with a long and carefully-cultivated moustache. He had also a musical taste, and could do a number of leger-demain tricks. While Chester and the cigar merchant went to the smoke room, Bertrand devoted himself to Rosa, amusing her and the others in the music room. He sang, and played on the piano, and accompanied her while she sang; afterwards they went together on the deck and did a little flirtation, finishing up the evening until the ladies' retiring hour, by showing her some pretty tricks with the cards.

Rosa felt she had made a conquest when she left him that night, with a tender and lingering squeeze of their hands, and, therefore, went to bed satisfied with her day, while he, equally satisfied, strolled along to the smoke room to have a final cigar and liquor.

When he got there he found Chester, the cigar merchant, and another of the passengers playing cards, and as Arthur wanted to have a chat with him, and the other man was just leaving off, Bertrand was easily persuaded to take his place in the next game.

They played for a few games at shilling points, most of which Chester won, then they passed down to the bar and had a drink or two, and afterwards went on deck. Here Chester proceeded to draw his young friend out on the duties of a mining expert, and soon found him to be one of the most confidential of Queenslanders.

"D'ye want to go in for that line?—for if you do, I can put you up to all the mysteries in no time. In fact, I'll introduce you as my man of business when we get there, if you like, and make it easy as drinking champagne for you."

Chester had told him he was a lawyer and wanted to combine that with the other if it could be done; therefore the bargain was at once clenched between them, and the husband of Rosa also went to his berth satisfied with his day.

The next night while the two were again walking the deck, this confiding young man remarked:

"What do you think of our friend the cigar merchant? — he seems a bit of an eccentric, don't you think?" "Yes, but he gives away remarkably fine cigars."

"You are right there, and if he is to be believed, he is inclined to give more away than cigars." "What do you mean?"

"Well, he tells me that his partner — you know the firm, doubtless, 'Sunthers and Green,' of Melbourne?" "Oh, yes, I have heard of them. Good, safe people."

"He is Green. Well, Sunthers is a bit of a philanthropist, and intends to endow an hospital up in Coolgardie, and Green has asked me to act for his partner and hand over a sum of money."

"Why can't he send it on?" asked the lawyer suspiciously.

"That's where his eccentricity comes in. He wants to do it anonymously, and he cannot do this if he sends a cheque, while he has got the notion into his head that postal orders ain't safe up there. What would you advise? Should I take this job on hand?" "I don't see why you shouldn't." "Neither do I." They walked along for a few moments silently and then Bertrand suddenly said:

"Look here, Chester, what's to prevent you acting in this instead of me? I daresay he'll be as ready to trust you as me with this anonymous commission, and it's more in your line. By Jove! it would be a first-class introduction, as they are sure to think it your own gift."

"I won't say 'No'if he offers it to me," answered Chester with a laugh; "and gives me a commission for my trouble, of course."

"Of course that is understood. Well, I'll touch him to-morrow before we land, and let you know."

Next day the matter was talked over between the three men, when Mr. Green, the cigar merchant, said:

"Well, Mr. Chester, as you are a lawyer, I can depend upon your discretion, and if Mr. Decrow, whose name I know well as a Townsville mine-owner, is agreeable to vouch for you—excuse my bluntness, but business is business——"

"Of course I'll vouch for our friend Chester, but what will satisfy you?" answered Bertrand impatiently.

"Well, I'll give you my cheque for a thousand pounds, or if you like to come with me to the bank at Adelaide, I'll give you cash. Meantime, I expect you to hand over a sum of money, say two hundred and fifty, to Mr. Decrow, as a guarantee that you are above the temptation of actual want."

"I suppose Mr. Chester's cheque will do for me to hold?" said Bertrand Decrow, laughing; "particularly if I have to hold it for any length of time."

"Yes, if the cheque can be cashed at Adelaide."

"Well," answered the astute lawyer, "I don't happen to have a bank at Adelaide, but I am able to produce the coin if it is necessary."

"In that case I'll make my cheque payable at Adelaide for eleven hundred pounds, one of which you will keep as your commission, and the thousand you will deliver to the Mayor of Coolgardie."

The Swampers

Soon after this they arrived at Port Adelaide, and Rosa accompanied the three gentlemen to the city, Chester taking with him the cash required as a guarantee of good faith.

Leaving Rosa to take a walk, the friends went to a hotel, and after a bottle of champagne, Mr. Green filled up and signed the substantial cheque. Having done so, he bade them both good-bye and went away. "There's a singular old card for you, Chester; you go over to the bank and see if it's all right; if it is, get them to make out an order on their Perth branch, and then we'll have a turn round the town. There, take back your coin."

He pushed the chamois bag which had been given him a little way across the table, and Chester half reached out his hand to take it; then he drew back with a sheepish feeling lest the other should think him suspicious. "No, you look after it for a few moments, Decrow; I won't be long away."

He wasn't outside the hotel before he repented leaving the bag of sovereigns, yet he still held on to the bank. The cashier looked at the cheque and said: "We have no account with that name, sir."

Chester rushed back to the hotel, but Mr. Decrow had just gone out, so had the two hundred and fifty sovereigns.

The Swampers

Chapter XIX. Jack Milton is Taken in Charge.

IN that cautious glance which he cast behind him, Jack Milton saw that his pursuers were provided for a considerable journey, and that he need not entertain any hope that they would relinquish the hunt now that they had sighted him. In a city he might have shaken them off, but not in this primeval waste. For a day and night they would probably rest their horses, and during that respite he might perhaps forge ahead forty or fifty miles, but the day after, the trackers and their masters would be rushing along his trail like resistless Fate, leaving their pack-horses to follow, sure as they were to be supplied with his provisions when they came up to him.

He would keep on until he was again sighted, then he would abandon his water and provisions to them and so gain another brief respite, while they once more freshened themselves with what he relinquished, as he and his horse went on famishing and hopeless. It was useless to think of escape by abandoning his horse, since he could not baffle those lynx-eyed trackers. The time would come, indeed, he could almost calculate the hour, when faint, hungry and parched, he took his last stand and waited for those remorseless riders to come up to him.

Then it would be the same story as had so often been read of other Australian refugees from justice. He would have the choice of dying by his own or their revolvers, since he had made up his mind not to be taken back alive.

The escaping prisoner from Siberia has several chances of eluding his pursuers, but Australia is nothing more than a vast prison yard, for even if they let him go now that they had seen him, it would only be to warn the South and West Australian police that he was coming, and on his first appearance at any point where humanity could live, he would be captured as surely as he then lived. There was no hope, no escape. He was a doomed man.

The Swampers

Yet he had one more day to live, and feel free, perhaps two, and amongst his packages he had the means of enjoying these two days, therefore, casting care to the winds, he rode on, determined to make the most of his respite. He was now utterly regardless and resigned to his fate, and for the first time since leaving Sydney he felt a placidity steal over him that seemed almost joy.

The morning was exquisite. The sky above him all dappled with cream-tinted clouds through which the sunbeams poured warmly. A fresh light air wafted down the valley, and filled his lungs with its gracious purity. The dewdrops glistened on the grass and leaves, and lay like gauze on the bush spiders' webs. The water-holes gleamed amongst the bull-rushes and lily plants, while on each side of him towered quartz ridges, snowy white, with patches of rose-petal radiance. It was a scene as fair and dazzling as he could hope to find anywhere in Australia, and for the time it was his own to enjoy.

"My God, what a joke it would be if the floods came now and caught us all here," he cried aloud, as he passed along this narrow glen with its inaccessible sides. He could fancy it coming down upon him with a roar round the next turn; that yellow torrent with its white crest bearing everything before it, changing in an instant this green valley into tempestuous rapids like those of Niagara, and tossing him and his horses like broken branches down upon the doomed hunters. That would be a decided change from the everlasting monotony of having his brains blown out on the red sand. He laughed loudly at the idea of this novel ending of his trouble.

Still laughing and hopelessly happy, he urged his beasts round the angle of the glen, passing under the overhanging shelf of a lofty cliff to find himself in another moment surrounded by about a couple of hundred naked and armed savages who were evidently waiting for him at this spot.

Instinctively he drew up his horse, and looked at them. It was useless to think of breaking through these close ranks, and indeed at the moment he was in such a passive condition of mind, that he had no desire to make the effort.

The Swampers

They were a splendid lot of fellows, despite all the disparaging descriptions which have been given about aboriginals, muscular and tall, and nearly all young, at least, the majority had not passed the meridian of life. The foremost amongst them appeared an old man at the first glance, yet he was stalwart and upright. Jack looked at him for an instant in perplexity, and then he burst into a peal of wild laughter, as he saw his own discarded grey wig and beard framing this dusky face.

That he was not already pierced by a dozen spears satisfied our adventurer that for the present their intention was not murder. "Hulloa! you white fellow, him run away from the dam police?"

It was a question that the man with the beard asked in fairly good English, and Jack answered promptly: "You bet, mate, that was my idea." "Him wanted badly, eh?" "That's about it."

"Plenty black fellow trackers with him, no dam use for white fellow to run that way." Jack nodded in token of assent.

"You come along of us. We help you clear away. Hide tracks so that no dam trackers find you out. Where you want to go?"

"Perth," replied Jack, laconically.

"Plenty long way Perth. We take you there bymby. How much you got?" "Baccy, flour, whisky."

"All right. White fellow, come along of me. I show you safe place. No dam fear police catch you now—no dam fear you die for water out there. Black fellow your mate. Police after him too—you wait, bymby no police, no dam trackers left. Me know them, the blooming cows. Me know you too, see."

He stepped up to Jack, and pulling open his shirt, placed his finger upon some tattoo marks which he had on his breast.

The Swampers

"Me see 'em yesterday when you wash him in the water hole. That save your mutton. That make you friend. Now you all same as black fellow, and he not see you hanged by dam police."

Jack had meditated often about removing these tell-tale markings, which in the first flush of his pride in becoming a craftsman, he had got stamped upon his body, but he felt glad now that he had delayed the erasing. He now hoped that none of his hunters bore similar tokens upon them, or if so, that they would not be seen by the sharp eyes of these new friends.

Hope once more began to kindle in his heart, for only these black fellows could cover his tracks and help him to escape. His luck had not deserted him yet.

The leader now caught hold of the rein of his horse and led him up the valley, several others accompanying them, while the remainder stopped behind, trampling over the tracks as they knew how, so that not a trace would be left.

After traversing several windings they came to a part where the valley divided, or rather where another gully led from it in a westerly direction. Into this they turned and proceeded for five or six miles, the gully getting drier and stonier as they advanced. It ascended also towards the ridges, so that before long they crossed them, and came to a sandy plain from which the vegetation had been lately burnt.

Crossing this for about a mile and a half, they suddenly arrived at another dip or gully still trending westward, at the foot of which they turned abruptly to the north through a close-set mallee scrub which, however, had a wallaby-run cut through it, and then, just as Jack expected another dry tramp, they all at once arrived at their destination, the native camp.

Australia is a land of surprises; sometimes pleasant, more often otherwise. It is also the home of contradictions, inconsistencies and oppositions to what are regarded as natural laws in other parts of the

The Swampers

globe. The people are never happy unless they are disputing and contradicting everything that is told them. Where the stranger expects a welcome he gets snubbed, and vice versa. Its swans are black, its moles lay eggs, and its owls hoot during the day; even its bees are out of all character, for they are stingless. The women only are consistent to their sex's privileges, and as they should be as regards beauty.

The surroundings of this native camp were surprises to Jack Milton, and surprises of the agreeable sort. Perched upon the side of a sterile and treeless mountain was a cup-like cavity carpeted with the greenest of grass, in the centre of which was a mountain lake of pure and sweet water. All round, strangely fantastic masses of red sandstone, with outstarting croppings of quartz and conglomerate, rose into the air six and eight hundred feet high, from a dreary desert where not even the dreaded spinifex appeared to be able to find a footing. It was as terrific a scene of desolation, yet weird grandeur, as ever the young man had gazed upon.

The gully bore a certain semblance to those heated and deathly passes of Arabia, near the Red Sea. The rocks appeared as tumbled and rent, with toppling boulders placed on each other like Druidical stones, while the bed of the gully was composed entirely of loose sand, crumbling masses of red stone, flinty pebbles, and quartz that crunched under the tread like calcined cinders. As Jack stooped over his saddle to look at these, there was that about their appearance that made him resolve to examine this gully more minutely if he got the opportunity.

Alone, he might have gone up this pass and over these ridges a dozen times without suspecting the existence of that fertile gem in the midst of this dreadful waste; as a wall-like cliff rose up directly in front of the only entrance, round which the traveller would as likely as not pass without more than a glance at the narrow gorge that led up to it; in no way different from many other rents which split the mountain's breast. It was not until his horses had stumbled round several twistings that he could realize he was going anywhere else than into a cul-de-sac which would presently terminate. Then the

The Swampers

ascent became gradual and easy, and he found himself on the stony crest of the cavity gazing at a spread of loneliness.

Fancy an amphitheatre of the extent of the Colosseum, open at the one side and walled round by a semi-circle of wild bare rocks pierced by caves and with shelf-like ledges overhanging and casting cool shadows upon this secluded spot. An oblong pool of water of unknown depth, with sloping sides like a great Roman bath, and round it a level sward that terminated as abruptly all round as if it had been trimmed so far up the hard quartz sides, and you may realize the astonishing sight that broke upon the bewildered senses of this new guest.

Try to fancy also this astonishing scene, peopled by a crowd of men, women and children, as free from false shame as they were of any other covering, if conventional modesty will allow you to realise such a picture without blushing.

There they were of both sexes and all ages, lolling idly on the soft grass, or sitting in their caves where their fires were burning; they had no other shelter, and no need for any other shelter. Young girls, plump-bodied and lithe, with big, soft eyes, and snowy teeth that made them pretty in spite of their uncertain features and dark skins; they had plenty of water here to bathe in, and they evidently used it often, for they were sleek and satiny, and as active as young panthers. Naked mothers nursing naked babies. Old ladies skinny and ugly as Hecate. Old men like ancient baboons, young boys as pretty and vivacious as the girls. The young men and able-bodied husbands of the tribe, Jack had already met.

A wild scene of excitement took place over the advent of the stranger and his horses; they crowded round, chattering loudly and gesticulating in the most unstudied and abandoned manner. However, as soon as a little quietness was restored, the guide explained matters to their satisfaction, and Jack was made welcome with much effusion. Very soon he was off his horse, and the other animals unloaded and sent to grass. They were not entirely ignorant of white people or horses, Jack could see, although he had been

The Swampers

prepared for this by his friend speaking English so fluently. Bashfulness also was not an attribute of these maidens any more than it is of their colonial and usurping sisters, and the stiff ceremony of introduction was not called for to establish friendship and favour.

Jack had hardly flung himself at his ease on the grass before he was surrounded by a bevy of the nymphs, who showed him by unmistakable signs that his coming was agreeable to them, and that they were prepared to render his visit as pleasant as they could.

The packages also were opened and the contents spread out to their admiring glances, and as Jack told the guide they were his contributions for the favour shown to him, they immediately commenced preparations for a general feast.

The Swampers

Chapter XX. Rosa Gets Initiated in Mining Parlance.

IF there is one quality a Sydneyite prides himself upon possessing above all other created beings, and reverences above all other virtues, it is "'cuteness." He may have his failings as regards non-observance of the ten commandments, but, dash it! he is smart, or else he is nothing.

Arthur Chester, solicitor of the supreme courts of New South Wales, and embryo mining expert of the coming colony, almost swooned with unadulterated shame when he realized that he had been M. U. G. enough to be taken in with this thin and threadbare confidence trick. He fell limply into the chair that he had so lately occupied, and laid his head upon the table, feeling as if he could never lift it again. "Ain't you well, sir?" asked the waiter, who had followed him into the room. The lawyer pulled himself together and smiled in a sickly fashion.

"A sudden spasm. I often have them, but it is passing away; fetch me in a small bottle of champagne."

The loss of the money was the least of his troubles, although that also touched him deeply, but at the moment it seemed a trifle. It was the awful shock to his self-confidence that stunned him. "By George, if Rosa should hear of this, I may as well cut my lucky."

He must keep it dark from her and every one, also get her back to the steamer as soon as possible. As for Bertrand Decrow, or whatever the shark's name was, and his accomplice, he resolved to let them go; better the loss of the money than a shattered reputation.

He drank off the pint of champagne, then lighting a cigar, with the remainder of the match he set fire to the bogus cheque and watched it burn with sombre satisfaction. After this he went out to look for his bride, concocting a story for her benefit as he went along.

The Swampers

He met Rosa as he was crossing Victoria Square. She had seen as much as she wanted to see of the South Australian capital, and as there was nothing overpoweringly magnificent here to raise her jealousy, as there had been in Melbourne, she was in a genial mood, and declared it to be a sweet little town and well worth a visit.

"It is ever thus with woman," thought her husband bitterly. "When a man is in the dumps she is always in a merry mood, and vice versa."

He was diplomatist enough, however, to conceal his mood from her and affect equally high spirits; the wine he had taken helped him in this; therefore, it was quite in a holiday sort of manner that he proposed lunch, which she, with that ever ready appetite that youth and health has at command, assented to.

"Where is Bertrand?" she asked—an hour serves for a cornstalk to speak of the latest friends by their christian name.

"I don't know, nor do I expect we are likely to see either that card or his brother-sharper, Green, again." "What do you mean, Arthur?"

"What I say, Rosa, that they are a couple of Victorian sharks who tried to nibble New South Wales, only it didn't come off—not exactly, nor any way near it."

He told her about the game they had played, with a slight alteration which redounded a good deal to his credit as a smart fellow. "I saw through this dodge the moment they asked me to plank down the ready."

"I should say you did—any juggins of six years old could do that," replied Rosa, scornfully. Arthur winced and smothered a groan, as he continued playfully:

"I got the cheque into my hands and then gently told them I'd trust them after I had been to the bank. By George, you never saw such a pair of jays as they looked when I left the room—green—yellow—blue, with black murder in their eyes. I guess this favoured admirer of yours, Rosa, won't try that game on again with a Sydney boy—you thought him such a charming fellow, didn't you, eh?"

It was a mean retaliation, but it gave him a momentary surcease from his own hidden anguish to reflect it on her.

"I didn't think about him either one way or another," answered Rosa calmly. "He had his uses on the passage, and did for me what you could not—got me the best seat at the table and the most sheltered nook on the deck, also prevented me from absolute starvation; therefore, I used him as I would utilize any handsome and agreeable fellow, as I suppose that is what good-looking and nice men are made for, to amuse and serve pretty women." "And chisel greenhorns," snarled Arthur.

"Never mind, old boy, since he didn't chisel you. If he had, you would have deserved being put under restraint as an imbecile, therefore, don't you go and flatter yourself that you have done anything smart in evading that open ruse, for you haven't."

Chester drank a good deal of champagne that day before they went on board their steamer, and smoked a great number of cigars, the consequence being that as they had it pretty rough after leaving Albany and across the Bight, he was forced to confine himself to the limits of the cabin, and cultivate the friendship of the steward.

Rosa, however, had by no means a dull passage, for although it was her first experience of rough weather, she was the only lady who was able to show up at meal-times and on the deck amongst the adventurers going west.

There was no rushing on this boat, as the rough element was confined to the steerage.

The men who occupied the saloon were nearly all speculators, mine owners who had been to England to float their mines, and were returning with full purses, or young gentlemen accustomed to Piccadilly and Bond Street, who had come out to pick up what they

The Swampers

could, as their Norman ancestors had done in the dim and misty past.

Those exquisites had the natural polish of centuries on them, while their clothes gave Rosa her first insight of what a gentleman is like in his outward appearance and manners. The speculators and mine owners likewise had been often enough in England to get a coating of varnish over their original habits, while they also had patronised Poole, and as they all vied with each other in flattering her and paying her attention, the hours flew for her between Adelaide and Albany, however much they might have crawled for Chester, with his basin, below.

There were representatives from nearly every nationality there, and all were united together by the one bond—Gold. They spoke of it from morning to night, and as it was a subject which interested Rosa, her admirers initiated her into all the mysteries of the stock and share market. She quickly understood the quotations, and astonished her husband, when he joined her at King George's Sound, by her fluent gabble about the different mines and their chances.

"Hannan's," "Lady Loch's," "North and West Boulders," "Great Fingal Reefs," etc., etc., she had them all, as pat as a parrot. She also bewildered him with her remarks about "Soaks," "Swampers," "Sandgropers," "Speilers," and "Boomellers," and other strange expressions which were as yet darkly unintelligible to him.

"The hotel is the thing, Arthur, but we must order any amount of champagne, as my friend, the Hon. Billy Shatters, tells me it is the tipple for Kalgourlie. Twenty-five shillings a bottle up there they charge, and they suck into it like ginger-pop."

Arthur listened in a dazed way, for his head seemed empty and his stomach, likewise in the same condition, felt moving like a swing-boat, although they were now in the peaceful waters of the lovely Sound. "I could do a bottle myself just now," he muttered feebly, "only not at the price."

The Swampers

"Come and I'll introduce you to the gang, and you will get it for nothing, my boy," she said promptly. "They have drank enough the past three days to ballast a China clipper."

Chester was received with great civility by these scions of nobility, and capitalists, for Rosa knew them all by name—each had introduced the other to her—and her husband was delighted to find himself amongst men who could talk about hundreds of thousands as if they were shillings, or with gentlemen whose names and ages could be found in "Burke."

The champagne flowed, as Rosa had remarked, like ginger-pop at a Manly Beach Temperance pic-nic.

They were all exultant in spirits and full of humour and good-natured chaff. The land they were going to was every man's country for the time. The hell of fever, dust, condensed water and gold. It was not a country to boast about as a home, that is, the portion where they were bound for. No man would think of making it his home, therefore there was no patriotism nor even politics in their talk; the latest quotations or fresh discovery were all that interested them.

Albany is one of the cleanest, sunniest, sweetest, sleepiest and least go-ahead townships in Australia. As it was ten years ago it still remains. The people live on their visitors, and the visitors look at the town and bay, till the steamer or train leaves, and then they run on to other destinations, yet Albany as a sanatorium is delightful, and its government officials about as red-tapy as they can be and be permitted to live.

The natives will not move out of their confirmed habits for king or kaiser. They are accustomed to be sworn at by the maddened visitor, while they can blaspheme in return as fluently as could be desired. Their wants are few, their demands exorbitant, and their minds independent, therefore the visitor, not being able to get anything he requires, learns to expect little when he comes again.

The Swampers

The voyagers had not longer than a couple of hours to wait in this delightful and picturesque port of call, while the porters and wharfers leisurely loaded up the train, then they were off once more across the salt marshes to the capital of West Australia.

Many of the passengers continued by boat round the granite cliffs to Freemantle, but Chester had experienced enough of life on the ocean wave, therefore he took the train.

"That hotel idea of yours, Mrs. Chester, is a veritable stroke of genius," murmured the Honourable Billy Shatters in the ear of Rosa, as he stood on the platform waiting to see her away; he was going round by boat.

"It is what we want up Kalgourlie, almost as much as the electric light, to make us perfectly happy; a house where we can have the reforming influence of a lady to keep us straight. By Jove! I'll be your first lodger, so remember your promise and reserve a bed for me." "I won't forget," she answered, with one of her studied upward glances.

"You'll recognise me when we meet again, I trust, Mrs. Chester; we are all rigged out alike up there, you know, and high hats are strictly prohibited according to miners' law." "I'll recognise you by your eye-glass," she replied saucily.

"Alas, then I am forgotten, for that is the outward insignia of a mining expert, and none of us care to take such a responsibility."

"By your Piccadilly drawl then," she said with a vague remembrance of having read this expression in the Guillotine.

"The boys would lynch me, if I tried it on with them. I leave the eye-glass, high hat, drawl and other etceteras in my hotel at Perth until I come back again. Is there nothing else you will recognise me by, my dear Mrs. Chester?"

The Swampers

"Yes," murmured Rosa. "There is no fear of me forgetting you. I shall think often about you."

"And I of you—and our stormy passage across the Bight. Well, ta-ta, till we meet again at Kalgourlie the thirst-provoking."

"Here 'Duke,'they are wanting you over here, there a game of 'Two up'going on," were the last words Chester heard as the train rolled out of the station. He quickly banged his head over his wife's through the window to see where the "Duke" was, but could only see the Honourable Billy being dragged away by one of the other gentlemen. "Why do they call him the Duke, Rosa?" he asked.

"I'll tell you presently," answered his initiated bride, who was engaged waving her handkerchief and kissing her hand to the friends she was leaving behind.

"You must know, you guppy," observed Rosa, as she settled herself after the train had steamed out of sight of those on the platform, "that a man is called a 'Duke'on the gold fields who can throw double heads six times in succession at 'Two up.'" "And what the dickens is 'Two up?'"

"Oh, hang it, I cannot be bothered teaching you the A B C. Go to an infant school for that. Two up—if you must know—is pitch and toss with a slight difference. However, I don't doubt but you'll find it out yourself before long. I won a tenner on it the other night in the saloon in less time than you could have put down a whisky and soda."

Saying which Rosa took out of her bag one of half-a-dozen of the latest London novels, which Billy had given her, and settled herself down to a two hundred and fifty-six miles' read.

The Swampers

Chapter XXI. Jack Milton and His Coloured Friends.

ALTHOUGH the black fellow of Australia is neither the reasonless, nor hideous animal that it is generally the fashion to make him, he must be allowed to be one of the most improvident, in fact; in this particular phase of his character, he very closely resembles the literary, artistic and theatrical Bohemian, who at one period might have been seen prowling about the regions of the Adelphi Terrace, but who is now almost exterminated since the poet, novelist, journalist, critic, artist and actor have taken to frock coats, high hats, cigarettes, and the Stock Exchange for their inspiration. The aboriginal and the Bohemian have both to retire before the advance of civilization as represented by the Rothschilds and their fellow-capitalists.

Still, if the aboriginal is like the true and ancient Bohemian—an improvident fellow who acts on the early Christian principle of trusting in Providence for his next meal, when he has one before him, he is not stingy about sharing it with his friends, as he is not at all particular about sharing in his friends' goods. He bears no animosity to the white fellows for stealing his land from him, so long as they do not grudge him a few sheep now and again to keep him alive, for he believes in sharing the plunder. He would even share his water-holes with them if they would only be content to leave him a drain to quench his own thirst.

But his experience of the whites since they took forcible possession of his hunting-grounds has not been such as to conduce towards friendship or trust on his part. All his life he has been accustomed to fighting as a relaxation, and he has the same distaste to be conquered as any other created being; the only difference between him and other races is that whereas patriotism and property have been incentives to war and slaughter on their part, the stern necessity of having to fight for his bare existence has been the excuse of the aboriginal.

The Swampers

Explorers have gone over his ground and hunted him down as sportsmen do foxes. When he showed them his wells, they have emptied them without the least consideration for him, or his women and children. Settlers growing wealthy on his lands have laid poisonous baits for him, as they would for such pests as rabbits, rats and dingoes, arsenic being the favourite flavouring for these baits, although phosphorus and other merciful means were also employed for removing these original owners of the soil, who committed the crime of helping themselves to a sheep now and again from the hundreds of thousands that were feeding on their grass and drinking all their available water. Mounted troopers with their renegade serfs, the black trackers, have followed these natives to their lairs and shot them down, old and young, women and infants, exterminating the tribe, root and branch, who have been in too close proximity to the latest encroaching settlement. They call this Iraelitish system, "Dispersing the Natives," who may have been considered troublesome to the invaders. These Christianized land-robbers ever creeping onward and grasping another slice, call the easy-going and unpatriotic owners, treacherous, thieving and murdering beasts. I wonder what kind of beasts we, the builders of churches, would become, if we were robbed as we have robbed the aboriginal. I wonder what kind of outlaws we would show up, if we were treated as we treat them, and had only wooden spears, boomerangs and waddies to avenge our wrongs with, against revolvers, Winchesters, dynamite, and, most damnable of treacheries, the cold-blooded assassin's weapon—poison secretly spread over the land to destroy and torture us. If we were first robbed, next starved, and lastly poisoned when the pillagers could not get near enough to shoot us down?

We have given them blankets when their nakedness affronted our females, and kidnapped a boy or two to make servants of in return for the vast territory we have stolen from them, and when the blanketted scoundrels pilfer our trifles, and the kidnapped boys run back home, preferring liberty and rough times to pampered slavery, we call them ungrateful and treacherous beasts.

The Swampers

Aboriginals, Kanakas, Chinese, Japanese, Afghans, all who do not represent Western civilisation we treat like beasts, denying them any of the rights of man; yet we howl against them if they dare to remonstrate, retaliate or claim equal privileges as children of Earth. Our murders on them are acts of justice, their retaliations on us are atrocious murders. If a native, a Celestial or an Oriental kills a European, a holocaust hardly appeases our implacable rage. If a European kills or injures a coloured man, the most kindly will say, "Serve the dog right!"—and unless it is attended with peculiar features of atrocity or publicity, the law and the press unite in hushing it up. As for those native lords of the soil, from the evil day that the first white man accosted him down to the present hour, a ceaseless record of wrong has been presented to the Great Avenger dark and vile enough to damn to everlasting perdition the greatest race that ever struggled to be supreme.

As for treachery, vileness and atrocity, their acts seem like flakes of snow mingling with soot-smuts when compared with ours, when we remove the magnifying glass from them and the cover from us—hypocritical and ruthless savages as we are in spite of our pious pretensions.

The English-speaking guide, who had sworn brotherhood and introduced Jack Milton to his tribe, was the leader of the fighting-men and the eldest son to the chief. After seeing him safely placed, this splendid warrior left the camp, with those followers who had come so far with him. He told Jack on no account to leave the ground until his return, also promised to be back in time for the feast.

"Yarraman (horses) no good to you after this; only eat up all the grass, drink up all the water, and then die. Better kill and eat them before that. You see bymby when we leave this place."

Jack owned the wisdom of these remarks, and agreed to sacrifice his pack horses, as he reckoned they would be of little use after the crowd had taken its fill of his stock of provisions, but he pleaded for the life of his riding horse—the chum who had carried him so far. "All right, keep that one; we bring along some more to-night."

The Swampers

He gave some orders to the women who were looking after the fires, and then he went off and left Jack to amuse himself the best way he could.

This best way seemed to be sleep to Milton after his long and fatiguing journey, therefore, filling and lighting his pipe, he lay down under the shadow of the overhanging cliffs; and puffing gently he watched the smoke rings ascend into the still atmosphere, and soar lazily towards the blue, until sleep gradually claimed him as her own.

When he woke it was night, and the moon was high in the heavens. The camp fires also were burning brightly, and the natives all assembled and feasting. A pleasant perfume of broiling flesh was in his nostrils, and a tremendous vacuum under his belt, so that without any invitation he went over to the first group, amongst which happened to be his friend and helped himself to what they were devouring.

It was horse flesh they were indulging in. During the hours he had been unconscious they had killed a couple of his pack horses and transformed a bag of his flour into dampers, and were now putting them away as quickly as they could.

When his friend saw him he nodded, and made room for him at his side, then he said briefly, chewing vigorously at the same time, which gave his words a muffled sound: "These dam troopers and trackers no trouble you no more. See!"

He pointed to the open near the pond, and as Jack looked he saw a number of horses grazing, with the hobbles on them. "What have you done?"

"All same as they wanted to do to you. All same as they would do to us—what you call it on the dam stations when black fellow am shot down all round?" "Dispersed?"

The Swampers

"Yes, that am the word—they are all dispersed and sent to kingdom come. We went along down to their camp, and wait till bymby they all fall 'sleep 'cept one fellow. He watch with him gun. Then we creep round 'em and rush in. Some jump up and begin to shoot. That all right, only we no care one dam for him shooters, and him very soon shut up that game when our spears go into him. Not long and all lie same as him make black fellow when him get the square chance. That all right, you bet, mate."

"What have you done with them?" asked Jack, who now that the deed was done felt strangely relieved. They were his natural enemies, although they had only been doing what they considered to be their duty, so that he could hardly be expected to do more than regret the necessity of destroying them.

The aboriginal still talked with his mouth full and his teeth working, in a muffled, indifferent way, as if the subject had not much interest to him; yet there was a lurid glitter in his eyes that contradicted his assumed disregard.

"I did what this fellow, Cap'in George they call him, have done to my friends, once, twice, thrice. Leave him to rot, or for the birds and ants and dingoes to pick him bones clean." He pointed with his greasy finger towards the north.

"Over there him creepy up to our camp, and shoot him little lubras and gins when him all asleep two years ago, that am him game always. He dam sharp and not let many run away. Ha! ha!—not dam smart enough this time, though." "But this party will soon be missed, and a search made for them?"

"Bymby, yes, but we all gone by that time—no come back for a long time. We go along o' you over there." He pointed westward. "Plenty good places all long away there which men with big yarraman all miss. Plenty gold down there. Plenty gold where I show you bymby. Water and grub and gold and grass 'nough too for one yarraman, but no more. We kill them fellows to-morrow some, the rest another day, then we go on two days more."

The Swampers

The next morning a number of the natives went off on an expedition which, the young leader explained, was to carry the bodies of the troopers and trackers into the desert, where they would not be found, and to remove all traces of the conflict that had taken place.

The others who remained in the camp were busy dividing the packages into more portable baggage. Two more horses were slaughtered and cut up, while the women were busy preparing for another feast.

Jack and his friend went down into the dry gully, attended by about a dozen of the best-looking young girls, who were full of sprightliness and mischief. The young chief was already married and had a little son. The "gin" was his second wife, as the first, with her children, had been murdered by the troopers, whom he had just revenged himself upon so terribly. Possibly this was one of the causes why he had taken so kindly to Jack Milton.

The lubras, or unmarried girls of the tribe, were not available to any of their own tribe, as such were considered too near akin, and on this point they are very particular. They would be abducted by some other friendly or hostile tribe, as were the Sabine women by the Romans, therefore there was no more possibility of jealousy among the young men over the partiality shown towards Jack by the girls, than would be amongst brothers towards the stranger their sisters paid attention to. Jack in fact was the only man whom these fair ones could flirt with at present, therefore, it was no wonder that he was greatly in demand by the dusky, and in many instances, unmistakably comely girls. He had the run of the ranch without a present rival.

Jack had not gone far fossicking in this valley before he saw that he had a gold centre at his command. If it could have been possible to stay and exploit this, he might have stayed here and made his fortune, but as such an idea was out of the question he had to sigh and relinquish it.

The Swampers

One of the girls who were with him suddenly stooped and picked up a dark-coloured pebble about the size of a duck's egg. This she attracted his attention to, and then placing it on a hard boulder with a piece of quartz she struck it with her full force, and split it in two, then she held out the broken halves to him with the inner sides uppermost.

She laughed merrily at his loud cry of admiration, exhibiting all her snowy teeth as if they were better worth looking at than the prismatic-tinted milky centre of that pebble, pretty although it might be. Yet she was pleased at the eagerness with which he pounced upon her present.

It was an opal in the rough, that unlucky but exquisite gem, with its rainbow-coloured fires swimming and sparkling, now green, now red, now blue and purple in the sunlight.

Jack looked at the stone carefully outside and inside, then he forgot about the gold specks that he could see in the sand and crumbling quartz, and began to look all round him for other specimens of the same sort.

He found, as he supposed, many exactly on the outside like the one he held, but when he broke these open, despite the dissentient cries of his handsome attendants, they were without a glimmer of the colour he wanted. It was only now and again, at considerable intervals, when they brought him, or pointed out one stone from a heap of others that he found the opal vein crossing the kernel. They knew where it was to be found in all colours and shapes, but they could not explain their secret, and the leader, seeing him well protected, had left him to their tender mercies. They were merry girls, if somewhat forward and inquisitive, but already Jack had got used to their ways, likewise to their lack of apparel, for they seemed to have no consciousness as to its being unbecoming. Indeed, the young man had to own that nature here could not have been improved upon by dress.

The Swampers

Afterwards, when he saw these same beauties hiding their charms under the shirts, &c., of the troopers and trackers, he thought what a world of impropriety may be suggested by a shirt.

On the second morning they struck the camp, some of the boys and girls riding the spare horses and causing great sport as they rolled off or were sent flying over the animals' heads. That day they travelled sixty miles and brought up at a native well in the desert.

The Swampers

Chapter XXII. To Kalgourlie.

ROSA CHESTER and her husband, for as he was at present in the position of her pupil in Western ways, she had naturally taken the leadership of the expedition, therefore he became known at this point and ever afterwards, as her husband.

Rosa and her husband stayed for several days at Perth, looking after their goods and purchasing other articles required, and they lodged at the "Shamrock Hotel" in Hay Street.

Here Rosa, who was on the out-look for a barmaid, found one that just suited her, and as she offered much better wages than the girl was getting at Perth, she secured her services for Kalgourlie.

Mrs. Sarah Hall was a young widow with one child, a little girl of about three years old. Sarah was dark, remarkably good-looking, and exceedingly lady-like in her manner, therefore would make an excellent foil for her blonde and vivacious mistress.

They had written, previous to their coming, to their townsman, and found that Mr. Anthony Vandyke Jenkins, mining expert, who had secured for them a vacant area in Hannan Street, and acting on their orders, had also fixed up commodious premises in wood, corrugated iron and hessian canvas, so that all they had to do on arrival at Perth was to pay the bills for building, material, and painting, which their friend and agent enclosed in his last letter.

This was no light matter, for Jenkins had done the thing according to his customary style, when entrusted with a commission, and things were flourishing, that is, regardless of expense. A gang of workmen had invaded the rising township, with doorways, windows and frameworks all prepared beforehand. The foreman, under the direction of that enterprising little cornstalk, pegged out the ground and on it made his plan of rooms, store-houses, stables, and bars, etc. There was no stairway required, nor intricacies of that sort, as they

The Swampers

had plenty of space to stretch back if more apartments were required, and the plan of construction was simple in the extreme.

On the first day the workmen were busy erecting a fence round the block of ground and putting up the frame. On the second day the building was complete, signboard and all, and the first coat of paint laid on the woodwork. On the third day the "Chester Hotel" was an accomplished fact, and the workmen who had built and painted it were either rushing off to Coolgardie or other places to execute fresh commissions, or else striking out for themselves as explorers and gold prospectors, for this is how business is conducted in the West of Australia to-day.

A photograph of the new establishment was sent along with the accounts by the energetic Jenkins, likewise a preliminary advertisement and descriptive puff in "The Western Argus." A deep well had been dug and condensing plant erected, so that as the advertisement said, first-class mineral waters were to be manufactured on the premises. Billiard and concert rooms had not been forgotten. Stabling for horses and yards for camels were provided; in fact, Jenkins had proved his genius for business where money was no object, and had erected for them the most commodious and sumptuous establishment on the fields.

"We'll go partners," Jenkins wrote to Chester, "as you are posted up in legal matters. I've fixed up an office next door to the bar, where we can work together."

From the photographs Chester read on the sign-boards that ranged along the front, over the striped canvas awning of the verandah, "The Chester Hotel, Mrs. Rosa Chester, Proprietor, etc., etc.," and on the other "Jenkins and Chester, Mining Experts, Advisers, Arbitrators, Mining and Titles Agents, Accountants, Auditors and Solicitors, etc."

Arthur Chester was not at all averse to this partnership of the expert and legal combination, as it left him free to follow the profession he had been brought up to. Rosa also was pleased to have the hotel

The Swampers

entirely in her own hands, and everything so expeditiously managed.

"Tony is a little marvel with his brassy assurance, one of those sons that New South Wales should be proud of," said Rosa to her husband.

"Yes, he is smart—only I hope he won't speculate too recklessly now that we are partners," replied Arthur. "That land-boom experience of his is a trifle dangerous."

"Oh, you must keep him within limits, Arthur, only let him have a bit of line, for he is a lucky fellow, and even in the land-boom got out of it better than most. The mines are pretty sure, so don't be too cautious, for Jenkins knows the ropes, you bet. I'm also in luck to get such a taking help as Mrs. Sarah Hall. We ought to make a good business between us." "Yes, she is a most superior girl. Did she tell you what her husband was?"

"A remittance man—got his quarterly allowance from England and lived up to it, as these swells all do; then when he kicked out, she was left to make the best of her good looks and woman-wit. I only hope she won't be a fool and get married again up there too soon. She hasn't got over the loss of her husband and seems to live only for the little girl, so that this may keep her from entanglement for a time."

Sarah Hall was certainly all that they described her to be. A young woman of about twenty-five, stylish and lady-like in her get-up, with quiet, amiable manners about her. Her language was more correct than that of most colonial women, that is, she did not indulge in slang as Rosa so constantly did, and in this as well as her personal appearance, formed a decided contrast, which was likely to keep them the longer friends.

She was tall and superbly formed, as most Victorian women are, with a mass of jet-black hair which she wore discreetly coiled up. Her eyes also were intensely dark, and her eyebrows strongly

The Swampers

defined. Her features were regular and her colour fresh, giving her that peculiarly vivid look that characterizes the young daughters of Judah, and always suggests tropical flowers.

But she had a feminine softness which is not always present with those vivid Orientals, and although her dark eyes were penetrating in their glances, yet they were velvety and caressing as well. Her voice also was of a silky and musical texture, and the sensitive ripe lips curved pleasantly over the regular white teeth. She was in fact a very fresh and charming woman, who need not have gone far to find a lover, even with that encumbrance to which she was so devoted — her lovely little daughter, Alice.

This small maid of three years old was the most gipsy-like and flashing little elf that it was possible to imagine. Lively and quick as an eel, with all the vivacity and sharpness of a sun-bred colonial, she had passed her life in public-houses along with her mother, who could not bear to let her out of her sight. Dressed in the latest child fashions, her mother made all her dresses and was constantly using her needle when she was not drawing corks or pulling beer, and seemed to have no other desire or pleasure than that of making her child attractive and doll-like. Where she went, little Alice had to go also. They slept together at night, while during the day the inside of the bar was her playground, and the customers her only friends.

It was natural to expect that she would be oldfashioned and precocious, also that the language she heard was not the best education for a child, yet, to the credit of most of the customers, the presence of that little elf acted as a check on their profanity or obscenity, and it was but seldom that Mrs. Hall had to correct those who came for refreshment. A nudge in the ribs and a glance at the small listener generally stopped even the inebriate humourist from finishing his latest comic yarn.

It is astonishing how much the presence of a child in a bar can purify its moral atmosphere, to say nothing of such a barmaid as Mrs. Sarah Hall. When not wanted by the customers, she would sit quietly working at her seams, with an amiable smile for everyone, the child

The Swampers

at her feet playing with her toys. If men told their questionable anecdotes in a subdued whisper, she could be conveniently deaf or engage the attention of Alice by speaking to her. She had always an affable answer to every question or address, yet only the new chums ever attempted to compliment her on her good looks, and when they did this once it was seldom that they repeated the offence.

She was not stern with these poor new chums, indeed a considerable amount of mild if contemptuous pity blended in the glance which her black eyes threw over them, yet it never failed to stop the commonplace and idiotic nonsense which one hears so often addressed to barmaids. The "bounder" generally returned to the sucking of his walking-stick handle, with his fascinating warble trailed off to broken incoherence.

"A devilish pretty girl, but what a know there is in her eyes; turns one inside out in a flash."

That Sarah Hall was not one to be lured off her feet by flattery most of her customers knew after a little bar intimacy, and no one had as yet got beyond that stage in their friendship with her. What leisure she had was devoted to her child. It was seldom also that she had to say, "Stop that talk, will you, please?" as the men generally saved her the trouble, but when she did, the animal who provoked it did not soon forget the dagger-like look that flashed from her jetty eyes. If the masher read world-lore in the pitying glance, the filthmonger read a cut in the face if he persisted.

Rosa got a first-rate character along with Sarah. She could hold her own and keep order anywhere, and was withal a general favourite with the frequenters both old and young.

When it was known she was going up to Kalgourlie, little Alice got numerous presents, while general regret was expressed throughout the town. Detective Wilmore, who was one of her oldest and most attentive customers, came to say good-bye.

The Swampers

"Well, Sarah, I'll miss you, but I wish you luck. We have known each other a tidy time now, and the longer our friendship, the more I respect you. By George, little Alice there has done wonders."

"You have been very good always to me, Mr. Wilmore," answered Sarah, with quiet emotion.

"By George, not a bit more than you deserve, Sarah. Had anyone told me three years ago that a girl of your abilities could have knuckled down to the life you have, I wouldn't have believed them—don't blush, you are the cleverest woman in Australia, barring none, and it isn't many artists who could have strength of mind enough to give up old habits as you have done."

"Oh, love can work miracles, Mr. Wilmore," replied Sarah, looking softly at her child.

"Good luck to you, my dear, keep on as you are doing and there's no fear; the little one will grow to be a credit and a comfort to her plucky mother. I respect you, Sarah, because I know you; a deal more than I do some who consider themselves your betters."

And Detective Wilmore meant all he said, for it had been part of his secret duty to look after Sarah Hall since her coming to Western Australia, and he was now giving her her freedom from surveillance, and pledging himself to bury her past as far as he could.

There was a considerable amount of liquor consumed at the "Shamrock," indeed visitors were but coldly received who were at all disposed to temperance. Its locality also was not of the most law-abiding, particularly on a Saturday night, when free fights were an ordinary occurrence, so that both Chester and Rosa were glad when their business was over and they could leave their own crowded and evil-smelling quarters, even although the change meant dust, heat, and shortness of water, the auriferous sand desert.

The Hon. Billy and his friends joined them on their train journey and made things as pleasant as possible for the ladies. The carriages also

The Swampers

were comfortable, and the canvas water-bags which they carried with them a decided novelty to Rosa, who had never been through a waterless land before.

They had not proceeded many miles on their way before they seemed to be whirled into another land with many features different to unromantic Australia. Caravans of camels with their picturesque Afghan drivers could be seen lining the sandy landscape outside. New arrivals plodding along with their swags, bound for the gold centres, bullock teams, horses, cycles, coaches—every one in a mad hurry to get along, and all consumed with overpowering thirst.

The train was waited eagerly for at every station by such of the population as were not under the ground, so that the platforms were crowded. Introductions and hand-shaking, likewise liberal libations. Chester, Rosa, and Sarah Hall were made intimate with every man of consequence in the land, and each promised to visit Kalgourlie and patronize the new hotel. If Mrs. Chester ever entertained any doubt about her idea being a success, such doubts were laid for ever at rest now, when she beheld the evidence of that everlasting and slakeless thirst. The "sand-gropers" were like the sands they groped amongst, capable of absorbing moisture to an unlimited extent. The gold fields might yield a golden harvest, but nothing compared to the mine she was about to float—in champagne.

There is nothing to look at from the windows as they rush over that dust-filled country, while the flies swarm in such irritating clusters that any other occupation except constantly shifting them is out of the question; but this provides them all with exercise sufficient to make them long for rest when at last the journey is over and Coolgardie is reached, after which they drove the eighteen miles to Kalgourlie. A festive crowd met them as they entered the town, from the mayor downwards, and here Jenkins becomes a personage to be courted as the "boys" press forward eagerly, to be introduced to the pretty newcomers.

They are escorted to their new premises where they find everything in readiness for them, for Jenkins has done his duty and forgotten no

The Swampers

items. He had hired Japanese servants, and prised open several of the cases of provisions, wines and spirits, so that after a wash, Rosa and Sarah came down to find both bar, dining, billiard and concert rooms crowded with thirsty well-wishers. That night she acts the hostess for the first time, and as no charge is made on this evening, the "boys" assemble in force, and the "Chester Hotel" is declared a success.

The Swampers

Chapter XXIII The Swampers.

ALONG a portion of the coast between Eucla and Eyre within the great Australian Bight, a small schooner was beating as if on the outlook for a cove or bay to enter and bring to anchor.

A dreary and inhospitable portion of the coast this is, with those wall-like cliffs standing out of the surf that ever lashed whitely against them from these stormy waters, for the Bight is, like the Bay of Biscay, a place of storm, and the waves are mighty as they come from those antarctic wastes without any impediment until they fling themselves against the granite walls.

On the deck of this small craft several of my characters are gathered who have been too long neglected; yet, as they have been engaged upon a monotonous and uneventful sea voyage with retarding head winds, my readers have not lost much in leaving them alone.

The unfortunate Psychometrist, Professor Mortikali or Jeremiah Judge, who unconsciously has been made an accomplice of housebreakers, torn from his comfortable and lucrative practice and forced to endure the combined misery of sea-sickness and dread of capture, makes one of the group along with Barney and his brother and sister criminals.

They had intended to go to America when they started from Sydney with their loot, for the captain and his crew had as urgent reasons for leaving Australia as these passengers had—but deny it who will, we may have our reasons for cursing this home of the kangaroo and the cornstalk, yet there is something magnetic about it that seems to draw back again and again those who have once been there. England is delicious and restful with its green meads and sheltered lanes; Australia is arid, unpicturesque and monotonous in its scenery, yet to the convict-bred, or the restless adventurer, it is a magnet which he cannot long resist.

The Swampers

Perhaps it was some newspapers that the skipper had laid in to beguile the long voyage before them that did the trick. Perhaps because most of these criminals had never been out of the land of their birth, and America did not hold out a tempting or a fertile prospect, the competition in roguery being too keen in that great land, or the news of the gold-finding in Western Australia being too much for them to resist the fascination; but, whatever the cause, they yielded and sailed round the coast and approached the land instead of keeping out to sea.

Certainly Barney was the only man amongst them who knew that murder was amongst the things they were wanted for, and he kept the secret for the sake of his chief. He it was who had played upon their lust for gain and home-sickness, and persuaded them to seek the shores at this desert portion.

They had gone round Tasmania, as they did not wish their motions to be telegraphed about at Bass' Straits, and a long and wearisome voyage it had been round South Cape, and after many an argument they had resolved to land in the Bight, and go from there to the goldfields.

The captain knew the coast line well, also a good landing-place where they would not be more than a couple of hundred miles from the latest discovered fields, possibly less than half that distance from new fields which had been discovered. His idea was to make a joint company affair of it, bring the schooner to anchor at an old abandoned whaling station that he knew, and leave a portion of the crew to look after her, while the rest pushed on and prospected a bit.

Several of them had done some prospecting; the captain and Barney had both worked on different diggings in their time, while the Professor, albeit the mystical arts were his strong points, yet had matriculated as a mining engineer both in America and New Zealand, and although, like most other people, he despised the calling that he had been brought up to, his knowledge of geology was much less a sham than his knowledge of astronomy.

The Swampers

"I reckon the Professor there could put us right if we struck a goldfield," said the captain.

"Yes," admitted the Professor; "if the gold is likely to be there I can guess at it most likely; but what is that to be compared to the glorious knowledge the speruts reveal an' what the stars show us? Speruts are no good at finding out gold mines nor buried treasures—they despises filthy lucre."

"Never mind—you tell us what you know in your own line, and we'll believe what you want us arterwards about the speruts, when we has our mining rights made out and our ground pegged off."

I have seen men who were first-class mechanics pretend they know nothing about their craft, yet be weakly boastful over something which they were only amateurs in. Poets and painters who deprecated their inherent and acquired gifts, who boasted about their talent as cooks. The Professor was really a man to be respected as a mining expert, yet that was the last occupation he would have thought to make money in. Real knowledge gave him modesty on the only subject he was really an adept at.

His companions, however, had tested him by adroit questions, and felt confident that if he was with them there might be some chance of success in their quest; therefore the Professor was a man to be taken care of. They had provisions enough for all their wants for the next twelve months. In the galley also they had a good condensing machine, which although not very large, yet condensed enough for their purpose, therefore they made all their arrangements.

They would anchor in this secluded cove, and leave half the crew to look after the ship and work the machine during their absence, while they went up country prospecting as they went along.

If successful, they would send one of their number to the nearest warden and take out rights, also purchase camels, while the others camped on the ground, then they would establish a camp and bring up their water from both places—the nearest centre and the ship.

The Swampers

They had money enough to pay for what they required, and at an outlying field like this they need not fear surveillance. A camel can travel a hundred miles a day, and there were plenty of them to work the show. Let them once introduce a new field to the market, and no one would ask where they came from. They would become respected citizens. The gold of the pawnbroker's jewellery they had already reduced to ingots, while the gems were untraceable, therefore they considered themselves perfectly safe.

It is astonishing how even an habitual criminal craves to be regarded as a respectable member of society, so long as he can become so without disgorging the proceeds of his nefarious undertakings. To be mine owners and floaters of mines, seemed to these criminals much as the Church of England looks to a Dissenter who has been indulging in a course of the early fathers. When the Dissenter joins the Church of England, he has taken the first decided step in abnegation of personal responsibility, and the future paces from Low to High, and afterwards to Rome, are simple.

When a thief feels a craving to become a respectable member of society, yet has a lingering fondness for his old habits in Australia, he tries to discover a gold mine, then he floats it and becomes a member of society without relinquishing his old habits. He advances on his course in time as he becomes hardened to his new career, and takes office as a director of companies, next a magistrate or warden, to be afterwards put up as a member of parliament, and finally he may become that bulwark of society, a deacon in the church. After that stage, he is like Alexander when he had conquered the world, for earth has no more to offer him. If he can only steal a good position in Heaven, then indeed he is a master of his profession.

It was a laudable instinct that animated these bank-breakers to return to their native soil and face the hardships and privations of an explorer's life. The possession of a good capital had given them daring and respectable impulses. A thief with a thousand pounds is not the reckless ne'er-do-well that a thief is with thirty pieces of silver. The thousand-pound man will make a stern effort to take care of and increase his store. He will, if he has the chance, become a

The Swampers

careful speculator, particularly if placed as those men were on a rocky and uninhabited shore with no public houses near at hand.

About mid-day the captain descried the opening he was in search of, and then easily they sailed inside and brought to anchor in a small bay, with a good beach in front of them, and protecting head-lands all round.

In olden times this place had been a whaling station. There were even some remains of huts and sheds on the shores, but they had long ago been deserted, while this portion of the land the natives did not visit.

The telegraph line ran along close to the coast here, but there were no stations nearer than Eucla. Here in this quiet and secluded bay the vessel might lie for months, without having a visitor, and only then if an accident occurred to the wires.

It was decided therefore that meantime the captain, the Professor, Barney, and three others would do the prospecting, leaving the mate with the women who had accompanied them, and the sailors to overhaul the schooner and repaint her, also keep the condensing machine constantly at work, so as to supply those up country with water as they might require it.

The company was to be a joint-stock affair, so that those left behind would have the same profits as those who might find the field. Barney for the present was chosen leader of the explorers, and the mate left in charge of the ship.

They spent the first day landing their provisions and arranging their swags, and at daybreak on the second day they started for the desert.

By sundown they had covered twenty miles of ground, mostly sandy land and mulgee scrub, but hardly a sign of grass.

However, they were successful in finding several waterholes where they camped, in which a little muddy water still remained. With this they contented themselves, reserving the condensed water which they had for a more urgent occasion.

Throughout Australia perhaps there is hardly a worse track of country to traverse, than this over which they had resolved to go. They were fully aware likewise of the risks they were running, for, as the explorers' journals is the only history that Australia has yet to relate, the roving population are nearly all pretty familiar with the experiences or mistakes of those who have opened up the land. Along these precipitous cliffs, Eyre, and later the present Premier of Western Australia, Sir John Forest, had travelled and endured much hardship.

Farther inland they had not much hope of meeting anything but salt marshes, sand and wild scrub, and perhaps the coveted article they were after—gold.

But they were all colonial born, with the exception of the Professor, and well accustomed to roughing it, therefore they never forgot for a moment even in the midst of their plenty, the possibility of being reduced to famine point. They were treacherous and murderous hounds, but the instinct of self-preservation was planted strongly in them, and although they could indulge in a debauch when the way seemed clear to future refreshments, they had fore-knowledge and prudence enough to resist anything like over-indulgence now.

One pannikin of boiled tea was the allowance served out to each man, even with those half-dried waterholes round them, with a piece of damper and a slice of cold pork as flavouring, and then they lay down and smoked themselves to sleep, the tobacco keeping the mosquitoes from them while they were conscious of the annoyance; afterwards they did not mind these marauders taking their feast.

They carried with them a couple of bottles of three-star brandy, but that was for medicinal purposes only. They were not such idiots as to take any of this thirst-provoker on a journey like this, where a man requires to husband all the moisture he has about him. They were not reckless, although they were remorseless scoundrels.

The Swampers

Ten miles is a good day's walk over the ground they were passing, but they pushed on and doubled this during most days, that is, when the ground was fairly level.

They were also fortunate in the line they took, for luck is everything in such cases. Many explorers have passed water-holes and soaks a little way right or left of them, to suffer untold thirstagonies with water so close at hand. Science and experience are of no great help, for in this land both water and gold are found in the most unlikely places with no premonitory signs to guide the traveller to them. He may be walking over sand ridges, wading knee deep in the loose soil and all at once drop across a clay soak, a quartz outcrop with a cavity filled with water, or a fertile patch of ground fringing a pool crowded with water fowl, or he may miss all these by less than a quarter of a mile, and leave his bones to bleach on the arid desert.

That loose sand is as fertile as the loams of other countries, and in places as engulfing as the quicksands by the Solway. When the wanderer goes forth to the wilderness of Australia, he ought to pray constantly to his guardian angel to protect and watch over his feet.

The six adventurers who now trusted to the captain's sextant, chronometer and pocket compass, must have had many friendly demons accompanying them, for although the season had been such a dry and hot one, their water-bags never ran dry. Mirages surrounded them from dawn till dusk, spreading like cool lakes on every side. At night these burnt lambently and ghost-like. They trod over salt marshes with the crusted saline like frosted snow, and the gypsum shining like glass, while underneath lay fathomless bogs of blue-black slime. They touched on places where the quicksands quivered under their tread like badly-made jelly, and endured heat-fumes that might have sucked the vitality from any but a colonial. Mosquitoes, ants and sand flies bit them viciously, while countless myriads of flies and fleas covered them as they struggled on; what these desert plagues exist upon, who can say?—where animal life is wanting. Possibly they can live and die fasting, yet when they do get a chance they make the most of it.

The Swampers

On the sixteenth day, these explorers came to a series of ridges over which they struggled for about six hours to find themselves at the entrance of a deep gorge, leading between volcanic ranges. Then the Professor said as he looked about him: "If there is gold anywheres, boys, it should be hereabouts."

"Then let us camp," gasped the wanderers with one accord, for they were dog-tired with the heavy ground they had gone over, and at the words, swags were flung aside, and from the dried-up bushes that broke the desolation round them, they began to make their fire.

As yet they had seen no sign of natives or white men, although they knew that they could not be very far from the outskirts of that far-stretching civilization as represented under the elastic title of East Coolgardie, for they had kept in a direct line west-north-west from where the schooner lay; therefore as the smoke from their fire floated up into the afternoon atmosphere, they kept a vigilant watch for any answering signals.

They had finished their supper, and were sitting listening attentively to the Professor as he delivered a discourse on the causes of these abrupt and riven cliffs that surrounded them, when suddenly Barney started up with a loud cry and pointed down the gully.

There, plodding down wearily on horseback came the figure of a white man, with dark hair and dust-covered, tangled beard, attended by several black fellows.

He had been a considerable time out, judging by the tattered state of his costume, yet both rider and horse seemed well enough nourished.

"Coo-ee," came the friendly call from the rider, to which they responded and then waited on his approach. "I saw your smoke, boys, from my camp, so thought I'd look you up."

"By the Lord, it's Jack Milton," shouted Barney, springing forward to his old chief and gripping his hand.

The Swampers

"Barney—Professor—well, I am in luck—and so by Jingo, are you, for I have just struck a rich lode in this gully—give me a pipe and a billy of tea, for I've had nothing of the kind for the past month." Jack flung himself from his horse, and pointing to the natives with him, said:

"Be good to these, boys, for they have been right chums to me, during the past two months."

The Swampers

Chapter XXIV. Chester Takes a Month's Leave.

ROSA CHESTER could not possibly have fixed upon a better moment than she did to come to Kalgourlie and establish a hotel like this, and before a couple of weeks were over, she had proved that she possessed the necessary qualities for the post.

Before her advent, men had been satisfied with paying long prices for drink and food served up any way. Kalgourlie was yet in its embryo stage, its lights at night being paraffin oil and candles, although the Mayor, John Wilson, had just gone to London to arrange, with other matters conducive to the township's future welfare, the lighting of it by electricity.

Gas is an impossibility for the goldfields of Western Australia. They must have the latest and the best in everything. At present Hessian huts satisfy them, while they are arranging and waiting for the genius to utilize their waste quartz crushings and make these into sculptured domes and palaces. In olden times the mining owners employed geniuses to cut out their marbles. The West Australian money maker pulverizes every ounce of stone about him for the wealth it contains, leaving the future artist the finest of crushed powder to make casts of and bring back again to impervious stone. There are hundreds of thousands of tons out there of this magnificent powder, blowing about and choking the inhabitants at present, which will before long eclipse the marbles of Italy for purity and the bronzes for endurance. A very simple process will make it once more impervious quartz. The sculptor will cast columns, friezes, and statues which Time cannot destroy. Great and cool buildings, richly decorated, will rise out of this quartz débris. Streets will be paved with its enamel linings, watertanks coated with it, while gardens and terraces eclipsing those of Babylon will rise out of the sandy desert. West Australia has only commenced her career. She is building up her proppings and bulwarks with gold, by-and-by they will begin to decorate, for the men who are there like refinement and comfort because they have matriculated in England and are not over-colonial. The West Australian colonists are seldom

The Swampers

seen on the goldfields. It is the Rothschilds and other capitalist kings who rule the roost there.

Rosa went on the ordinary lines for the first few days, and found her customers content enough to take what she gave them, so long as she made no mistake about the quality of the drink. Then, having walked down Hannan Street in the cool of the evening, and looked from the outside at some of the Japanese refreshment shops, she held a consultation with her husband, Jenkins and her importation, Sarah Hall. "We must alter all this," she observed severely. "The boys know what they'd like, only they can't express their wants. Red hot lemonade at these Japanese slums isn't good enough for Europeans to indulge in long without surfeiting them. I'll tell you what, now, I'm going to run this shop. We'll have some good cooks imported. I can cook a little. Can you, Sarah?" "As well as a woman is expected to do," replied Sarah, modestly.

"That's right. Japanese girls are interesting. Sir Edwin Arnold found them so. We'll have Jap waitresses and a Jap chef. They can turn tinned meat into anything. We'll import fruit and vegetables. Have ice made on the premises, as well as aerated waters, and make this the flash hotel of the West."

Anthony Jenkins was enthusiastic, for he had a Napoleonic mind, and when Chester saw the results of the drawings, he also succumbed, and thought that Rosa might with all safety launch out a little, therefore, that indefatigable young woman began her operations, and in a couple of weeks had expended a considerable portion of the money they had brought, but she made the place a big success.

More bedrooms were added to the hotel, which was easy to do by canvassing the rear verandah and raising up fresh frames round the yard, for they had plenty of space to fall back upon. The kitchens were enlarged and carried farther from the house. Refrigerating machines were added to the condensers. Palms and other shady plants and shrubs imported to make the hotel comfortable and luxurious as well as roomy, and the public showed their

The Swampers

appreciation of these efforts to please them by coming often and staying long in this Hessian temple of Venus and Bacchus.

The taste for display which prompted Rosa to long to make a "splash" in Sydney, she was able to indulge in with profit at Kalgourlie, for although gentlemen will swallow champagne whether it is warmed or iced, they naturally prefer to have it cooled, also to quaff it from proper glasses instead of pannikins, and to have the surroundings clean and tastefully arranged. They enjoy their drink all the more if it is poured out for them by pretty young women instead of parded ex-prize-fighters, and the "Chester Hotel" was the one place in the district where all these comforts could be had without extra charge.

A wide verandah stretched along the front, covered on the top by striped awning, with Japanese blinds to pull up and down at desire. A line of tubs filled with good-sized palms were ranged outside, with pots of exotics inside to give it the look of a conservatory. Rosa had spent a lot on these feminine adornments, for, like most colonial women, flowers were a necessity of her existence. Lacquered tables, bamboo and canvas deck-chairs, with other pretty nick-nacks, filled the interior of the verandah, which, with the tasty hangings of beadwork and muslins, offered so strong a contrast to the other houses of the kind. The other portions of the hotel were furnished in the same tropical and artistic style. Punkahs waved from the ceilings of the public room, while the tables of the dining saloons were covered with the whitest of linen and brightest of glasses and other adornments.

The servants, of course, were all Japanese, as it was nearly impossible to get Europeans to serve as menials, and the Japs were strictly prohibited from acting as miners, but Rosa had to own, in spite of her colonial prejudices, that she could not have been better served than she was by these deft, silent and obedient hirelings. The girls were pretty, young, and adaptable, and the men industrious and unobtrusive; quick to grasp her orders, and giving her no trouble or cause for complaint.

The Swampers

She was much happier, acting as the mistress and hostess in this establishment, where she was flattered from morning till night by her customers, than she could possibly have been presiding over a mansion at Pott's Point and vainly trying to get inside the conservative rings of Sydney society. Sarah Hall also pleased her immensely, for while helping her mistress in every way, with her experience and quiet management, she never attempted to rival Rosa with the men. They were all respectful to the dark-eyed, black-haired manageress and fond of the sprightly little maid Alice, but when they wanted a bit of flirtation, they sought out the mistress.

Chester and Jenkins were up to their eyes in work, and coining money hand over fist. Litigation was common in a community like this, where gambling and speculation were the occupations of their lives, and bets and bargains were constantly being disputed, and legal arbitrations were required.

It is difficult for an Englishman who has not been on a new gold field, to grasp the colossal profits which may be made in a day by lucky speculation, although he may be able to comprehend the unwillingness to part with thousands to the one who may have speculated only a few shillings. The purchaser of twenty pounds' worth of possibilities will naturally expect his hundred thousand when the result turns up trumps, while the seller will as naturally hunt about for any loophole of escape from his liabilities. In such cases the lawyer steps in, arranges a compromise, and gets his own fat commission from both sides.

Jenkins brought customers of this kind constantly to his partner, and from the office to the bar, the litigants proceeded with their advisers, and over the flowing bowl settled the dispute to the satisfaction of all parties. What mighty cheques were drawn up and signed at these lacquered tables, while Rosa, in her cool, perfumed dress, went about smiling and gracious; the sedate Sarah, sitting behind the counter filling the till with sovereigns as the pretty Japs carried round the liquid and iced gold. It may have been arid and dusty outside, where Afghans, aboriginals, swampers, camels and horses lay about in the shadeless rays, blackened over with flies, baked in dirt, and with the everlasting thirst upon them all, but inside that verandah, shadow and comfort were to be found for all who could afford to push aside the rustling hangings.

The first outlay had been the strain, but Chester had brought sufficient money with him to cover all that, and leave a fair surplus for current expenses. This store he had no need afterwards to touch upon, for from the first day of his arrival, he was able to add to it by his own commissions and speculate also discreetly. He was not a plunger, like Anthony, who had the true gambler spirit, yet both were remarkably successful in all their speculations, therefore their business was a stable one, and themselves highly-respected citizens of Kalgourlie, in spite of all the chaffing of that anti-Sydneyite and mine-owner, Wallace.

In about six weeks' time the Chesters were considered to be old hands in this mushroom population, and knew all the residents, and all the ropes, when an event happened which caused the solicitor to pack his valise and apply to the Municipal Council for a month's leave of absence from his public duties. He having been appointed to several vacant posts and holding leases, required this public announcement of his intention and permission, otherwise his rights would have been forfeited, and himself possibly stopped from proceeding further than Albany on some charge of debt.

The event that hurried him off at a moment's notice was a telegram which he received from Sydney, informing him that a fire had taken place there, and that his house was burnt to the ground.

He did not tell Rosa, although she guessed it from his concern, where he had hidden the last plunder, but he felt devoured with anxiety to be on the spot, therefore promptly wiring back to his agent to permit no one to touch his property, he posted with all speed back towards his native town.

Rosa was quite complacent about her husband's absence, not that he interfered with her liberty in the slightest degree, but his constant presence about the hotel made her friends shyer than they might be

The Swampers

when his back was turned. The boldest admirer is apt to feel awkward in his attentions to a married lady, before even the most blind and complacent of husbands. Now all such foolish restraints were removed with him, and she could begin to have a high old time of it. Rosa liked admiration, adored presents, and appreciated perfect liberty of action; if she got these she did not mind letting Sarah Hall carry off the barren respect of their customers. Mr. Chester drew a good sum of money from the Kalgourlie bank before he left, and reached Adelaide with due expedition. Here, however, he received a shock which forced him to change his intention and destination.

It was an announcement in the papers of the discovery of stolen property by the police at Sydney. With eager eyes and a heart filled with agony and fear he read the full account as it was at that time known. And as he read, he cursed his own stupidity in placing Jack's share of the pawnbroker's jewellery beside the bullion and stamped gold, through which the hoard had been identified. His house was mentioned as the place where the plunder had been discovered, but no word showing that they suspected him was as yet printed.

The wisest course and the one a bold man might have taken, would have been to proceed openly to Sydney, and deny any knowledge of this plant. It would not have been impossible to place the blame on the shoulders of the missing housebreaker; at least, if he had courted investigation it was possible to evade conviction.

For a moment he thought of doing this, then he remembered his fatal wire ordering his agent to let no one disturb the burnt ruin; and as he remembered this, he shuddered with horrified anticipation.

He had taken his ticket to Melbourne, and was just waiting on the train leaving when he read this item of news. With a muttered curse he caught up his valise, and leaving the station, took a cab and drove down to the port.

In the offing lay two ocean liners, both ready to start; one represented the Orient Company and the other the German Lloyd. The Orient steamer would call at Albany for the mails, he knew, but

The Swampers

this was the last Australian port that the Prinz Luitpold would touch. In a few more moments the second husband of Rosa was being rowed towards the German mail steamer.

The Swampers

Chapter XXV. Jack Milton's Discovery.

JACK MILTON and his dusky friends camped that night with his old pals, and it was a long story he had to relate of his wanderings.

Rapid and long journeys day by day from water-hole to water-hole; in this, however, he had been more fortunate than most explorers, as the blacks knew where these were to be found, with such food as Nature furnishes for her desert children. Jack made a grimace as he recalled some of those feasts after his own provisions had been exhausted.

"Sometimes we lived like fighting-cocks when wallaby was about, or when we camped at water-pools where fish, fowl and other game were plentiful, sometimes we came down to snake, lizard, grubs and such-like delicacies; one thing I can tell you, mates, I seldom fell asleep fasting—and if those F.R.G.S. coons had only the natives with them, there wouldn't have been so many bungled expeditions across Australia. They go out with all their scientific instruments and blunder along, treating the natives as if they were fools, and never trying to make friends of them. They see the fires ahead of them, and never guess that they are being treated as Napoleon was when he crossed Russia, and that the people they've made enemies of are starving them out, and hiding their camping places from them.

"Any fool can cross Australia if the natives are his friends, as I have just proved, but I guess it will be a feat if they happen to be turned against him."

It had not been by any means an uninteresting journey, nor one devoid of pleasure. Corroborees and love-making, hunting and fighting had filled out their days and nights, all of which Jack had taken a share in. At one time the marriageable young men had gone on a love raid, bringing back wives and wounds from their expedition; at another time the marriageable girls had been abducted from their own party, all taken as matters of course by the parents on both sides, and expected by the girls. Jack had qualified as a fighting-

The Swampers

man when he knocked out those couple of front teeth, which considerably altered his appearance.

The evening passed while he narrated his adventures, and told how faithfully his friends had acted up to their promises and brought him safely to his journey's end.

"Beroki here said he would show me a gold mine, and, by gum! he has done it with a vengeance. I have looked on that to-day, which, when you see it, boys, to-morrow, will make your mouths water. No more need for us to break into any more banks. We can start one of our own now as soon as we can secure miners' rights. I never saw such a wonder in my life." He was glad that Australia had been too strong a fascination for them to leave, and that they could keep this discovery in their own hands; also delighted to hear that the vessel was on the coast to be a refuge in case of discovery.

"There are only two of us need be afraid of arrest over that last job, and those are the Professor there and myself. I saw all the papers about it before I left New South Wales, and we are the only ones whose descriptions they have and know anything about, therefore we must lie low until my beard grows a bit longer and I can alter your appearance, if it can be done with such an uncommon physiognomy as yours is."

"Well, Jack, I don't think there is anything peculiar about my face outside its brainy expression," retorted the Professor.

"That's it, you know, Professor, we may shave your beard and cut your hair, but it's the forehead that'll give you away."

"And the heyes, Jack. It's the heyes that reveals the man of intelleck—yet there's nothink so much again me as I knows of."

"What, d'ye think Australians will ever get over those racing prophecies of yours, Professor?"

The Swampers

"Ah, I knowed that business would ruin us, Jack," groaned Jeremiah dolefully. "Never you mind how they may be thirsting for your blood, Jerry. The place that I'll show you to-morrow is as safe as quad to hide in."

"But my occupation and spear of usefulness as a Psychometrist is gone; what can I do in a gold mine, I'd like to know, except tell you where the lode is likely to travel?"

"That's what many a man calls a real good business in these parts and likely to give you more popularity than fortune-telling by cards," replied Jack earnestly. "However, we'll keep your skill for our own private use, and give you occupation enough, don't fret about that. You reckon from what you've already seen of these ranges and this gully, that gold ought to be found here."

"Yes," answered the Professor firmly. "It's all round us from where this chain begins to where it ends, and I should say should be richer lower down, only it ain't fossickin' ground, for the best of it lies deep, and all you get on the surface won't hardly pay. That's my opinion, knowing as I do how them rocks happen to be sticking out here among the sand hills." "You are right, Professor. We'll want machinery—boring and crushing, eh?" "Yes, and I'll tell you what you are likely to find arter you get down far enough." "What?"

"A stratum of all sorts, through which that fused quartz was shoved, leaving the bulk of ore behind it." "Then it would be best to tunnel the range at its lowest depth?"

"Yes! I am of that opinion," answered the Professor modestly; he always gave his opinion on geology with diffidence, although so blatant over the card-lore and palm lines.

"Professor, you are a greater man than I ever gave you credit for. Every word you utter is gospel, and what is more, the tunnelling has been done for us." "Then you have jumped a discovered and worked mine?"

The Swampers

"Yes, but God only knows who or where the discoverers and workers were and are. I should say, that Beroki there and his tribe, with their ancestors, are the only human eyes that have looked upon it for the past thousand years, until it was shown to me. Listen, boys, to a fairy story, which you can prove for yourselves to-morrow. My friend, Beroki, who has chummed with me for the past six weeks, brought me to this gully this morning and took me into a cave or tunnel which I could never have discovered myself, for the entrance is no wider than what a man can squeeze into. Inside we went down at a pretty steep slant, until we came to a part where a deep well had been dug. Who dug it, or how deep it is neither Beroki nor anyone else can tell, but there it is, filled to the brim with cool sweet water.

"Of course we had to make a light to see all this, but at this part, where the well lies, is a pretty large chamber, with borings in all directions, like passages spreading from it. Where they all take to I don't know yet, but the one I went down brought me to just such a stratum as you described, Professor. See! I picked up that specimen and brought with me."

Jack took out of his shirt a piece of quartz so thickly impregnated with gold, that the metal predominated over the stone. This was passed round amidst cries of admiration.

"I saw lots more like it all round me, and as easy to pick out as plums from a bit of Sunday duff. If the other tunnels show up like this did, Mount Morgan isn't in it with this one. There isn't a Jack amongst us as won't be Vanderbilts in no time, only we must have our miners' rights, and the place pegged out without a day's delay. I could hardly tear myself from it." "What made you leave it?"

"One of our watchers outside came in to tell us that there were white fellows close at hand, therefore I hurried off to find out who you were, and mighty pleased I was to drop upon you instead of strangers."

All were now in a passion of eagerness for the night to pass, for the fury of gold was upon them. Seeing that sleep was out of the

The Swampers

question, they discussed how the business was to be managed, and it was finally decided that the Captain and Barney would start as soon as possible with the blacks to guide them and get to the nearest warden. There they were to take out miners' and explorers' rights for the whole party, including those left on the ship, purchase camels and stores, with tools, and hurry back, while those left were to peg out the ground on each side of the ancient tunnel, and erect a hut in front of it.

"We'll load the vessel before we spring our mine and make a rush; then we can show our specimens and purchase the ground. Fortunately, we have the rhino to pay our preliminary expenses."

At the first sign of approaching day they were up and following Jack and the natives down the gully, fearful lest some other prospectors might have already discovered their find, but all was as he had left it—a solitude, and, as yet, their own.

At this point the bottom of the stream bed was reached, and the valley branched round a lower range of hills. The punctured mountain rose above those round it, the upper portion bare and gleaming quartz, and the base clothed with dwarfed yet pretty close scrub.

Experienced prospectors would possibly have paused here and fossicked about amongst the sands, as it was a likely place for gold to be found in pockets, but with the bushes covering it and filling it up, it was unlikely that they would have discerned the hole, which the natives used for the water it contained, regardless of the other treasures.

Fortunately they had a fair supply of candles with them, therefore, leaving the blacks to mount guard outside, and the horse with its hobbles on to feed on what it could find, they crawled one after the other, Jack leading the way, into the tunnel.

It was no chance aperture they could see, for it had been roughly cut by the hands of some ancient miners through the solid rock, and was

The Swampers

therefore firm and dry, and as Jack had told them, slanted downwards at a steep angle in irregular and rude shelves or steps.

To reach the chamber where the well was a considerable distance had to be crawled, for it was impossible for any one to have gone down it in an upright position, the roof not being more than four feet from the ground, but once here they could all stand and look about them. They were now more than fifty feet below the bed of the gully.

"By George, Jack, when rains do come to this district and the creek rises, this hole will be swamped out unless there are some outlets to drain it off," observed the Professor, as he looked round him.

"Yes, it would be rather a bad trap for a man to be caught in during a flood, only there isn't much of that sort of thing in this part of the colony."

The well was a large one, almost like a plunge-bath, and from the blackness seemed to be fathomless, yet the water was good, fresh and cold. It stood in the centre of the chamber or vault, with over six feet of rock margin round it. The roof also was about fifteen feet above their heads, while there were five passages pierced in the walls at different angles, as if the unknown miners had gone several directions in search of the gold. These passages all slanted downwards to lower depths.

No markings on the sides gave them any clue as to what race of people had done this engineering, although there were several native paintings on the rocks, which had been executed by the tribes visiting this abode of fresh water and mystery. It was an unornamented mine and nothing more.

Jack led his companions with their lighted candles into the passage which he had previously penetrated where, after going with stooping heads for several hundred feet, they came to the vein he had spoken about. Before they quitted the rock-cutting, however, the Professor stopped at one point and cried:

The Swampers

"I say, boys, here is something that strikes me is a discovery, if we could make it out."

He held his candle close to a portion of the quartz upon which some marks had been cut.

Where the Professor had paused, they were still within twenty yards of the termination of the quartz-reefs, so that the sides, floor and top were composed of solid granite.

On a portion of this solid mass, the marks were engraved, deep, bold and rugged. It was only by going a little way from them that their connection could be seen, and then they looked thus:

The men, eager as they were to see the gold, stopped before this strange device, if device it was, and regarded it with curious eyes.

"Well, Professor, what do you make that out to be?" enquired Jack, a little sneeringly.

"Them's Howrografficks, that's what them are," replied the Professor solemnly. "If you asks me what they mean I answers: 'Just wait till I consults my sperrut guide,'but if you asks me who printed them on this ere stone, I says: 'The lost tribes of Israel.'They is the boys as made these 'ere cuttings, for why?—they always managed to find out and boss the 'oof'business when they got a square show, the same as they do at present."

"Bother the Sheenies now or in the past," replied Jack, passing his candle carefully over the outer edge of this singular device. "I'll have another examination of this part later on; meantime, come and have a squint of the pretty show of ore that lies a few paces farther on."

The Swampers

Chapter XXVI. The Courtship of Bob Wallace.

LITTLE ALICE had been ailing for the past few days, and her illness caused a terrible shade of anxiety to rest over the frequenters of the hotel, with whom she was a general favourite.

When the doctor declared it to be a case of typhoid fever, twenty strong men volunteered to nurse their infantine favourite back to health.

Her mother, however grateful for the proffered services of these honest boys, with whom time meant literally gold, declined their offers and determined to do the best she could herself.

Rosa wanted the child to be sent over to the hospital, but this suggestion the mother would not listen to; where she was, her daughter would have to be tolerated also, therefore if Mrs. Chester was frightened about the infection, she was willing to leave.

Typhoid is a common complaint about the goldfields, as it has been in Sydney of late years; most of the residents had either passed through it, or lived in its proximity, so that they had come to regard it as incidental to the climate, like the mosquitoes and the flies. The fact therefore of a patient being in the hotel made no falling away in the custom, no man believing nor caring about infection. They were sorry for the sake of Sarah, as well as for the youngster, and drank their liquor in a more subdued manner. "Mexican Joe" told newcomers gently about the inevitable funeral that followed the pulling out of his "shooter." Sailor Bill nursed his chin with his ringed hand, and looked moodily into his glass, and the rest of the worthies tried to give as little trouble as possible, yet they stuck to the bar and verandah with heroic fidelity, and drank as deeply if more silently than before.

Bob Wallace, however, bustled in on the fourth night of the trouble, and seeing that Sarah was looking pale and jaded, he told her that he had a fortnight of idleness on his hands before going farther West,

The Swampers

and as he had nursed his mates without catching it, he reckoned himself fever-proof, therefore, whether she liked his services or not, he was going to look after little Alice.

Wallace was a favourite with Sarah, for although fond of yarning and chaffing, he was one of the most respectful of the visitors, treating her with a great deal more reverence than he did her coquettish mistress. Indeed, the boys had come to regard it as a settled thing that this lucky mine-owner was paying serious attentions to the handsome barmaid, and intended to become a stepfather if he could. Sarah tried to resist his determination, but was too fagged to hold out long; therefore, that night he took her place at the bedside of the little sufferer, while she got the sleep she so much required.

He was a good nurse, and as he had watched the different phases of this disease before, he knew exactly what to do, which Sarah quickly saw. A woman might have been more correct under the circumstances, for, as the hotel was crowded with sleepers, Sarah was forced to take her rest in the same apartment as the patient and this volunteer help, but the few women who were at Kalgourlie had their own sick to look after, while it would have been the last place to expect to see Rosa. Besides, cosmopolitans who have travelled over the world of waters in ships, and lived in canvas houses where only Hessian partitions separate them from their neighbours, do not think so much about the conventionalities in such trivial matters as do dwellers within brick-built walls.

Bob Wallace had watched Sarah quietly, but with great interest, since her arrival in Kalgourlie, and felt that he could easily make a big sacrifice to intérest her equally in him. Men had spoken freely enough with and about Rosa Chester, but the circumspect conduct of the barmaid had been the subject of only respectful admiration. He was a plain fellow, was Bob, but he had the desire and ambition of his sex, to marry a woman whom he could trust. Sarah to all appearances seemed to have this quality, as well as the pleasing charms which attract a man. That she was a woman of the world,

The Swampers

with experience, was an additional attraction in the estimation of the miner.

He had many opportunities after that first night, while both child and mother slept so close to him, of thinking the matter out; and long before little Alice was declared out of danger, he made up his mind to try his luck as soon as possible, and offer his hand and fortune to the first woman who had taught him to believe in her sex.

"There's grit in that girl," he said to himself, "and, by George, there are few that can hold the candle to her for looks."

It is a dangerous thing for a man to be much with a woman, even if they only meet during the day, whether she is ugly or handsome; but to be as they were then placed, in a sick room, the chances pointed strongly towards matrimony, if both parties were heart-whole and free before, or misery to the one who was inclined that way if the other was not.

Now whether Sarah was satisfied with her first experiment, for some women are constituted that way, or that her heart was buried with her dead husband, or that she was too much used to men, Bob could not determine. She was kind to him, and had grown wondrous free in this close intimacy—too free, by a long way, for his newly-awakened sentiments to glean much encouragement from, for it was the unconscious freedom of a sister towards a brother, united with the grateful tenderness of a doting mother towards the man who has aided her to push back the grim tyrant, Death. The kind of tenderness and freedom which a woman will display towards a self-sacrificing and devoted physician. He knew that she trusted him utterly after the first night. That first night she had been restless and watchful, only dropping asleep from sheer fatigue by fits and starts, and waking up often. He had felt angry at this suspicion, yet owned it was only natural on her part.

Since then, however, she had given him her confidence, and lay down on the couch calmly to take her needed repose. She came to him with a loose dressing-gown on, as she left her day costume in

The Swampers

her mistress's room. There he had her before him through the night as she reclined on that couch only a few yards distant. Her heavy black tresses, loose and falling to her knees in rippling waves when she stood beside him bending over her child, lying like a dark cloud in all directions when she slept.

He heard her low, regular breathing, for she was a quiet sleeper. He saw her red lips part sometimes in a smile, and her white teeth gleam between, as she tossed round towards him in that unconscious abandon, then the longing came upon him almost beyond his strength to resist, to take the kiss that those red lips seemed to ask.

Then, filled with shame and fear of himself, love made him do what he had not done since he was a boy at his mother's knee, kneel down by the side of the child, and, taking her hot, thin hand in his, say his prayers with a passion and earnestness that so few threw into the words: "Keep us from temptation and deliver us from evil."

The child did him good at such moments of agony. Half conscious as she was and listless with the awful prostration of typhoid, the wan little fingers pressed his, and sometimes the other hand was passed gently down his face. The evil fled at the touch of those fevered fingers, and manhood poured into his heart and made love revive.

Oh, yes. He loved her now as a man loves once in his life, if no more. It may be that this kind of love comes more than once to a man, yet it is doubtful, for the woman who is loved in this way seldom appreciates it, and men get to learn the standard that women are content with.

He went in and out during the day, but none of the boys chaffed him about his vigils, for they had an instinct that it was likely to be a serious business, and they all liked Sarah too well to make a joke of such a subject. They enquired after Alice gravely and wished him success with their eyes, but they would have smashed the eyes of any bungler who dared to make a joke of that sick nursing yet. When the time came for Bob to announce his engagement, then he would run "amuck," meantime they were not the kind to frost a young bud before it was far enough grown to stand the blast. These diggers are wonderfully intuitive, if they are at times rough and inclined to burn effigies when they cannot get at their enemies with their boots. Champagne and whisky are not like absinthe in their effects. They don't blunt the sensibilities.

Rosa also could afford to let Sarah have this man, who abhorred Sydneyites so heartily. He wasn't a favourite of hers, that is, he had never shown any desire for her society, and she had plenty to pick and choose from, without him; therefore she could afford to be generous.

She had read the account of the discovery in Sydney, and as her husband had never written, she guessed that he had shown the white feather and absconded. She had been interviewed also by the police, and told them she knew nothing about the business. If Chester knew anything they had better find him, as she would like to know where he was, and so matters stood at present. Meanwhile she was enjoying herself and making money, therefore her mind was easy.

"If I don't hear from Arthur very soon, I'll apply for another divorce, and get spliced again," she said to herself complacently, as she dressed herself to go for a moonlight drive into the desert with the Hon. Billy.

Sarah Hall was very, very grateful to her friend, Bob Wallace. He was a good-looking and an honourable, as well as a wealthy, man, and she wasn't indifferent to that last fact either.

She was woman enough to see that she could do with him as she liked. Alice was fond of him, as she had good cause to be, for without his help and experience she would have lost her treasure. If she married him, herself and her daughter would be placed beyond the buffets of fortune for life. That was an inducement to tempt any fond mother. Did she like him well enough to accept these blessings with him tacked on to them? Yes. Leaving one man out of the

The Swampers

question, whom she had lost for ever, Bob Wallace was more, in her estimation, than any other man in the world. She felt, if she took him, her fate ought to be happier than that of most women who marry, for he had proved himself to be a good and a true man. Alice would never want.

If he had not nursed her child and told her so much of his past, if he had asked her over the bar before she knew him so well, she might have said "Yes," but now— —

With a shuddering moan she thrust the temptation from her. He was too good a fellow to curse. She had only respect and gratitude to give—not love, which makes a woman reasonless and remorseless. Alice was up and about again, so Bob's occupation was gone as a sick nurse.

One afternoon he came with a buggy to give her a drive, and as the hour was a slack one she got leave and went with him, knowing what that drive meant.

They drove into the sandy waste and there under the twilight sky, Bob asked her the momentous question, flinging a bit of eloquence into it and introducing Alice as an inducement for her to say Yes, and become a life partner in his profitable speculations. She felt that he was in deadly earnest, and they were familiar almost as man and wife already.

"See here, Bob," she said after a pause, and an intense look at him out of her dark eyes. "You have told me all your past life, and it's been an honest one, but you know nothing about mine."

"I don't want to hear about your past so long as you are at liberty to marry me and care for me enough to do so."

"Ah, I am a free woman as far as that goes, Bob," she replied, bitterly. "And I like you well enough." "That's enough. Then we will reckon it as settled.

The Swampers

"Not yet, my friend. Give me a night or two to think of it. I'll marry no man unless he knows all about me first, and I cannot tell you that story to-day. To-morrow, perhaps, I'll tell you it, and if you are willing then to have me, I'll be your wife." "My darling!"

He put his arms round her waist and kissed her, while she didn't resist the embrace. Then they silently returned to the hotel.

That night, as Sarah was waiting at the bar and Wallace was sitting on the verandah with his friends, two visitors came, the captain and Barney.

After securing their beds and ordering their supper, they went into the bar for a drink. Sarah started as she saw Barney, but at a sign from him she became calm as before. In a few minutes she managed to get him where they could talk without being observed, then she said: "Do you know anything about Jack?"

"Yes," replied Barney; "he is with me, a hundred miles from here, and doing well." "Thank God. See, Barney, what do you think of that?"

She pointed to Alice, who was sitting in a pillowed chair at the farther end of the bar. "Yours?" he asked laconically.

"Yes—and Jack's. Tell him when you see him that he has got a piccaninny waiting for him at Kalgourlie."

Alas! for the hopes of Bob Wallace. He sits happily shouting champagne for all and sundry, while Sarah flits about the bar with a bright glitter in her eyes—but not for him.

The Swampers

Chapter XXVII. The Meeting of Jack and Rosa.

AS might be supposed, the captain and Barney did not waste any time at Kalgourlie after they had secured their own miners' rights with those of their comrades by proxy. The more rights they had, the more ground they would be able to prospect and purchase. The quicker also they were on the ground, the better for the security of their property.

They hired twenty camels with their Afghan drivers meantime, as a preliminary piece of business; and as they had ready money to pay for what they ordered, they were treated with corresponding complaisance and respect—for ready cash is always the visible sign of a man's respectability and worth in the eyes of people who have wares to sell, no matter how much poverty-stricken and debt-laden Robert Burns declaimed against it! "The man is not a man for a' that," unless he possesses the gold, stamped or otherwise. In fact, he becomes a very poor and abject tool without it when his creditors begin the hunting-down game, and his butcher, grocer, baker and milkman refuse to let him have any more credit. The fine and poetic sentiment of being "a man for a' that," may be sung over the drink his friend treats him to, but it is difficult to feel it while he has to borrow.

Independence would be a very noble kind of feeling if it could only be carried out, but alas! for poor humanity, it is utterly impossible to keep it up and live. Burns was far from it all his life, although he wrote so much about it; and as he was, so are we all, abject slaves to circumstances. Man is a borrower from the hour he first indulges in the luxury of living; the very air he breathes being an obligation which he accepts from his Creator. He has only two courses left open to him from his birth to his death. To be a debtor or to be a robber, in spite of all his protests and foolish pride. Which is the most degrading and unmanly is beyond me to decide. I only know that the possession of money is the nearest approach to that condition which all men court and respect.

The Swampers

Barney and the captain, flashing their stolen sovereigns, commanded the position, and when they set out with their caravan, they were sent off with a hearty God-speed, and their return looked for with eager expectation.

Meantime, while they had been absent, Jack Milton and the others settled down in the gully. They raised a branch-and-leaf hut in front of the mine entrance, which completely covered and protected that secret. They also pegged out the ground and broke the surface in several different places, under the Professor's instructions, to serve as blinds to inquisitive people, keeping the half-dozen natives with them as outposts to warn them of the approach of any strangers. The main body of the tribe had stopped a couple of hundred miles to the east, and only Jack's friend, the son of the chief, with a few of the adventurous young men, had accompanied him so far.

After building the hut and storing their provisions, Jack Milton and the Professor explored the mine, while waiting on the return of their emissaries, and found enough there to comfort them after all their privations.

The other passages had been merely experimental borings, and not carried to any great extent, yet in each of these were indications of interbedded lodes and cross veins, which in some places were particularly promising. The original miners, whoever they were, evidently must not have had crushing appliances, and therefore looked for "off-shoots," "blows," and "alluvial deposits."

The first passage which they had discovered was where the original miners had found what they could extract easily from the decomposition of the rocks and the mixing of clay, which permitted them to extract the ore almost purely and easily. They had reached a "show" of extraordinary richness, and had contented themselves with working that at the time they were interrupted or left off.

That this lode had only as yet been broached was clear to the Professor after a careful investigation.

The Swampers

"I tell ye what, mates," he exclaimed joyfully. "Them lost tribes left off afore they got to the best part of their discovery. They only got the thin end of the wedge so far, the heavy part lies below. I reckon we'll get enough out of this dip to make us all dooks if we want to, and leave plenty in the mountain to float the biggest mine in the West arterwards. Lor'! this rock is saturated with it; meanwhile our game is to make what we can out of the gravel gold fust."

Jack knew he could trust the Professor's geological knowledge, and indeed, soon picked out sufficient specimens to satisfy his mind that they need go prospecting no farther, but on the second day he made a discovery which nearly sent every member off his head.

That portion of the wall where the lettering was engraved fascinated him so greatly that he devoted most of his attention to it, with the result that on this second day he saw what appeared like a cut division in one portion of it. That was quite enough to set this professional safe-opener's sharp wits at work.

"I'm going to try a little gunpowder blasting here, Professor. Are the walls safe to stand a mild charge?"

"Yes," replied the Professor, "they'll stand all the powder you have in the camp without shaking the tunnel."

"All right, we'll do it at once then, for I'm mighty mistaken if this ain't a door which a little powder will open for us." Together they set to work and soon bored a hole between the crack at the bottom, then charging it, they made a running train to the chamber outside, and lighted it. In less than a minute the explosion occurred, and the sulphur smoke came pouring out towards them.

As soon as the atmosphere was cleared they went forward with their lighted candles, and saw that Jack had been correct in his surmise. The rock on which the hieroglyphics, or writing, had been, was broken and lying in the passage on a mound of débris, while beyond lay a dark cutting.

The Swampers

With eager steps Jack plunged into the cavity, holding his candle in front of him, the Professor following as quickly as he could after the young man. "What do you think of that, Professor Mortikali?"

"By golly!" gasped the Psychometrist, as he gazed round with starting eyes. "The store-house of the lost tribes."

Yes, whatever ancient adventurers had been here, and whatever treasure they had taken away, they had locked up sufficient in this cutting to reward handsomely those coming after. There the gold reposed on the quartz floor, as it had been picked and packed ready for transportation. Pure nuggets of all sizes from a few grains up to pounds in weight; lumps of quartz and hornblende veined like black and gold marble, with the dim tinted ore clinging to each piece in delicious filigree tracings. There were camel loads of it, all selected and arranged ready for the packing.

"Hoorah!" cried the Professor. "We don't need even to dig this yere mine. The lost tribes have saved us the trouble."

"Good chaps, these lost tribes were," responded Jack. "But why didn't they come back for it, I wonder?"

"They was too greedy and kept it all to themselves. I guess they got wrecked with the first shipload they took from here, and so the news never got back to their own country. It's a legacy of the past, that's what it is."

They troubled no more about the digging out for the time, but carried the nuggets and quartz-lumps to the hut, packing them up carefully and placing them ready to be forwarded to the ship. This occupied them till the arrival of the captain, Barney and the camels.

A fortnight passed and the caravan was sent off loaded to the schooner. Jack went with the load and saw it shipped carefully, while Barney went once more to Kalgourlie, and took out purchase rights for the company.

The Swampers

They were rich already, and could afford now to be generous with their information, therefore, having secured the full rights of the mountain, they took in specimens to the warden, calling their mine "The Lock Up," after that ready find, and the range Mount Berrima, after a place of seclusion which some of them had tender recollections of. Australia is mostly named in a sentimental fashion of this kind: Mount Hopeless, Cape Desolation, Fly-blown Flats, Gallows Gully, Cold Water Creek, Starvation Scrubbs, etc., etc. The time is yet to come when they will fix upon euphonious, or at least, less significant, and more taking titles.

There was such a mad rush to the district of Mount Berrima as had never been to its original namesake, and Jack Milton, or, as he now called himself, John Milroy, as the recognised head of the concern, was now regarded as a man to be courted.

His beard was long enough to serve as a disguise, while the Professor, with a clean shave, a false set of teeth, close-clipped hair, and blue glasses, felt that even his own wife might well have passed him by. Jack then determined to pay a visit to Kalgourlie, and arrange matters for his gang.

He had received splendid offers for shares; already a host of men were working the lodes. Capitalists were haunting him. The caravans were constantly travelling between Kalgourlie and Berrima; therefore, one day, he mounted a camel and rode into the mining centre.

All went well; he arranged his programme, saw the chief men of the place, and according to the custom of the place, put up at the "Chester Hotel."

Barney had told him about Sarah Hall and her child, yet knowing nothing about Rosa, it was not to be expected that Jack would associate her with the hotel. It was therefore a shock to him when they came face to face, and he knew that his land-lady was his divorced wife.

The Swampers

Rosa recognised him the moment she saw him, for although a mother may forget her child, he was too big a man now for his wife who had so lately divorced him, to pass him by.

Sarah, at the moment he called at the hotel, was off duty, so that he didn't see her, but Rosa, who was in the bar, looked up with a gasp as he ordered his drink, then a glance passed between them, and that was all. "You are Mr. Milroy, I believe?" she said, as soon as she recovered herself. "Yes," replied Jack quietly, "and you are Mrs. Chester!" "The same—come, let me show you your room."

There were a number of people in the bar at the time, and Jack, after finishing his liquor, followed the hostess inside. She did not take him to his own room, but led him towards hers, and when she got him inside, she shut the door, and then turned towards him with the one word: "Jack!" "Yes, Rosa, I've turned up, you see." "I'm glad of it, Jack. We are friends, I hope." "I trust so, Rosa—you have me in your power, as I have you!" He spoke easily, yet he did not feel so confident, knowing her as he did.

Rosa looked at him with pathetic eyes in which she had thrown her old dove-like witchery.

Chester was gone—she hadn't heard from him since he left, and there was no man so much talked about as John Milroy at present on the diggings. Why shouldn't she win him back and have him again as her slave, the richest man about the Coolgardie district? The room where they were was only a small one but it was well furnished.

The bed was tastefully arranged, and Rosa sat now upon it, as a couch, while Jack stood a little way from her. It was only a few months ago since they had shared one room, surely her task was an easy one—charming woman as she was.

"Don't speak that way, Jack. If you knew how I have regretted my foolishness in the past, you would forgive me. I did not think. I was tempted, but you were my first love, Jack, and I would have died had any ill befallen you."

The Swampers

"I daresay, Rosa—only since then there has happened a good deal. You have got a divorce and married again. That makes a difference, doesn't it?"

"I don't know—there is no difference in me. I am the same as I ever was, where you are concerned."

The Swampers

Chapter XXVIII. Jack Milton at Kalgourlie.

JACK MILTON stood looking at his former wife with a good deal of admiration blent with a little amusement. She was very charmingly dressed, very pretty and innocent-looking with that contrite expression on her soft, cream-tinted features, as if she had been a child who was full of sorrow for having broken her doll or dirtied her pinafore.

"What an opinion she must have of me and my love, if she thinks she can wheedle round me after what has passed," he mentally said, while he quietly stroked his beard with his strong brown hand.

He glanced round the room where they were, and saw more than the usual number of skirts hanging about, with the linings outside. An everyday suit of the absent Chester also dangled from a peg, while on the dressing-tables lay in trays a profusion of bangles, rings, and other costly nick-nacks, presents, most of them, from her admiring friends.

"Eh, is it quite safe for us to speak here, Rosa, with those Hessian walls? They are a little more revealing than even weather boards, don't you think?"

"Oh, that's all right," replied Rosa. "There is no one about the bedrooms this time of day. My servants are all Japs, with the exception of my manageress, Mrs. Hall, and she has gone for a drive with her little girl, and her spoony man, Bob Wallace." "Ah! but the customers in the bar, what of them?"

"Oh, they can cultivate a thirst till I get back, or help themselves; they are all honest boys at Kalgourlie, who don't go in for bilking landladies. They fly at higher game. Won't you sit down, Jack?"

Jack glanced round the apartment again, but the two bamboo chairs were at present filled with feminine articles of attire. Then Rosa, following his glance, laughed lightly as she said:

The Swampers

"Here, I mean, beside me; there is no room on the chairs, but there is lots here, if you ain't frightened to sit beside your wife." "That was," murmured Jack under his hand, then he replied gently:

"No. I'm used to standing; besides, I just remember some business I have to look after with the warden, before office hours are over, so I'll stand for the few moments I can stay, if you don't mind, Rosa."

"As you please," answered Rosa, with a pout and a shrug of her pretty shoulders, then instantly recalling her rôle of penitence, she continued sadly:

"I did badly by you, Jack, in Sydney, but you ought not to have left a young girl so long alone." "No, that was wrong of me," murmured Jack reflectively.

"I know since, that it wasn't entirely your fault, Jack, since you were locked up and couldn't get to me." "Well, perhaps that might be some excuse, Rosa."

"I didn't know it at the time though, dear, and Chester, my cousin, whom you trusted instead of me, was always about me putting bad ideas concerning you into my head." "Ah!"

"Yes, I never liked him, Jack, as I loved you, and — and as I'm afraid I do still, more's the pity for poor me, if you won't forgive me and be friends."

"Oh, I forgive you, Rosa, more than I can forgive myself, and am willing to be friends with you, therefore say no more about it." "But can you trust me ever again, dear?"

Jack flashed only one look at her, then he fixed his eyes on the wall opposite and smiled.

"Yes, Rosa, since you have seen your mistake, I think I can trust you again; besides, I'm going to make over some shares to you in my

The Swampers

mine as a sign of our mutual good faith." "Oh, my darling Jack, how real good of you."

She sprang from the couch with girlish vivacity, and made as if she would have flung her arms about his neck, only that he stepped back a few paces, smiling still and saying softly:

"Wait, Rosa, with your thanks until I can give you those shares. I have only just floated the mine, or rather accepted terms from the agents of a London syndicate. It has all to be arranged yet and—it's on that business that I have to see the warden to-day." "But surely, Jack, you are not going to refuse a kiss from your own loving wife?"

"Hush, Rosa! Judge Jeffreys finished all that between us, you know. Let us be good and faithful friends, if you like, only remember that your kisses now belong to—Chester."

"Oh, bother Judge Jeffreys and Chester also. I have chucked him now," cried Rosa impatiently.

"I read about his plant being discovered by the Sydney police, therefore I guessed he would clear out, but I suppose he hasn't left you in the lurch, eh?"

"No," answered Rosa vindictively. "The craven skunk has skedaddled, I suppose. But I've got the hotel in my own name and am doing well enough. It isn't that, Jack." "If you need any money at any time, Rosa, you know where to come to for it. While my secret is kept, I'll always be able to help you."

"Thank you, Jack; and is that all you have to say to me?" asked Rosa, fixing her blue eyes on him with a slight flush rising on her creamy cheeks.

"Anything else you want, Rosa, and I can give you—I'll only be too pleased to serve you," stammered Jack, looking uneasily towards the closed door. "Look here, Jack Milton——" "Milroy, my dear Rosa," corrected Jack gently.

The Swampers

"Well, Milroy if you like. I've done wrong and I've confessed my fault and been forgiven, as you say." "And mean, Rosa."

"All right. We were both brought up in the Catholic Church and married from it, and you know there are no divorces there. My divorce and marriage with Chester do not count with our faith. I am still your wife in the eyes of our Church, and nothing can alter that."

"Perhaps not, Rosa, in the eyes of the Church; yet I fear we are both pretty bad Catholics."

"I've repented, Jack, and been forgiven by you. I can get another divorce easily from Chester, and we can be married again legally under your new name and no one be the wiser." Jack looked at her, trying hard to conceal his disgust, then he said lightly:

"Oh, dash it, Rosa! we've had enough of marriages—let us be real good friends for the rest of our lives."

"But I love you, Jack. I have loved you all along, though I forgot myself at one time. Take me back again, and I'll be a good faithful wife to you."

Jack looked at the trinkets on the dressing-table and laughed silently while he muttered to himself bitterly: "Faithful? what a fool she still takes me to be." But he felt that he must temporize.

"I must go now, Rosa, or I shall miss the warden. Let us discuss this matter next time I see you." "Very well, only you must show that you have forgiven me by kissing, as husbands and wives, and good children do, when they have made up their quarrels."

She spoke jestingly, and raised her face while Jack stooped over her and brushed her lips-with his moustache. Then she caught him round the neck, and holding him firmly she whispered:

"Oh, Jack, Jack! why was I such a foolish girl when all my heart was yours? Oh, cruel Jack, to leave your Rosa that way." Jack during this

The Swampers

pretty speech had separated her arms from his neck and pushed her gently from him, so that she sank, as if overcome with grief, on to the couch, while he made towards the door hurriedly, looking at his watch as he ran. "By Jove! just time to catch the warden. I'll see you by-and-bye, Rosa. Ta-ta!" Rosa sat for a moment listening to the retreating steps, then she sprang viciously to her feet, and darting to the mirror, looked for a full moment at her own reflection.

"Has he got another since he left me?" she cried to her own reflection. "By Jingo! if I thought so, I'd give the square tip to the police. What are a few shares or a gift now and again when I ought to have the bang lot? Ah, Jack, I'll have another try to win you; and if you repulse me, then I'll fix you to a worse fate than taking me, you bet."

That lucky mine-owner, Jack Milroy, just reached the hotel front as Sarah Hall returned from her afternoon drive, and as Mr. Bob Wallace was engaged at the moment with the horse, it became Jack's pleasing duty to help the mother and child to the ground. There was nothing uncommon about this, as he chanced to be the only gentleman near at hand, but it gave both Sarah and him the opportunity of looking at each other and exchanging a whisper free from observation.

"Yours, Jack," she whispered as she gave him Alice to hold, while she arranged herself before descending.

A thrill passed over him as he received and set Alice upon the ground, then he turned to her mother. "I must see you, Jack, to-night." "All right, I'll be outside here at nine o'clock."

They looked at one another, these pair who had not met for nearly four years, and although their eyes spoke volumes, no one could have said they were more than two strangers looking with interest on each other.

"Let me introduce you, Mr. Milroy, to my friend Mrs. Hall," said the jovial Bob Wallace, who had now given his horse to the charge of a

The Swampers

stable-boy. Jack lifted his hat and the pair shook hands. "You are staying at the 'Chester,' I suppose, Milroy?" asked Wallace.

"Well—I'm going to have dinner here, but I must be off again after it. Are you dining here?" "Yes, of course." "All right, I'll see you then." With another hand-shake Jack left them and hurried along Hannan Street.

He had meant to have stayed a few days at Kalgourlie, before he met Rosa, as, since Barney told him about Sarah and Alice, he had thought a good deal about them both, about the grit and fondness of the mother while they were together in Melbourne, about his responsibilities respecting the child which he had burdened her with.

They had both in the old days come together as confederates in dishonesty—in fact, Sarah originally was his teacher in crime, and she always had loved him better than he had done her then. They had parted as criminals as well as honest people must part sometimes, however fond. The cause of that parting was the incarceration of Sarah, while Jack sought pastures fresh in Sydney. Here he had seen Rosa and forgotten his old and faithful pal—for a time.

Respectability in petticoats had betrayed him, while Dishonesty had been true all these years, for he had enquired a little about her from those who visited the mines, and some knew her both in Perth and Kalgourlie. He was known in Melbourne as Jack Hall, for gentlemen of his profession have as many names as royalty, and so he heard of her still wearing that alias, which struck him as a compliment in itself. No man had a word to say against her, not a scandal was attached to her name.

The men who praised the virtues of Sarah, spoke likewise about her mistress in a way that men will speak about those ladies whom they do not honour, yet condescend to admire at times. Why Jack did not connect her with his former wife was, he had no idea that she had

The Swampers

even left Sydney until he saw her. Chester is not an uncommon name in the colonies, any more than Plantagenet and Montmorency are.

Sarah also had no idea that her giddy mistress had been the wife of Jack. That was, as yet, a misery spared to her.

He passed along Hannan Street thinking of his past false wife, and faithful past mistress.

Had he wedded Sarah she would never have played him that trick, for they were pals as well as lovers, and the school that Sarah belonged to counted treachery towards friends as the unpardonable sin.

What a vile beast Rosa was, he thought, and what a lot of wiping he would have to do with his lips before he could let them rest on Sarah's, after that hypocritical and politic embrace.

"I'll give her the whole yarn to-night before I go back to Berrima" (he meant Sarah, the ex-pick-pocket, not the woman that Judge Jeffreys wept his maudlin tears over, before he granted her the divorce). "If she will have me after that, I'll splice her right away, and take her and the kid over to America, where we'll be safe. If she prefers Wallace, I'll make little Alice comfortable for life, for hang me if I'm worthy of her."

It was a proper and wholesome condition of humility for this millionaire, for after all, he wasn't worth such a woman as Sarah; few men are worth the love of a woman who can lift herself out of the mire with all the dead weights that society puts upon her. It is easy for a cold-blooded woman to keep respectable, but oh, how hard for a woman who has given her all and tasted life to sit down once again to the distaff.

Jack had found no difficulty in disposing of the mine, and all that was settled before his present visit. Each of the original owners could now retire when and where they liked, and live like princes on the purchase money. The mine was now being worked only to keep the

The Swampers

property until valuable plant was transported from England, and what Jack had come to Kalgourlie for was to get stores for the gold-loaded schooner, as yet unknown to anyone outside the discoverers of the mine.

These stores he had already ordered and forwarded. His own camels and Afghan attendant now waited for him at another house of call, so that he could go at any hour.

He went to the warden first and took out permits of absence for himself and his partners for six months. It was only natural that having made their "piles," they should want to rush off from the sands, condensed water, tinned meats and willywillies of the desert. No man wants to stay an hour longer in that Sahara than he can help. The warden gave him the permits, and wished them all a merry time in the clubs of London and the lively cafés of Paris.

Jack next went to his Afghan driver and gave him his directions about starting that night at ten o'clock, and the Indian promised to have all things ready.

He was now finished with business, so he went back to the hotel and had dinner and a few convivial drinks with the many acquaintances he met there.

He managed to keep Rosa at bay during the evening, for as she expected him to stay all night, she did not trouble herself so much about him in the earlier portion.

At nine o'clock, while sitting on the verandah, he saw Sarah leave the bar and Mrs. Chester take her place; then he got up, and making an excuse to his new friends he also passed out into the night.

He made his full confession to Sarah, of all his sins against her, and woman-like she forgave him after a little cry on his breast. Women, when they love, are always forgiving angels. Yet she said some hard things about Rosa, vowing that she would leave her at once. Of course she would marry him and go to the world's end with him if he liked. The devotion of Bob Wallace was not thought of. "When can you come?" asked Jack, when they had arranged these matters.

"As soon as she can let me go. She'll want another barmaid up from Perth. I must wait till then, I suppose. She'll think I'm going to marry poor Wallace." She had also told him all about Bob Wallace, and how she had put him off.

"I'll see him to-night, Jack, and tell him as much as I dare about us. He is a good man and will see the rights of it. He saved the life of Alice—poor Bob." They were both so much engrossed with each other that they did not see the dark figure that had followed them to the rear of the hotel and heard all their plans. They passed that crouching figure on their way back, yet Rosa had time to get into the bar before Sarah said good-night to Jack.

"I'll send you word before I come, Jack, and will keep my eyes open meanwhile," said Sarah, as she bade good-night to her lover, and saw him stride away to join his Afghan.

That night Sarah Hall told her story to Bob Wallace under the moonlight, after the bar was closed, and broke his honest heart—at least, as much as a man's heart can be broken nowadays. He didn't do anything selfish or extravagant. He only said she was an honest girl, promised her his aid if she wanted it, went into his bedroom and finished a bottle of brandy that he had there. That is how men behave now when their hearts are broken.

Rosa had a bottle of champagne sent up to her room, and drank that off to her own cheek, then she lay down and went to sleep, vowing to herself that she would do some real business in the morning.

The Swampers

Chapter XXIX. "Where the Weary Cease to Trouble and the Wicked are at Rest."

IT was late the night following when Inspector Wilmore drove into Kalgourlie from Coolgardie, and put up at the "Chester Hotel."

A quiet and amiable man of about forty-six was Inspector Wilmore, with sallow skin, clear, grey eyes, and close-cropped, dark brown beard. He was well known over the gold fields, as he often came on the search after missing sheep. He was temperate and methodical in his habits, yet could be capital company when he liked.

Rosa had retired when he arrived, therefore Sarah did the honours, and saw the chef about his supper, then she returned to have a chat with her old friend while his supper was being prepared.

Wilmore had been here several times since the "Chester Hotel" opened, so that Sarah, although slightly uneasy at his presence so soon after the visit of Jack, did not attach too much personal importance to it. Wilmore was generally pretty communicative with her, as he believed in her cleverness and discretion, while he honoured the unflinching stand she had made during the past three years. He knew her, as only Bob Wallace now did in this place, and he had shown himself a good friend before now.

"Well, Mr. Wilmore, and what has brought you up this time?" Sarah asked, as she gave him his sherry and bitters.

Inspector Wilmore looked through his glass at the lamp for a moment, and then he suddenly turned his eyes on her and gave her a searching glance. Sarah in an instant was on the alert, and knew that she was being read—and warned by her friend with that look. Folding her hands over each other on the counter, she met his glance steadily, and waited quietly on his coming words, her heart standing still and all her faculties attentive.

The Swampers

They were both subtle students of human nature, and were reading one another in that mutual swift glance. What he read made him resolve on a sacrifice, the hardest to a conscientious criminal-hunter. What she read filled her heart with gratitude and terror. At that moment she could have laid down her life for Inspector Wilmore. "How is Alice?" he asked after a pause. "Much better, thank you," replied Sarah with shining eyes. "Past all danger of a relapse, I suppose?" "Oh, yes; she has been out several times." "I'm glad to hear it." This was said heartily, then, with a slight shrug of his shoulders, he continued his queries, which were to her as plain as directions. "Mrs. Chester, I suppose, has gone to bed?" "Yes."

"Good. She believes in having her beauty-sleep, the giddy girl. Good sherry this, I think. I'll have another glass, but without the bitters."

As he was sipping his second supply he said indifferently: "You were asking what brought me up here, friend Sarah. Nothing that I expect to make much kudos or coin out of. A red herring trailed over an old scent I guess it will turn out to be. An affair that happened in Sydney some months ago, which will give me a long ride to-morrow for nothing, so I reckon it will be with me as it was with the Duke of York, I'll have my ride there and back again. No news yet about Mr. Chester, is there?"

"None," replied Sarah huskily, as she clutched at the counter to keep herself from falling.

"Try a glass of this same sherry, Sarah; you look tired-out, poor girl. I reckon you've been nursing and working too hard lately," said Wilmore kindly.

"Thank you, Mr. Wilmore," answered the barmaid gratefully, accepting his suggestion and pouring out some wine from the decanter into a small glass. Her hand trembled as she poured out the liquor, and a good deal of the contents were spilt as she raised the glass to her dry lips, but she set it down steadily enough. The wine had done her good. "Your supper is ready now, Mr. Wilmore."

The Swampers

"And I am ready for it, and for my bed as well. Order me a good staying dromedary for ten o'clock to-morrow morning. I won't start before that hour, as I need a proper sleep to-night. I'll have a bottle of that same sherry with me. Nothing could better that tipple for a long journey. By Jove, there is the moon rising, and making Kalgourlie look almost pretty. Good night, old pal, and take care of little Alice." "Good night, Mr. Wilmore."

She put out her white slim hand and grasped his closely, then she turned to another customer, who happened to be Bob Wallace, while Wilmore went into the dining room. "You want me, Sarah?" asked Wallace in a low voice, as he bent over the counter.

"Yes, Bob," she answered in a hurried whisper. "I must go to-night and take Alice with me. Wilmore has given me ten hours' start of him. Can you lend me your swiftest camel?"

"Yes. I'll go and get all ready now, and wait for you outside the town. Give me a bottle of brandy and some wine." "I'll bring them with me, and join you in an hour's time." Bob Wallace drank his champagne slowly, then, lighting a fresh cigar, he strolled leisurely outside to the moonlight, where the camels, dromedaries, and Afghan drivers were lying, and making the township look picturesque. The canvas tents and Hessian huts gleamed pale under the silver lustre and cast brown, deep shadows over the sands. Paraffin lamps and coloured lanterns burned richly inside the open Japanese shanties, where sights and sounds of debauchery helped the picturesqueness, and blent with the doleful shrieking of the desert-ships. Ghostly gum trees started from the waste, with the skeletons of the mine scaffolding, making altogether a weird and foreign-looking picture.

Bob Wallace knew where to find his own camels and drivers, therefore he steered towards that quarter, and gave his orders; then, while the drivers were getting ready for the approaching journey, Bob went to the store and purchased the needful provisions.

The Swampers

Sarah meanwhile saw Wilmore safely to his room, and looked after the closing of the hotel, then, when all these duties were over, she went to her own room and got herself and her child ready.

At last all was quiet inside the hotel, although the street outside was by no means silent, nor would it be all through the night. Wrapped up, however, warmly, for the night was chilly, she led her little girl from the side door, and with hasty steps passed out of the town to the point where her friend, Bob, waited for her with his three most valuable animals and most discreet of drivers.

Onward through the night they travelled at full speed, Sarah and her child on one beast, Bob on another, and the driver in advance with the provisions.

They went in line—Bob's dromedary bringing up the rear, so that there was not much opportunity for conversation, except at such places as they stopped to rest. Even then they did not converse much, for Sarah's heart was too full of gratitude and sorrow for her companion, and his too doleful, for words. Alice slept most of the way, wrapped up in warm rugs, and lulled by the cradle-like motion of these shambling, but soft-footed, enduring and swift animals, who have found a home in the western wilds of Australia, and made it a possible land to journey over.

Bob Wallace was only an ordinary type of the gold-finding element. A cynical story-teller and hard imbiber of spirituous fluids. Ready to plunge into a swimming time of it in London or Paris. Keen as a vulture where speculation or adventure were concerned. Sceptical on religious questions, and dubious concerning questions of morality, virtue or humanity at large. He had made his pile, therefore was placed beyond the necessity of plundering, yet he had no serious scruple about shaking hands, drinking, or dining with a plunderer, whether he was on the Stock Exchange, in Parliament, or only carrying on a small game on his own private account. In fact, he was not unlike the Great Social Reformer in his ideas of associating with publicans and sinners.

The Swampers

He enjoyed champagne, three-star brandy, special whisky and mineral waters. He likewise preferred a dinner at the "Savoy," or the "Maison Dorée," to tinned meat, for his digestive organs were still in good order, and he was able to sleep calmly through the night, after a heavy club evening, without waking up at four o'clock in the morning and thinking of his sins. He could also rise and enjoy a good breakfast without a preliminary vomit, no matter what the night before had been, and Remorse, as yet, did not peck, raven-like, at his liver. In fact, as yet, "Carter's Little Liver Pills" possessed no attraction for him, while saline draughts were not to be compared to a whisky and soda.

But, while enjoying all these gifts of our beneficent civilization, he could take to condensed water and tinned meats without much regret. He wasn't a man to whine over misfortune or hard lines any more than did the other adventurers of his class, nor did the possession of gold wake up any particular humanitarian, philanthropic or moral responsibilities. If a chum needed a five-pound note or a hundred, he shelled them out. If any unfortunate beggars appealed to him, whether male or female, he didn't stop to investigate their merits or virtues. He chucked them the shilling or the sovereign without saying afterwards, "What a good fellow am I."

In fact, Bob Wallace was a very ordinary sort of man of the Californian or Westralian type of diggers, who was as ready to assist a thief or a demi-rep if he was interested in them, as he was to help one of the unfortunate redeemed. Readier perhaps, as he didn't believe in parsons or their ways.

He didn't consider he was doing anything noble, self-sacrificing, or virtuous in helping Sarah to meet her housebreaker lover. He was dreadfully down in the mouth because he had to run away with her for another man instead of on his own account. But he recognised that this fellow had prior claims to the woman he adored. He knew that nothing else than Jack would make her happy, and he was interested enough in her welfare now to make him regard the riches of Ophir as dross compared to a grateful thought from Sarah. He had

had his innings and lost the game, and he wasn't going to act mean, no matter how much he suffered by the loss.

All through the night he watched the dromedary in front of him with its precious burden. He was looking at her now for the last time, and bidding her a long farewell under the moonlight, and these with other thoughts kept him subdued and silent.

In the early morning they rested and had breakfast together; in a couple more hours they would be at Berrima Mountain. The Afghan had fed his animals and himself, and now lay looking skyward and smoking a cheroot. Alice had fallen asleep on the sands after her meal, and the pair were together silently watching the breaking of the day.

"Bob, I can never forget you, you have done for me what no woman can forget—and I have nothing to give you in return."

"Oh, yes, you have, Sarah. Give me a lock of your purple hair to set with my gold, and a photo of yourself and Alice to—pray before when I am that way inclined. That'll do for me when I get a bit hipped."

Sarah seized his brown hand and kissed it passionately, then loosening one of her long tresses she said: "Cut off what you want, Bob, for it's little you ask for all you have done." "D'ye mind me biting it off, Sarah? My teeth are as sharp as a knife at present." "Certainly not, Bob—my brother."

"Ah," he grunted as he stooped forward, and separating a sable tress, began gnawing it through with his teeth.

He was leaning over her left shoulder with the tress end trailing out of his mouth, while she glanced sideways at him with brimming eyes. His teeth were sharp, yet it took a little grinding to get through that massive tress. "I wish to God, Bob, that I could have made you happy."

The Swampers

"Don't—for Christ's sake, don't! Sarah—say words like these. Give me one kiss, and I'll try to content myself with that."

She turned like a panther and flung her arms round his neck, and then their lips met for an instant only; when they withdrew their faces, each cheek was wet with the tears which had burst from the hot eyes. Sarah wiped that moisture away with her handkerchief, but Bob left his to soak in and dry.

Jack Milton received them at the camp hospitably, and, when he heard the news, at once held a consultation with his mates.

Barney, the Professor and the captain decided to flit at once, but the others decided to hang on and look after the concern. Therefore, after a hurried lunch while the caravan was packing, they set off towards the schooner.

The parting of Bob Wallace and Sarah was of a formal character, merely a few bottles of champagne shared round—some good wishes—a shake and a waving of hands. Then they were off—Jack, his child and future wife; while Bob Wallace remained to look over the mine, and arrange about its success. He had taken pretty heavy shares in it, therefore he was within his rights to be on the spot.

He was there when Inspector Wilmore came in on the following day, and replied to all that investigator's questions with discretion. The pair rode back to Kalgourlie mutually pleased with each other—doing well.

Mrs. Rosa Chester is thriving and has secured a fresh manageress. She has not yet applied for her second divorce, for she is doing well enough without.

Anthony Vandyke Jenkins is coining money as a mining expert and arbitrator. His enemy Bob Wallace has returned again to England. The Berrima and Lock Up Mines are things to conjure with, on the Stock Exchange and elsewhere.

The Swampers

Arthur Chester is still at large, and Inspector Wilmore is looking after other criminals who are constantly springing up, while fresh "Swampers" are rushing to the field. Westralia is the land, at present, of golden possibilities.

In a certain part of the globe—and I am not going to say where, as this is an extremely up-to-date romance—although Bob Wallace knows—a little colony are living comfortably and honestly, respected by all who supply them with the comforts of life since they can meet their responsibilities.

Jack is there with his wife Sarah, and their child. The Psychometrist Mortikali is there and appreciated for his occult powers. Barney is there and all the rest of them, and if mosquitoes predominate, and quinine is required as a tonic, at least that bugbear of civilization, the detectives, have no chance of extradition.

They are all happy and virtuous in that paradise "where the weary cease to trouble, and the wicked are at rest."

THE END

The Demon Spell

The Demon Spell

It was about the time when spiritualism was all the craze in England, and no party was reckoned complete without a spirit-rapping seance being included amongst the other entertainments.

One night I had been invited to the house of a friend, who was a great believer in the manifestations from the unseen world, and who had asked for my special edification a well—known trance medium. 'A pretty as well as heaven-gifted girl, whom you will be sure to like, I know' he said as he asked me.

I did not believe in the return of spirits, yet, thinking to be amused, consented to attend at the hour appointed. At that time I had just returned from a long sojourn abroad, and was in a very delicate state of health, easily impressed by outward influences, and nervous to a most extraordinary extent.

To the hour appointed I found myself at my friend's house, and was then introduced to the sitters who had assembled to witness the phenomena. Some were strangers like myself to the rules of the table, others who were adepts took their places at once in the order to which they had in former meetings attended. The trance medium had not yet arrived, and while waiting upon her coming we sat down and opened the seance with a hymn.

We had just furnished(sic) the second verse when the door opened and the medium glided in, and took her place on a vacant set by my side, joining in with the others in the last verse, after which we all sat motionless with our hands resting upon the table, waiting upon the first manifestation from the unseen world.

Now, although I thought all this performance very ridiculous, there was something in the silence and the dim light, for the gas had been turned low down, and the room seemed filled with shadows; something about the fragile figure at my side, with her drooping head, which thrilled me with a curious sense of fear and icy horror such as I had never felt before.

I am not by nature imaginative or inclined to superstition, but, from the moment that young girl had entered the room, I felt as if a hand had been laid upon my heart, a cold iron hand, that was compressing it, and causing it to stop throbbing. My sense of hearing also had grown more acute and sensitive, so that the beating of the watch in my vest pocket sounded like the thumping of a quartz-crushing machine, and the measured breathing of those about me as loud and nerve-disturbing as the snorting of a steam engine.

Only when I turned to look upon the trance medium did I become soothed; then it seemed as if a cold-air wave had passed through my brain, subduing, for the time-being, those awful sounds.

'She is possessed,' whispered my host on the other side of me. 'Wait, and she will speak presently, and tell us whom we have got beside us.'

As we sat and waited the table moved several times under our hands, while knockings at intervals took place in the table and all round the room, a most weird and blood-curdling, yet ridiculous performance, which made me feel half inclined to run out with fear, and half inclined to sit still and laugh; on the whole, I think, however, that horror had the more complete possession of me.

Presently she raised her head and laid her hand upon mine, beginning to speak in a strange monotonous, far away voice, 'This is my first visit since I passed from earth-life, and you have called me here.'

I shivered as her hand touched mine, but had not strength to withdraw it from her light, soft grasp.

'I am what you would call a lost soul; that is, I am in the lowest sphere. Last week I was in the body, but met my death down

The Demon Spell

Whitechapel way. I was what you call an unfortunate, aye, unfortunate enough. Shall I tell you how it happened?'

The medium's eyes were closed, and whether it was my distorted imagination or not, she appeared to have grown older and decidedly debauched-looking since she sat down, or rather as if a light, filmy mask of degrading and soddened vice had replaced the former delicate features.

No one spoke, and the trance medium continued: 'I had been out all that day and without any luck or food, so that I was dragging my wearied body along through the slush and mud for it had been wet all day, and I was drenched to the skin, and miserable, ah, ten thousand times more wretched than I am now, for the earth is a far worse hell for such as I than our hell here.

'I had importuned several passers by as I went along that night, but none of them spoke to me, for work had been scarce all this winter, and I suppose I did not look so tempting as I have been; only once a man answered me, a dark-faced, middle-sized man, with a soft voice, and much better dressed than my usual companions.

'He asked me where I was going, and then left me, putting a coin into my hand, for which I thanked him. Being just in time for the last public-house, I hurried up, but on going to the bar and looking at my hand, I found it to be a curious foreign coin, with outlandish figures on it, which the landlord would not take, so I went out again to the dark fog and rain without my drink after all.

'There was no use going any further that night. I turned up the court where my lodgings were, intending to go home and get a sleep, since I could get no food, when I felt something touch me softly from behind like as if someone had caught hold of my shawl; then I stopped and turned about to see who it was.

'I was alone, and with no one near me, nothing but fog and the half light from the court lamp. Yet I felt as if something had got hold of

The Demon Spell

me, though I could not see what it was, and that it was gathering about me.

'I tried to scream out, but could not, as this unseen grasp closed upon my throat and choked me, and then I fell down and for a moment forgot everything.

'Next moment I woke up, outside my own poor mutilated body, and stood watching the fell work going on—as you see it now.'

Yes I saw it all as the medium ceased speaking, a mangled corpse lying on a muddy pavement, and a demoniac, dark, pock-marked face bending over it, with the lean claws outspread, and the dense fog instead of a body, like the half formed incarnation of muscles.

'That is what did it, and you will know it again.' she said, 'I have come for you to find it.'

'Is he an Englishman?' I gasped, as the vision faded away and the room once more became definite.

'It is neither man nor woman, but it lives as I do, it is with me now and may be with you to-night, still if you will have me instead of it, I can keep it back, only you must wish for me with all your might.'

The seance was now becoming too horrible, and by general consent our host turned up the gas, and then I saw for the first time the medium, now relieved from her evil possession, a beautiful girl of about nineteen, with I think the most glorious brown eyes I had ever before looked into.

'Do you believe what you have been speaking about?' I asked her as we were sitting talking together.

'What was that?'

'About the murdered woman.'

The Demon Spell

'I don't know anything at all. Only that I have been sitting at the table. I never know what my trances are.' Was she speaking the truth? Her dark eyes looked truth, so that I could not doubt her. That night when I went to my lodgings I must confess that it was some time before I could make up my mind to go to bed. I was decidedly upset and nervous, and wished that I had never, gone to this spirit meeting, making a mental vow, as I threw off my clothes and hastily got into bed, that it was the last unholy gathering I would ever attend.

For the first time in my life I could not put out the gas, I felt as if the room was filled with ghosts, as if this pair of ghastly spectres, the murderer and his victim, had accompanied me home, and were at that moment disputing the possession of me, so instead, I pulled the bedclothes over my head, it being a cold night, and went that fashion off to sleep.

Twelve o'clock! and the anniversary of the day that Christ was born. Yes, I heard it striking from the street spire and counted the strokes, slowly tolled out, listening to the echoes from other steeples, after this one had ceased, as I lay awake in that gas-lit room, feeling as if I was not alone this Christmas morn.

Thus, while I was trying to think what had made me wake so suddenly, I seemed to hear a far off echo cry 'Come to me.' At the same time the bedclothes were slowly pulled from the bed, and left in a confused mass on the floor.

'Is that you, Polly?' I cried, remembering the spirit seance, and the name by which the spirit had announced herself when she took possession.

Three distinct knocks resounded on the bedpost at my ear, the signal for 'Yes.'

'Can you speak to me?'

The Demon Spell

'Yes,' an echo rather than a voice replied, while I felt my flesh creeping, yet strove to be brave.

'Can I see you?'

'No!'

'Feel you?'

Instantly the feeling of a light cold hand touched my brow and passed over my face.

'In God's name what do you want?'

'To save the girl I was in tonight. It is after her and will kill her if you do not come quickly.'

In an instant I was out of the bed, and tumbling my clothes on any way, horrified through it all, yet feeling as if Polly were helping me to dress. There was a Kandian dagger on my table which I had brought from Ceylon, an old dagger which I had bought for its antiquity and design, and this I snatched up as I left the room, with that light unseen hand leading me out of the house and along the deserted snow-covered streets.

I did not know where the trance medium lived, but I followed where that light grasp led me through the wild, blinding snow-drift, round corners and through short cuts, with my head down and the flakes falling thickly about me, until at last I arrived at a silent square and in front of a house which by some instinct, I knew that I must enter.

Over by the other side of the street I saw a man standing looking up to a dimly-lighted window, but I could not see him very distinctly and I did not pay much attention to him at the time, but rushed instead up the front steps and into the house, that unseen hand still pulling me forward.

The Demon Spell

How that door opened, or if it did open I could not say, I only know that I got in, as we get into places in a dream, and up the inner stairs, I passed into a bedroom where the light was burning dimly.

It was her bedroom, and she was struggling in the thug-like grasp of those same demon claws, and the rest of it drifting away to nothingness.

I saw it all at a glance, her half-naked form, with the disarranged bedclothes, as the unformed demon of muscles clutched that delicate throat, and then I was at it like a fury with my Kandian dagger, slashing crossways at those cruel claws and that evil face, while blood streaks followed the course of my knife, making ugly stains, until at last it ceased struggling and disappeared like a horrid nightmare, as the half-strangled girl, now released from that fell grip, woke up the house with her screams, while from her releasing hand dropped a strange coin, which I took possession of.

Thus I left her, feeling that my work was done, going downstairs as I had come up, without impediment or even seemingly, in the slightest degree, attracting the attention of the other inmates of the house, who rushed in their nightdresses towards the bedroom from whence the screams were issuing.

Into the street again, with that coin in one hand and my dagger in the other I rushed, and then I remembered the man whom I had seen looking up at the window. Was he there still? Yes, but on the ground in a confused black mass amongst the white snow as if he had been struck down.

I went over to where he lay and looked at him. Was he dead? Yes. I turned him round and saw that his throat was gashed from ear to ear, and all over his face—the same dark, pallid, pock-marked evil face, and claw-like hands, I saw the dark slashes of my Kandian dagger, while the soft white snow around him was stained with crimson life pools, and as I looked I heard the clock strike one, while

The Demon Spell

from the distance sounded the chant of the coming waits, then I turned and fled blindly into the darkness.

THE END

The Vampire Maid

The Vampire Maid

It was the exact kind of abode that I had been looking after for weeks, for I was in that condition of mind when absolute renunciation of society was a necessity. I had become diffident of myself, and wearied of my kind. A strange unrest was in my blood; a barren dearth in my brains. Familiar objects and faces had grown distasteful to me. I wanted to be alone.

This is the mood which comes upon every sensitive and artistic mind when the possessor has been overworked or living too long in one groove. It is Nature's hint for him to seek pastures new; the sign that a retreat has become needful.

If he does not yield, he breaks down and becomes whimsical and hypochondriacal, as well as hypercritical. It is always a bad sign when a man becomes over-critical and censorious about his own or other people's work, for it means that he is losing the vital portions of work, freshness and enthusiasm.

Before I arrived at the dismal stage of criticism I hastily packed up my knapsack, and taking the train to Westmorland, I began my tramp in search of solitude, bracing air and romantic surroundings.

Many places I came upon during that early summer wandering that appeared to have almost the required conditions, yet some petty drawback prevented me from deciding. Sometimes it was the scenery that I did not take kindly to. At other places I took sudden antipathies to the landlady or landlord, and felt I would abhor them before a week was spent under their charge. Other places which might have suited me I could not have, as they did not want a lodger. Fate was driving me to this Cottage on the Moor, and no one can resist destiny.

One day I found myself on a wide and pathless moor near the sea. I had slept the night before at a small hamlet, but that was already eight miles in my rear, and since I had turned my back upon it I had

The Vampire Maid

not seen any signs of humanity; I was alone with a fair sky above me, a balmy ozone-filled wind blowing over the stony and heather-clad mounds, and nothing to disturb my meditations.

How far the moor stretched I had no knowledge; I only knew that by keeping in a straight line I would come to the ocean cliffs, then perhaps after a time arrive at some fishing village.

I had provisions in my knapsack, and being young did not fear a night under the stars. I was inhaling the delicious summer air and once more getting back the vigour and happiness I had lost; my city-dried brains were again becoming juicy.

Thus hour after hour slid past me, with the paces, until I had covered about fifteen miles since morning, when I saw before me in the distance a solitary stone-built cottage with roughly slated roof. 'I'll camp there if possible,' I said to myself as I quickened my steps towards it.

To one in search of a quiet, free life, nothing could have possibly been more suitable than this cottage. It stood on the edge of lofty cliffs, with its front door facing the moor and the back-yard wall overlooking the ocean. The sound of the dancing waves struck upon my ears like a lullaby as I drew near; how they would thunder when the autumn gales came on and the seabirds fled shrieking to the shelter of the sedges.

A small garden spread in front, surrounded by a dry-stone wall just high enough for one to lean lazily upon when inclined. This garden was a flame of colour, scarlet predominating, with those other soft shades that cultivated poppies take on in their blooming, for this was all that the garden grew.

As I approached, taking notice of this singular assortment of poppies, and the orderly cleanness of the windows, the front door opened and a woman appeared who impressed me at once favourably as she leisurely came along the pathway to the gate, and drew it back as if to welcome me.

The Vampire Maid

She was of middle age, and when young must have been remarkably good-looking. She was tall and still shapely, with smooth clear skin, regular features and a calm expression that at once gave me a sensation of rest.

To my inquiries she said that she could give me both a sitting and bedroom, and invited me inside to see them. As I looked at her smooth black hair, and cool brown eyes, I felt that I would not be too particular about the accomodation. With such a landlady, I was sure to find what I was after here.

The rooms surpassed my expectation, dainty white curtains and bedding with the perfume of lavender about them, a sitting-room homely yet cosy without being crowded. With a sigh of infinite relief I flung down my knapsack and clinched the bargain.

She was a widow with one daughter, whom I did not see the first day, as she was unwell and confined to her own room, but on the next day she was somewhat better, and then we met.

The fare was simple, yet it suited me exactly for the time, delicious milk and butter with home-made scones, fresh eggs and bacon; after a hearty tea I went early to bed in a condition of perfect content with my quarters.

Yet happy and tired out as I was I had by no means a comfortable night. This I put down to the strange bed. I slept certainly, but my sleep was filled with dreams so that I woke late and unrefreshed; a good walk on the moor, however, restored me, and I returned with a fine appetite for breakfast.

Certain conditions of mind, with aggravating circumstances, are required before even a young man can fall in love at first sight, as Shakespeare has shown in his Romeo and Juliet. In the city, where many fair faces passed me every hour, I had remained like a stoic, yet no sooner did I enter the cottage after that morning walk than I succumbed instantly before the weird charms of my landlady's daughter, Ariadne Brunnell.

The Vampire Maid

She was somewhat better this morning and able to meet me at breakfast, for we had our meals together while I was their lodger. Ariadne was not beautiful in the strictly classical sense, her complexion being too lividly white and her expression too set to be quite pleasant at first sight; yet, as her mother had informed me, she had been ill for some time, which accounted for that defect. Her features were not regular, her hair and eyes seemed too black with that strangely white skin, and her lips too red for any except the decadent harmonies of an Aubrey Beardsley.

Yet my fantastic dreams of the preceding night, with my morning walk, had prepared me to be enthralled by this modern poster-like invalid.

The loneliness of the moor, with the singing of the ocean, had gripped my heart with a wistful longing. The incongruity of those flaunting and evanescent poppy flowers, dashing the giddy tints in the face of that sober heath, touched me with a shiver as I approached the cottage, and lastly that weird embodiment of startling contrasts completed my subjugation.

She rose from her chair as her mother introduced her, and smiled while she held out her hand. I clasped that soft snowflake, and as I did so a faint thrill tingled over me and rested on my heart, stopping for the moment its beating.

This contact seemed also to have affected her as it did me; a clear flush, like a white flame, lighted up her face, so that it glowed as if an alabaster lamp had been lit; her black eyes became softer and more humid as our glances crossed, and her scarlet lips grew moist. She was a living woman now, while before she had seemed half a corpse.

She permitted her white slender hand to remain in mine longer than most people do at an introduction, and then she slowly withdrew it, still regarding me with steadfast eyes for a second or two afterwards.

The Vampire Maid

Fathomless velvety eyes these were, yet before they were shifted from mine they appeared to have absorbed all my willpower and made me her abject slave. They looked like deep dark pools of clear water, yet they filled me with fire and deprived me of strength. I sank into my chair almost as languidly as I had risen from my bed that morning.

Yet I made a good breakfast, and although she hardly tasted anything, this strange girl rose much refreshed and with a slight glow of colour on her cheeks, which improved her so greatly that she appeared younger and almost beautiful.

I had come here seeking solitude, but since I had seen Ariadne it seemed as if I had come for her only. She was not very lively; indeed, thinking back, I cannot recall any spontaneous remark of hers; she answered my questions by monosyllables and left me to lead in words; yet she was insinuating and appeared to lead my thoughts in her direction and speak to me with her eyes. I cannot describe her minutely, I only know that from the first glance and touch she gave me I was bewitched and could think of nothing else.

It was a rapid, distracting, and devouring infatuation that possessed me; all day long I followed her about like a dog, every night I dreamed of that white glowing face, those steadfast black eyes, those moist scarlet lips, and each morning I rose more languid than I had been the day before. Sometimes I dreamt that she was kissing me with those red lips, while I shivered at the contact of her silky black tresses as they covered my throat; sometimes that we were floating in the air, her arms about me and her long hair enveloping us both like an inky cloud, while I lay supine and helpless.

She went with me after breakfast on that first day to the moor, and before we came back I had spoken my love and received her assent. I held her in my arms and had taken her kisses in answer to mine, nor did I think it strange that all this had happened so quickly. She was mine, or rather I was hers, without a pause. I told her it was fate that had sent me to her, for I had no doubts about my love, and she replied that I had restored her to life.

The Vampire Maid

Acting upon Ariadne's advice, and also from a natural shyness, I did not inform her mother how quickly matters had progressed between us, yet although we both acted as circumspectly as possible, I had no doubt Mrs Brunnell could see how engrossed we were in each other. Lovers are not unlike ostriches in their modes of concealment. I was not afraid of asking Mrs Brunnell for her daughter, for she already showed her partiality towards me, and had bestowed upon me some confidences regarding her own position in life, and I therefore knew that, so far as social position was concerned, there could be no real objection to our marriage. They lived in this lonely spot for the sake of their health, and kept no servant because they could not get any to take service so far away from other humanity. My coming had been opportune and welcome to both mother and daughter.

For the sake of decorum, however, I resolved to delay my confession for a week or two and trust to some favourable opportunity of doing it discreetly.

Meantime Ariadne and I passed our time in a thoroughly idle and lotus-eating style. Each night I retired to bed meditating starting work next day, each morning I rose languid from those disturbing dreams with no thought for anything outside my love. She grew stronger every day, while I appeared to be taking her place as the invalid, yet I was more frantically in love than ever, and only happy when with her. She was my lone-star, my only joy—my life.

We did not go great distances, for I liked best to lie on the dry heath and watch her glowing face and intsense eyes while I listened to the surging of the distant waves. It was love made me lazy, I thought, for unless a man has all he longs for beside him, he is apt to copy the domestic cat and bask in the sunshine.

I had been enchanted quickly. My disenchantment came as rapidly, although it was long before the poison left my blood.

One night, about a couple of weeks after my coming to the cottage, I had returned after a delicious moonlight walk with Ariadne. The

The Vampire Maid

night was warm and the moon at the full, therefore I left my bedroom window open to let in what little air there was.

I was more than usually fagged out, so that I had only strength enough to remove my boots and coat before I flung myself wearily on the coverlet and fell almost instantly asleep without tasting the nightcap draught that was constantly placed on the table, and which I had always drained thirstily.

I had a ghastly dream this night. I thought I saw a monster bat, with the face and tresses of Ariadne, fly into the open window and fasten its white teeth and scarlet lips on my arm. I tried to beat the horror away, but could not, for I seemed chained down and thralled also with drowsy delight as the beast sucked my blood with a gruesome rapture.

I looked out dreamily and saw a line of dead bodies of young men lying on the floor, each with a red mark on their arms, on the same part where the vampire was then sucking me, and I remembered having seen and wondered at such a mark on my own arm for the past fortnight. In a flash I understood the reason for my strange weakness, and at the same moment a sudden prick of pain roused me from my dreamy pleasure.

The vampire in her eagerness had bitten a little too deeply that night, unaware that I had not tasted the drugged draught. As I woke I saw her fully revealed by the midnight moon, with her black tresses flowing loosely, and with her red lips glued to my arm. With a shriek of horror I dashed her backwards, getting one last glimpse of her savage eyes, glowing white face and blood-stained red lips; then I rushed out to the night, moved on by my fear and hatred, nor did I pause in my mad flight until I had left miles between me and that accursed Cottage on the Moor.

THE END

CPSIA information can be obtained
at www.ICGtesting.com
Printed in the USA
BVHW081352201120
593806BV00001B/79